empire

SHERIDAN ANNE

A DARK SECRET SOCIETY REVERSE HAREM

Sheridan Anne

Empire: Empire (Book 1)

Copyright © 2022 Sheridan Anne

All rights reserved

First Published in 2022

Anne, Sheridan

Empire: Empire #1

This book is a work of fiction. Names, characters, places, and incidents are products of the author's imagination. Any resemblance to actual events or persons, living or dead, is entirely coincidental.

Cover Design: Sheridan Anne
Photographer: Tatyaby
Editing: Fox Proof Editing
Formatting: Sheridan Anne

To Liam Hemsworth,

I don't care what everyone else says, you are the superior Hemsworth.

PROLOGUE

Zade

The burning smell of rotten flesh assaults my senses as my father's body goes up in flames, the blood of The Circle surrounding his burning corpse. I step up, taking what was once my father's position at the head of our society, my gaze shifting around the dark tomb. Pillars circle the ancient room, the resting place of the countless Empire heirs who have ruled before me.

The flames flicker, casting long shadows across the polished stone and over the emotionless faces of The Circle members watching me through dead, expressionless eyes, their long black cloaks as equally fucked up as this whole ritual.

I've always hated these bastards. They're The Circle, the assholes who lay claim to my Empire, who believe they govern what will be mine. They're nothing without me, and now that my father's body burns at their feet, I'll step up as their leader—the only rightful heir.

Outside of this room, this society, they're nothing but ordinary people—judges, police, politicians—but they harbor dark secrets, all of which will now rest on my shoulders, giving me the power to destroy each one of them.

With thick smoke billowing to the roof, I get the ritual underway. Raising the dagger, I place the ancient blade in the palm of my hand before closing my fingers around its intricate, gothic design, the eyes of The Circle locked on me. Tension builds in the tomb. The send-off of a blood heir is one of our most sacred rituals. If I fuck this up, I could be dead beside the bastard. But they won't dare. Maybe thirty or forty years ago, they would have had what it takes to end me, but I'm too strong, too relentless, too fast. I'm untouchable, and every fucker in the room knows it—even my father knew it. Hell, he sure as fuck knew it when I dragged my blade across his throat. Though these fuckers don't need to know that.

Squeezing my hand around the blade, I feel its sharp bite digging into my skin, and I stretch my arm out, watching as my blood—the blood of the new leader—stains my father's burning flesh. "The flesh of my flesh will perish in flames, but the blood will forever reign."

As one, The Circle repeats my words, their murmured chants chilling me to the bone. *The flesh of my flesh will perish in flames, but the blood will forever reign. The flesh of my flesh will perish in flames, but the blood will forever reign. The flesh of my flesh will perish in flames, but the blood will forever reign."*

My blood continues dripping over my father's corpse, the flames blistering my skin, but I don't stop or pull back until their final words have been spoken. Only then do I lift my gaze to The Circle and lower my hand, the sacred blade clattering to the ground as I release my grip on the dagger, blood running down my fingers and dripping by my feet.

"It is done," I announce. "The reign of my father, Lawson Michael DeVil the Third, has ceased, and I, Zade Alexander DeVil, stand before you, as the heir of the founding Circle, and proclaim my intention to rise in my father's wake and claim what is rightfully mine as the *only true heir* of Empire."

Each member of The Circle bows their head, their hands coming together at their chests. As one, they speak. "Your intentions have been acknowledged."

I watch them carefully. This culty-ritual bullshit really isn't my style, or probably any of theirs, but back when Empire was built from the ground up, this shit would have been seen as a privilege, as power. Now, it's nothing short of fucked up, but it's these kinds of fucked-up traditions that have kept us going.

The flames roar, quickly sucking the oxygen out of the small tomb, but we still have one more part to go. The initiation.

Anticipation burns in my chest. Only those of The Circle know what the initiation entails. It's not one of those secrets passed down from father to son, but a challenge presented to the new initiate to test his determination and loyalty to the cause. It is said to bind the ruling heir to Empire and ensure a lifetime of servitude to our people, something my father always described as an honor. To me, it sounds like a load of horseshit, probably something they'll be able to use against me if I ever decide to walk away. But that won't be happening. I've waited too long for this, watched my father hold a type of power over the world he never deserved or even knew how to use. Such wasted potential.

With Empire in my hands, the world is mine to bend and manipulate. Whatever I want will be thrust at my feet, and I do whatever it takes to make it so.

"You cannot flourish in the power of Empire without first giving your soul," The Circle member standing directly across from me says, his voice chilling and raw. "You will be challenged to prove your loyalty to our cause by making the greatest sacrifice of all, a sacrifice the heirs before you have each made."

"I'll do whatever it takes."

"In sixty suns and sixty moons, you will sacrifice the heart of an innocent. You will bring her to us, and in the hour before dawn in our sacred fortress, you will carve out her still-beating heart and offer it as your sacrifice to your people. Her heart will be placed on a pedestal and will remain until your reign shall cease. It is with this sacrifice that you, Zade Alexander DeVil, will be bound to Empire and rise as our rightful leader."

I nod, accepting what will be. Without another word, The Circle files out of the tomb, all except one. "Zade," he says, and I turn my attention to him, looking away from my father's burning body and into the eyes of Nikolai Thorne. His dead, emotionless stare from earlier completely gone, replaced with the familiarity of my best friend's father. "Are you sure you know what you're doing?"

I nod, more than ready to take this on. "My father did this?"

"He did."

My brows furrow, and I try to think back to the days before my father was initiated as the heir of Empire, but I was just a kid, still stricken with grief over the loss of my grandfather. "Who did he sacrifice?"

A fond smile pulls at his lips before that heavy darkness returns in his eyes, and I can all but see the images etched into his memory. "The love of his life," Nikolai tells me, his tone void of all emotion. "He sacrificed your mother."

My chest constricts as lead pulses through my veins, weighing me down. "No, you must have that wrong. My mother left us. She wasn't sacrificed."

"I'm sorry," Nikolai says, bowing his head. "Remember, sixty suns and sixty moons. Bring the innocent. If no sacrifice is made, Empire will not accept you as their ruling heir, and with no other, well . . . God be with us all."

CHAPTER 1

Oakley

"Would you rather fuck your dad in Thor's body or Thor in your dad's body?"

My jaw drops, gaping at my brand-new roommate. I mean, fuck! What must circle her brain to make that sentence fall out of her mouth? And before she's even said hello.

Holy shit, this chick is either going to be my new best friend, or she's mentally unstable and I'll need to sleep with a knife. "I, umm . . . my dad died when I was a kid," I stumble out, my hand still raised after knocking on the wide-open door.

"Was he hot?" She stares back at me from the small kitchen, watching me through a narrowed gaze as though my response is going to tell her everything she needs to know about me.

I consider her question, thinking back on the few old photographs I managed to salvage from our home before social services ripped me out of there. "I suppose so," I admit. "Tall, dark, and handsome with an edge of *touch my kid and you'll fucking die* . . . If you're into that shit."

She bites down on her bottom lip, her eyes glimmering with excitement. "Oh, I'm into that shit," she says, waving me deeper into the small college-owned apartment. "You didn't answer the question."

I scoff, dropping my bag at my feet and kicking the door closed behind me. "Does it really matter? As long as Thor's got that big hammer, I'm good."

"Right," she says, nodding as she leans back against the counter. "So, your dad in Thor's body then?"

"I . . . huh? How do you get that?"

"If you want the hammer, you have to have Thor's body, too. Process of elimination, babe. You're fucking your dad in Thor's body."

I stare back at her, unsure how we got here. "I don't know how I feel about that."

"I mean, it's not set in stone," she says, strutting across the kitchen and grabbing a bottle of wine out of the fridge before searching for glasses. "We can always change your answer. You can fuck Thor in your dad's body, but just between you and me, I think Thor would be hung like a horse, and girl, he's a god. He'd know how to use it. It's a no-brainer to me. Unless your dad was rocking a giant cock too. Do you happen to kn—"

"Oh God," I groan, cutting across the living room to the kitchen as she pours two glasses of wine. "One of those better be for me because there's no way I'm about to start discussing my dad's dick without at least feeling a buzz first."

She laughs and scoops up one of the glasses before reaching out over the counter to hand it to me. "Do you really think I'd let you talk about your dad's dick sober? Of course it's for you. Girl, we're roomies now. We need to have each other's backs. Besides, I find people need to drink while they're around me. You know, takes the edge off."

I lift the glass to my lips and tip its contents right down my throat before placing it back down on the counter. "I'm gonna need more."

She takes the glass from me with a wide smile. "You passed, by the way," she says as she refills my glass, my gaze shifting over her face and realizing she's basically a shorter version of Kendall Jenner. "Most people don't know how to answer that without sounding like either a prude or a fucking weirdo."

"I can't imagine why," I laugh.

She raises her brows and nods before lifting her glass and clinking it against mine. "I'm Cara, by the way."

"Oakley, or just O."

"Congratulations, O. You just became my number one bitch."

I press my hand to my chest, grinning back at her, absolutely dazzled by her gorgeous smile. "The honor is all mine."

"Damn right, it is."

"How long have you been here?" I ask, gazing around the apartment at the small living room and even smaller kitchen.

Her brows furrow, trying to do the mental math. "Ummm . . . little under two years maybe," she says. "I was lucky to snag this place.

I registered late and all the closer apartments were already taken, but the couple who lived here had this horrible break up and the girl left, leaving the guy to cover the rent, and when he couldn't, he bailed for campus dorms. I mean, damn, I jumped on this place faster than I'd jump Jason Momoa. It's perfect, apart from the fact rent is single-handedly destroying my life. Come check it out."

Cara skips around the side of the island counter, taking her wine with her, and I follow along, taking in the sights as she leads me down the hallway to the bedrooms and bathroom. "You saw the living room and kitchen. They're not much, but they're a shitload better than the campus dorms. Though be warned, this is still a college apartment complex, so there's always a party going on, and you'll never be able to sleep with all the music."

Cara grabs the handle of the bathroom door and pushes it open as she keeps walking by. "Bathroom," she says, quickly pointing inside before continuing toward the spare bedroom. "Clean up after yourself. Don't leave shit stains in the toilet, and please, for the love of God, don't leave your dirty ass tampons for me to clean up because I promise, you will wake up in the morning with it wedged between your ass crack."

"Promise," I tell her. "You won't need to worry about my used tampons, and in return, I'm hoping I won't come home to find you've been using my toothbrush because I promise that you'll be the one waking up to find my whole foot up your ass."

Cara stops and looks back at me with a fond smile. "Ahhh, healthy boundaries. I love it," she says before pushing open another door.

"This is your room. You're allowed to decorate it however you see fit, but be warned, the college likes to spring random inspections on us and they get pissed if things are messed up. Apparently, a few of the people upstairs painted walls and nearly got evicted."

"Noted," I say, glancing into my room and loving it. "No paint."

"It's not much, but it's decent enough," she says. "Oh, and the guy who lives in the apartment next door and shares a wall with you is kinda a manwhore . . . actually, kinda isn't doing it justice. He's a flat-out slut, so I recommend investing in some noise-canceling headphones unless you're into that soothing, rhythmic thumping. The repetitious sound can be quite calming if you block out the moans and grunts."

We make our way back out to the living room, and I drop onto the couch, more than prepared to put off the unpacking until tomorrow, or maybe next week. "Let me guess," Cara questions, detouring to the fridge for a second bottle of wine. "Business major?"

"Ooooh," I laugh, almost offended. "Psychology major. I'm two years in and just transferred from out of state."

"Ahhh, sounds like a lot."

"You're telling me," I mutter. "I'm also doing a Bachelor of Arts, but I'm thinking of putting it on hold for a while. This shit is too expensive to keep up with. I couldn't get a campus dorm room, which is how I ended up here, and after the move and having to pay rent on top of tuition, you're looking at the brokest bitch under the sun."

"You're preaching to the choir, girl," she says, dropping down beside me on the couch. "If you know how to mix drinks, there's a bar just at the end of the street. It's a shithole, and the boss is an ass, but they're always looking for extra hands. It's crazy busy on Friday and Saturday nights, and if you shake your ass a bit, the tips are great."

"You work there?"

"Nah, not anymore. I couldn't handle the ass grabbing, so I forced my way into this little indie bookstore and demanded a job until the owner couldn't say no."

Laughter bubbles up my throat, and I can't help the smirk stretching across my face. I hold up my glass and she clinks hers against it. "That's one way to get things done."

"Worked like a charm," she grins. "Stick with me and you'll never have to want for anything. But shit, are you a reader? Because I can hook you up with some good smut. I'm practically the smut expert, the Smutxpert. Actually, I like that name." Her eyes widen like saucers and she tears her phone out of her back pocket, madly unlocking the screen. "Holy shit. It's decided, I'm starting a bookstagram and that'll be my new handle. Smut_XPERT. Or should it be The Smut Doctor? No, no. I was right the first time. Definitely Smut_XPERT."

"What the hell is a bookstagram?"

Cara gapes at me, her hands pausing for just a moment. "Oh, girl. I'm about to blow your mind."

We spend the next hour scrolling through Instagram, and by the end of it, Cara's created a whole list of books and set me up with a Kindle account. Apparently, it's called a TBR and the size of it is already freaking me out, but if these books are anything like their covers suggest, I'm all in.

"Hungry?" she questions, once her new bookstagram @Smut_

XPERT is all set up, but before I have a chance to respond, loud music blasts from the next-door apartment, rattling the walls. Cara rolls her eyes before letting out a heavy sigh. "Welcome to Faders Bay."

I scoff, leaning back into the couch, the music already grating on my nerves. "More like welcome back!" I mutter darkly before indicating to the rattling wall. "Is it always like this?"

"Yeah," she says. "If it's not music, it's sex, and if it's not sex, it's wild parties. But you'll get used to it. It's the full college experience. Besides, every now and then, the guys in this complex prove themselves useful. Especially after a night of reading when there's an itch that needs to be scratched and the buzz of my battery-operated friends simply won't cut it."

I laugh and hold my glass to hers again. "Cheers to that."

She clinks it right back before tipping the rest of her wine down her throat and refilling once again. "So, you grew up here?" she questions, picking up on my earlier tone.

"Kind of," I mutter, wondering why the hell I even said anything. It's not exactly something I like to talk about. "I lived here with my dad before he died and then I was whisked away to Missouri to live with my aunt."

"Oh, shit. That sucks. I'm sorry about your dad."

I shrug my shoulders, brushing it off. "Thanks. I was only eight, so I don't remember much. All I know is one day, he was pushing me on the swings, and then the next, he was gone and I was being shoved into the back of a car. Next thing I knew, I was starting over in Missouri with my mom's sister."

"I can't even imagine how shitty that must have been," she says, just as something smashes into the wall from the adjoining apartment, making us both jump. "Shit. It's gonna be a long night," she murmurs. "I'm ordering in. You want noodles?"

Cara gets busy, and by the time the UberEats driver is knocking on the door, I've gotten most of my bags out of my car and dumped them in my room. The rest of my stuff is going to have to wait until tomorrow, or until I can convince Cara how desperately she wants to help me carry the heavy stuff.

I eat with Cara, and after knocking the Missouri noodle place off the leaderboard for the best noodles I've ever eaten, I quickly wash up and head to my room.

It's just after 8:30 p.m., and if I plan on being able to survive in Faders Bay, then I need to get my shit together.

Scrambling through my bags, I pull out an old pair of black jeans and match it with a black tank. It's not exactly my usual outfit of choice, but if I intend on scoring a job at the bar down the street, I need to fit the part. Screw the ass grabbing and rowdy assholes, I can handle that. They'll quickly learn what it means to fuck with me, until then, I need this. And I won't be walking out of that bar until I've secured a job.

After tying my golden curls back and slipping my phone into my pocket, I walk out of my room and find Cara curled up on the couch already deep into a new book, somehow able to ignore the booming music coming from next door. "Where the hell are you going?" she questions, looking over the back of the couch at me, her gaze raking up and down my body. "Shit, who would have known you had such a nice ass under those sweats?"

I laugh and pass by the kitchen, scooping up the keys she'd given me earlier. "I'm heading down to that bar to get myself a job."

"Damn straight you are," she says, turning her attention back to her book. "Give 'em hell."

A wave of determination flourishes in my chest, and I hold my head high as I make my way to the door. "Oh," Cara calls after me as I pull the door open, the music from outside spilling into our small apartment. "Whether you get the job or not, do me a favor and bring me back one of those extra cheesy burgers they have."

"What?" I laugh. "You just ate."

"And I'll eat again," she cheers.

My laugh fades as I step into the hallway and face the crowd of partiers with red solo cups wandering between open doors. Girls in short skirts linger in doorways as guys squeeze past them, carrying all sorts of booze under their arms. As I try to squeeze through the masses, a figure appears in the doorway directly opposite mine, and the fear that rocks through my body is like nothing I've ever felt before.

I don't know what it is about him, but the guy is bad news. He's tall and built like a fucking linebacker, and goddamn, he's the sexiest thing I've ever seen. I feel like those big hands alone could end a life with barely a flick of his wrist, and the darkness in his eyes is almost daring me to make him.

Jet black hair falls forward into his eyes which are equally as dark, like two hollow pits of nothingness just waiting for their next victim to fall into their rotten trap. His lips are full and drawing me in, but as he clenches his jaw and I see just how sharp it is, I know I need to back away.

A hint of tattoos peeks out from beneath his shirt, winding up his neck and arms, and the intricate designs have me needing to see more. But I don't dare stare a second longer than necessary. He leans against the doorframe, watching me with curiosity as I shrink away, a strange anxiety pulsing through my veins. Chills sweep over my body, and I swallow hard, the intensity of his stare too much for me to handle.

This guy isn't just dangerous, he's lethal. He's the type of man you'd find lingering in the shadows following you home, and I don't like it one fucking bit.

Fear settles into my stomach, and I force my stare to the ground before hurrying down the hall, squeezing past the bodies while feeling his curious stare locked on my back. I make a mental note never to walk these halls alone, and I pray there's a deadbolt on my front door, but I doubt a simple lock would be able to stop someone like him from getting what he wants.

With plenty of bodies between me and who I can only assume is some kind of serial killer, I find myself glancing back over my shoulder, my curiosity getting the best of me. Hell, this isn't just dangerous territory, he's straight out of a nightmare, and I shouldn't find him so alluring. But I guess that's just part of his plan.

His eyes are still locked on mine, and I watch as a friend moves into his side. The newcomer looks relaxed and ready to party, messy blond hair and bright green eyes, looking like some kind of sexed-up surfer dude. He looks like the kind of guy I could probably get down with, only when the scary dude tilts his head toward his friend and mutters something, the friend's back stiffens before his lethal stare sweeps toward me. His fun party-boy demeanor quickly morphs into something stony and cold.

They watch me and it's like they've been waiting for something—*waiting for me*—and it sends a bout of fear blasting through my chest. I move my feet faster, reconsidering my entire move to Faders Bay, but I wouldn't be my father's daughter if I let something keep me from getting where I need to go.

Continuing down the hall, I finally reach the exit that leads out onto the street. As I shove my shoulder into the door and push it open, I look back one more time and regret it immediately. The two guys from across the hall are now standing in front of my neighbor's apartment with another guy, the three of them huddled together, each with their hollow, wicked stares locked on me. This must be the neighbor Cara warned me about, the one I share a bedroom wall with . . . the one who's always fucking.

I don't doubt it for one second. The guy is gorgeous in a scary, gothic kind of way, kind of like the first asshole, but what really gets me is the small black snake weaving between his fingers as though it couldn't be happier there. And goddamn, I'd like to weave all my bits around those fingers too.

His hair is cropped short, and those dark eyes warn me not to look at him twice. He's scary as fuck, but he didn't terrify me in the same way the first guy had. This guy is trouble, but for some reason, I don't think I need to fear him murdering me while I sleep. I do need to fear him though.

Swallowing hard, I bust out through the door, putting space between us. I've never once been afraid of the dark, but in these unfamiliar streets with the chill of their stares still lingering on my skin, that could very well change.

I try to put it to the back of my mind and raise my head high. I'm not here to fuck around, and I'm sure as hell not here to let three scary as fuck assholes intimidate me. My daddy didn't raise a quitter . . . Well, technically he didn't raise me at all, but I can only assume that's what he would have wanted.

Making my way down the street, I follow the noise of the bar, more than ready to make this place my bitch.

CHAPTER 2

Oakley

anny's Bar is nothing but a glorified wasteland, but it's going to be my wasteland, no matter what anyone has to say about it.

Bodies fill every available space, and as I make my way through the door, I'm not surprised that no one checks my ID. It's definitely not that kind of bar. This is the type of place for bottom shelf drinks and bad decisions.

The dim lighting mildly disguises the stained carpet and the questionable plates of food served over the sticky bar. There's a stale smell, but I've quickly come to learn the majority of college bars tend to smell like this. Laughter pulls from every corner of the room as half the douchebag guys hit on every last girl in sight and the rest of them shout and curse at some big college football game I couldn't give two shits about.

It's just before nine on a Friday evening and most of the people here are only just starting to write themselves off after another long week of studying bullshit they'll never understand and disappointing their parents. It's going to be a long night for them, and if I have my way, it'll be an even longer night for me.

The bar is situated directly in the center of the room with a crowd packed around it like sardines. It's hard to see from here, but it looks as though there's only one girl working the bar, and she's completely run off her feet. There's another girl madly rushing around, collecting empty glasses and trying to get them back to the bar without tripping over her own feet or allowing some drunk asshole to make a joke out of her.

One thing is clear though, they could use all the help they can get.

Squeezing my way through the overcrowded bar, I pass the live band and take a moment to actually listen to what they're playing. They sound great and are smashing out covers of old 90's soft rock hits. Though, among this crowd, they'd be better off singing something from this century.

Reaching the bar, I find my way around to the staff entrance and unlatch the small gate, separating the employees from the zoo animals, and without a second of hesitation, I put myself to work. Scooping up a fresh apron off the bar, I tie it around my waist and head straight for my first customer.

"What can I get ya?" I call, hoping I can be heard over the sound of the busy bar.

He nods, acknowledging me, and holds up two fingers, saving me from having to try and hear him over the noise. Glancing around, I find the beer glasses and scoop two up before getting straight to work filling them. I'm just about done when the other chick running the bar glances my way. Her eyes bug out of her head, not having expected to see me here. "Umm . . . can I help you?" she questions, not bothering to ask me to stop.

"No, but it looks like I can help you," I tell her, putting the two beers up on the bar in front of my customer. I glance his way. "Ten bucks."

The guy shoves two five-dollar bills at me, and I gracefully take it before shuffling over to the cash register to quickly ring it up. He leaves a few dollars as a tip, and I shove it into my apron before moving on to the next guy. His order is the same and I get busy again.

"I don't think Danny is gonna like this," she tells me, straining to be heard over the live music and the game. "He's an asshole."

"From what I can tell, it doesn't look like he's got many options," I say, shoving the beers up on the counter and taking the guy's money. "Do you usually get left to work the bar by yourself?"

"No," she says, busily ringing up someone's order. "There's usually a few of us, but Cat, Jess, and Reb were no-shows tonight. It's just me and Hannah trying to hold down the fort. To be honest, you shouldn't have a problem convincing Danny to hire you, but it won't be on good terms and the pay is shit."

"No wonder you're not putting up a fight."

"Tell me about it," she says. "No one really lasts around here. Most people stick around for a few months before fucking off."

"What about you?"

She shrugs her shoulders and grabs another glass from beneath the bar. "Been here six months and had half of it off for exams and family shit. Even with all of that, I was still promoted to bar manager, simply because there wasn't anyone else to do it."

"I can't tell if you're trying to convince me to stay or scare me out of here."

She laughs. "Honestly, I've got no fucking clue myself," she says. "Just be prepared. This place isn't known for its high standards. You'll have assholes grabbing your ass and you'll be hit with dirty slurs and catcalling from the start of your shift right up until you fuck off at the end of the night. Girls will assume you're trying to steal their men and try to fight you out back while random assholes will try and drag you into the bathroom to fuck."

I nod, taking cash off another customer and cringing when the whole bar erupts into cheers from the football game. "I can handle it."

"Good, because I don't want to waste my time training you if you can't hack it," she tells me. "I'm Heather by the way. Don't get in my way, and don't fuck with my tips. If you can stick to that, we won't have a problem."

The other girl, Hannah, appears at the bar and dumps a bunch of dirty glasses over the side, smirks at me, and shakes her head. "Hope you know what you're getting yourself into," she says, leaning over to put the glasses into the sink to make space on the bar, clearly understanding that I just hired myself under my own authority. "This place isn't for the weak-minded."

"Yeah, well, my rent really doesn't care what kind of bullshit I have to suffer through as long as it gets paid."

"I hear ya, girl," she says, reaching over the bar and offering me her hand. "I'm Hannah."

I take her hand and give it a quick shake. "Oakley."

"Nice to meet ya," she says. "Hopefully you'll stick around long enough so I can actually get to know you."

"That's the plan," I tell her, pulling out all my party tricks and proving that I belong. "Is Danny here?"

Heather shakes her head. "Not yet. He usually shows up around ten and stays til midnight. Just long enough to show his face and raid the cash register. He won't be happy to see you working, but like you said, I don't think he really has a choice. Not unless he wants all his customers to fuck off and head down to Arthur's because they couldn't get served fast enough."

"Yo, bitch," some asshole says from across the bar, slamming his hand down to get Heather's attention. "Hurry up with my fucking beer."

Heather barely spares him a glance before grabbing the nozzle for the beer and pulling out the hose. She hits him square in the face, drenching him in seconds. "Get the fuck out or learn what it means to have respect. Either way, you're fucking cut off."

"The fuck?" he shrieks, squealing like a little bitch as beer drips off his face and people rush to get away from the spray. "You fucking whore. You're gonna pay for that. You can't touch me."

"I can and I did," Heather tells him, simply moving on to someone else's order, not giving two shits about the dripping asshole taking up space at our bar. "Whatchya gonna do about it?"

Heather raises her head and motions to the security guard waiting by the door, and like clockwork, he strides through the bar and grips the asshole by the arm. "You're done," he tells the dripping asshole. "Wait and see what happens if you try and get back in."

"You can't fucking—" he tries to pull his arm free, his words getting lost in the crowd, and before I know it, the guy is out on his ass and yelling obscenities from the street.

I laugh, watching as the girls get straight back to work as though nothing ever happened. Heather runs a washcloth over the bar, cleaning up the spilled beer as Hannah ducks round to our side to quickly wash up the glasses and get them back under the bar to be used again. For the first time in so many years, I feel like I might've just found a place I can call home.

This bar is a complete dive, filled with the worst kind of people, but there's something charming about the chaos. I can't help but love it.

An hour passes, and I quickly learn that the more I smile and flirt with the customers, the bigger they tip, and for a while I even enjoy it, until a chill sweeps over my body. My brows furrow and I glance up to find the three guys from my apartment complex, each one of their stares already locked on me.

The two less creepy guys look vaguely interested, but the third guy, the one I'd first seen across from my apartment, looks as though he's about ready to tear my head clean off my body. My heart races as I fumble with the glass I'm holding, spilling cheap beer up my arm. I've never felt fear like this in my life.

The way they look at me . . . it's as though they want something from me, but I have no fucking clue what that could be. I only just moved back here, and I doubt I owed these guys something before I left. I was eight years old. Surely I couldn't have racked up some kind of debt with them back then.

Hastily dropping my gaze, I get busy cleaning up the spill and making my customer a fresh beer, but my hands just keep shaking. The three guys don't try to approach me, don't even come up to the bar to ask for a drink, just simply hover in the darkest corner, keeping their lethal stares locked on me.

They murmur between themselves, and I'd give everything I have just to hear their conversation. I don't even know these guys, don't know anything about them, only that the dude holding the black snake likes to fuck. Though I know with complete certainty, whatever is being said over in that dark corner of the bar, it's about me.

It chills me to the bone. What do they want with me?

My hands shake profusely, and I try to get back to work, tuning them out and focusing on what I'm doing. I concentrate on the cash handed to me, making sure I give my customer the correct change, but my mind is boggled, and as I glance back at the row of rowdy people before me, I can't even figure out which one I was serving.

"Yo, what the fuck is this?" a man's voice sounds across the bar.

My head snaps up, and I watch as the older gentleman narrows his gaze on me as he walks around the bar, the customers stepping out of his way as though he's some kind of big deal around here. He's gotta be in his mid-forties and looks like an exhausted version of Chris Hemsworth, only where there should be muscle, it's nothing but skin and bone.

He makes his way right down to the side entrance of the bar and passes through the little gate.

I immediately offer him my hand, assuming this is Danny. I've got one shot to make a good impression, and despite the way my heart races, I won't be fucking this up. "Hey, I'm Oakley," I say, hoping I can be heard over the crowd. "Your new bartender."

"I don't need any more bartenders," he says, disregarding my hand. "I've got plenty."

"Sorry to break it to you, Danny," Heather says, not letting our conversation keep her from doing her job. "But you don't. Cat, Reb, and Jess were no-shows, and this girl is good. Give her a chance. She's even been overcharging on beer. Made you a nice little profit. Plus, she's hot and flirts with the customers. They've all been tipping well with her here."

Oh fuck.

"Overcharging?" I cringe, glancing at this chick who's supposed to be the manager and has knowingly allowed me to overcharge for the past hour and a half.

She shrugs her shoulders. "Yep. Friday night, game night. Three dollar special on our house beers, but no one's complained about it yet.

If they're willing to keep paying, then I'm willing to let it slide."

Danny grins at Heather, more than down with ripping off his customers. "They really didn't show up?" he questions, glancing around the bar as though magically hoping the three no-shows will just turn up.

"Yeah, not even a call," Heather says. "Oakley didn't think twice about it. Saw we were swamped and put on an apron."

Danny glances my way and his gaze sails up and down my body. "Oakley, huh?" he questions with a heavy sigh, clearly seeing he's backed into a corner. "How old are you?"

"Twenty-one," I lie. Well, kinda. My birthday is three months away, but it's close enough. It's not like I'm going to suddenly become responsible the day my birthday rolls around. As far as I'm concerned, I'm just as much of an adult as anyone else in this bar.

Danny's lips press into a hard line. He knows I'm lying, but he nods anyway. "Right, well here's the deal," he tells me. "This is a college bar. It's falling apart, but it's the best bar in town. Rowdy as fuck and the customers are assholes. If you can't hack it, don't waste my time."

"I can handle it."

"You sure?"

I nod, getting back to work while he talks. "A little ass grabbing is nothing compared to the shit I grew up with. Trust me, I'm good."

"Alright," he says as I risk a glance across the room, finding the three creepy stalkers still watching me, and quickly look away again. "I'll give you a shot, but like you saw tonight, we run through bartenders like the men's bathroom runs through shithouse paper. You last three months and prove you can handle it, then I'll put you on the books. Until then, you're getting paid cash, minimum wage, and whatever tips you make are yours to take home. The more you work, the more you make. It's simple."

"Got it," I say, sliding three beers up onto the counter and taking the customer's twenty-dollar bill.

"Keep the change," the customer says with a flirty wink, trying to scoop up all three schooner glasses between his fingers at once. I smile at him and shove his change into my apron before hastily moving on to the next guy.

"What can I get ya?"

I get busy with the new order as Danny continues with his run down of how he expects this to work. "Four shifts a week minimum," he says. "Newbies don't get lucky. You'll be rostered on Friday and Saturday nights unless you can get someone to cover your shift. Bar closes at 2 a.m. If it's still busy, it stays open. The only acceptable excuse for skipping out on a shift is if you're on your deathbed or you've got an exam the next day, in which case, I'll need to see proof. Other than that, you're working. This is a business, not a daycare. I don't wanna hear about your problems, and I sure as fuck don't wanna see your problems coming into my bar. Is that understood? You leave that shit at home."

"Understood," I say with a firm nod before my eyes discreetly wander back to the three strange guys—my problems already making their way into Danny's Bar.

Danny catches my eyes and holds my stare for a while as if really thinking this over. "Why do I feel like I'm going to regret this?" he mutters under his breath before letting out a heavy sigh. "Alright, you've got the job, but you're on probation. One fuck up and you're out on your ass."

"Fair enough," I say, "and for the record, you're not going to regret it."

Danny scoffs and strides past me, heading for the overflowing cash register. "That's what they all say." He opens the till and starts going through the cash, pocketing the majority of it and leaving us just enough to give us a comfortable cash flow for the next few hours. Though at this rate, the register will be full again in a little under an hour. He turns around, his pockets bulging from the cash. "Heather will revise the roster sometime tomorrow. Make sure you give her your number and she can tell you when you're expected to come in."

A smirk plays on my lips, feeling as though I just got away with something, but I try not to let it show. "Thanks. I'm down with taking as many shifts as you've got," I tell him. "Apparently, student loans and rent don't pay themselves."

"You got that right," he says before striding past me. "I'll be in the office if anyone needs me."

Danny takes off, leaving us to our customers, and we quickly get back to work. A newfound confidence ignites in my chest, burning away all the stress of not knowing how I was going to pay my way through college. I suppose this job isn't set in stone, but I won't be doing anything to fuck it up.

Ignoring the laser-sharp stares from across the room, I focus on what I'm doing, making a point that Danny can trust me working his bar, and by the time 3 a.m. rolls around I'm utterly exhausted. My feet hurt, and despite the late hour, I've really had a great night.

My apron is heavy with tips, though I'd be stupid to assume every night is going to be like this. Tonight is game night, and because of that, there are bound to be a shitload more customers here than on a weeknight, though that only goes to show that I can't be stupid about my shifts. Every Friday night, this is exactly where I'll be, and hell, on game nights, I might even go all out on makeup and fake flirty smiles.

After securing Cara's extra cheesy burger, I make my way out of the bar while Heather and Hannah lock up behind me, promising that by my next shift, there will be a set of keys just like theirs with my name on them.

CHAPTER 3

Oakley

The night breeze wafts around me, sending goosebumps spreading over my skin as I walk back toward my apartment complex. I get all of two steps from the bar when I get the feeling I'm not alone, and I know without a doubt that those three guys are still here, lurking in the shadows, ready to fuck with me. Chills sweep through my body, and my hands shake by my sides. I pick up my pace, my feet slamming down on the pavement as I immediately regret the decision to get a job that has me walking home alone in the dead of night.

Glancing over my shoulder, I peer into the darkness, my heart racing like never before, but I don't see them. Every last bit of reason tells me I'm imagining it, tells me they left ages ago and I'm making it all up, but deep in the pit of my stomach . . . I know they're out here, stalking me, watching me, waiting for me to make one wrong move.

But why? What is it about me that's caught their attention? Do they have some sick gang rape fetish? Am I about to be slaughtered in the street for pleasure?

Fuck.

I see the entrance of my apartment complex and breathe a short-lived sigh of relief, finding a man standing by the door under the streetlight. A cigarette hangs from his lips and as I get closer, I can see the puff of smoke billowing from his mouth.

I can't trust this guy either, but the likelihood of my three stalkers going all Jack The Ripper on my ass is significantly reduced by his presence alone, and I make a mental note to thank him if I ever see him again, though I have absolutely no intention of stopping to tell him now.

Keeping my stare locked on him to avoid thinking about the three men in the shadows behind me, I try to calm myself.

This is all in my head.

I'm not about to be raped and slaughtered.

I'm okay.

With each step that brings me closer to this man, I quickly realize just how attractive he is. Hell, he's fucking gorgeous with his tanned skin and bright blue eyes. He's got that whole smoldering *Flynn Ryder* thing going on and, judging by the flirty smile he gives me when his head snaps up, I'd dare say this guy is one hell of a ladies' man.

I give him a tight smile before averting my eyes to avoid making things awkward and then go to step around him as I search for the keys to the building.

"Woah, where are you going off to in such a rush?" he questions, his eyes lighting up like Christmas as he drops his cigarette and stubs it with his boot.

A rush of butterflies surface in my stomach, and I feel a flush spreading over my cheeks. "Bed," I tell him. "Where do you think I'm going? It's after three in the morning."

"Sounds like the night's just getting started to me," he says, the corner of his lips kicking up into a flirty grin. I have to give him credit, he's keeping his distance to avoid making me uncomfortable. "You new around here? I haven't seen you before."

I nod as I slip the key into the door while trying to juggle Cara's cheesy burger. "Yeah, moved in today," I tell him, glancing up at him from beneath my thick lashes. "You?"

"Same," he says before reconsidering his response. "Well, not exactly. Been here a week or two, but still feels new. I'm in 107."

"No way," I say, my eyes lifting to his before discreetly checking over my shoulder again. "Then I suppose that makes you one of my new neighbors. I'm in 106."

"Well, in that case, maybe I should start making a habit of asking my neighbors for a jug of milk," he says with a flirty wink.

"A jug of milk?" I laugh. "What is this? The 1920s?"

"Oh, shut up. You know what I mean," he says, rolling his eyes and almost looking embarrassed, though the confidence radiating off him suggests that being embarrassed is not something this man is familiar with. He offers me his hand. "I'm Dalton, by the way. Dalton Eros."

Not wanting to be rude, I slip my hand into his and get a rush of warmth the moment my fingertips brush against his skin. "It's nice to meet you, Mr. Eros. I'm Oakley," I tell him, drowning in the rush of feeling his warm, calloused hand against mine.

His hand tightens around mine, and in one swift move, he pulls me into his chest, my other hand bracing against his pecs to keep from tumbling right into him. His blazing blue stare locks onto mine, and I suck in a shallow gasp, not understanding this strange rush I get from simply being in his presence. I'm completely captivated, completely mesmerized by this gorgeous man.

He smells incredible and towers over me, yet I feel safe in his arms, and damn, it's clear from the way he feels beneath my fingers just how strong he is. His eyes become hooded, and I watch the way his gaze drops to my lips. "Would I be too forward if I asked to take you home?"

Well, shit. My heart kicks up a notch, and I'm sure he can see the desire flashing in my eyes.

"Way too forward," I say, trying to laugh it off. "I don't know about the girls you're used to fucking, but I'm not the girl who's going to spread my legs for a pretty face."

"You think all that's in it for you is nothing but a pretty face? What do you take me for?" he questions, those deep rumbly tones causing havoc between my legs. "I'm no two-pump chump, baby. I'll have you crawling out of my apartment, your throat raw from screaming my name, and your ass so sore you won't be able to sit down for a week.

Trust me, Firefly," he murmurs, his hand snaking around my body and lowering to my ass. "When I tell you I'll fuck you until the sun comes up, I mean it."

A smirk pulls at my lips. "If it weren't already after three, that'd probably impress me. The sun will be up in just under two hours. The douchebag I dated in junior high could fuck longer than that. Besides, after working for the last six hours straight, a marathon isn't exactly on my night's bucket list. Now, if you said you wanted to fuck me up against this building and make me come in three seconds flat . . . now that I would consider, but like I said, I'm not the girl who's going to spread her legs for some stranger she just met on the street."

"You see, that's our problem," he rumbles, his eyes sparkling like two blue flames in the night. "You're too fucking gorgeous to be a stranger. So what better way to get to know someone than feeling her come on your cock while she's moaning your name?"

"Sounds promising," I say, feigning consideration before I push against his chest, putting a little space between us. "But like I said, I'm not that girl. Take me out first, treat me like a lady, spoil me a little, and maybe then I might get on my knees for you. But until then, you're nothing but the stranger I met in the street."

"Ooooft," he laughs, giving me my space as he presses a hand to his chest. "Baby, that one stung."

"I'd apologize, but something tells me you get off on the pain."

"See? How could you call me a stranger when you already know me so well?"

I push the door open and step over the threshold before quickly searching the shadows again and coming up empty. "I'm going to bed, Dalton Eros. Let's hope you get the pleasure of meeting me again"

"Oh, something tells me I will," he says, those eyes sparkling so bright they almost light up the night sky.

A wide grin stretches across my face, and I shake my head, unable to believe this human exists. He's everything. Gorgeous, strong, tall, and looks that could kill. There's a hint of danger about him, but not in the same way as my three stalkers. This is much worse. A man like this has the ability to reach right into my chest, take my heart, and shatter it between his fingers, and because of that, I need to keep my distance.

But damn . . . Maybe I'll let him have his no-strings-attached fun for just a while and then cut my losses before it gets too deep. After all, skipping out on a treat like that would be a sin, and I pride myself on being a good girl. At least, I'll be a good girl for the right man.

Not bothering with a goodbye, I let the heavy door close between us and all but skip down the trashed hall. The party here tonight must have been huge to have caused this type of chaos, and to be honest, I kinda figured the asshole guy directly across the hall was hosting the thing. Though how could that be true if he skipped out on the party just to stalk me all night with his equally creepy friends?

Quickly hustling my ass down the hall, I become all too suspicious of the doors around me, expecting one of my neighbors to jump out at me and drag me kicking and screaming into one of their apartments. Only, I know without a doubt those bastards are lingering out in the darkness of the street, Dalton Eros being the only reason I was able to escape with my freedom.

God, I really do owe him.

Finding apartment 106, I slip my key into the lock and push the door open before hastily locking it behind me and flicking each of the deadbolts. "Shit, are you only getting in now?" Cara asks from the couch.

I whip around, wide eyed as I find Cara exactly where I left her, Kindle still in hand. "It's after three. How are you still up reading?"

"Call it a gift," she says, sitting up straighter on the couch and eyeing the takeout bag in my hand, excitement drumming in her stare. "Is that my extra cheesy burger?"

"Yup," I say, walking through the apartment and placing it on the counter as she pounces on it like a starved lion.

"I'm assuming since you've been gone all night, you got yourself a job?" she questions, pulling out her burger and getting stuck into it. I nod and she grins as though we've just gotten away with something. "Danny still an asshole?"

I really consider her question before responding. "I wouldn't call him an asshole," I muse. "More like an over-tired businessman who's sick of having to deal with college students running his bar."

Cara laughs around a bite of her burger. "So . . . still an asshole?"

"Yeah," I admit. "A fair asshole though. The guy gave me a job when he didn't have to and because of that, I can now pay my rent. Plus, the tips are pretty good."

"Yeah," she says with a heavy sigh. "I forgot about the tips. It was game night, right? I always used to rake it in on game night."

"Sure was," I tell her, walking around the island counter and finding a glass before filling it with water. "Bet you don't get those kinds of tips working in the bookstore."

"True," she says, a grin stretching across her face. "But I also don't get minimum wage in the bookstore."

"Ooooh, checkmate," I laugh, pulling out the chair beneath the counter and dropping my ass into it. "Hey, what do you know about the guys who live around us? Like, the scary as shit dude directly opposite and the guy just down from us—the one I share a bedroom wall with."

"Apart from the fact they like to party and fuck? Not much," she tells me, her burger hovering in the air in front of her. "They all moved in a few weeks ago at the start of the term, and apart from their parties, they keep to themselves. The guy directly opposite us gives me the creeps so I keep away from him, but he's friends with the guy just down from us."

"The one who likes to fuck?"

"No, no," she rushes out. "Well . . . yes, he's friends with him too, and don't get me started on that guy. He's a different kind of breed. He has this little black snake and it just—"

"Weaves through his fingers?" I finish for her.

"SHIT. YES!" she blurts out. "Is that not fucked up?"

"So fucked up," I agree. "I saw him with it on my way out. I didn't know whether to scream or shit my pants."

"When in doubt, always shit your pants, girl," she tells me, her burger long forgotten. "That guy gives me the shivers. I think his name is Cross, or maybe that's his surname. . . I could be wrong. I don't know, but either way, I try to keep my distance."

"Good to know," I say, chills sweeping over my body. "But if he's not the friend you were referring to, then who is?"

"Oh, umm . . . I meant one of our other neighbors. I'm sure you'll meet him soon enough. Shaggy blond hair, looks like a surfer dude. He will more than likely try to get you in bed at some point. His name is Sawyer, and he lives a little further down the hall."

"Oh yeah, I know the one you're talking about," I say, picturing him as clear as day, sitting next to the two others at the bar and watching me all night. "So this creepy guy directly opposite us, what's his name?"

Cara shrugs her shoulders, and I watch as her brows furrow. "I, uhh . . . I actually don't know," she says, staring off at the wall, deep in thought as though the name will magically come to her. "I don't share any classes with him, and apart from the guys I see him with from our building, I don't think he talks to anyone else."

"Right, okay," I say, not sure how to feel about that. If people knew about him, knew his name and what he was like, then I could get a better picture of the guy. I could find out if he's a man-slut, or if he's someone I need to be wary of, but the fact he's a mystery, even to his closest neighbor, doesn't sit well with me. Wanting to shake off the unease, I flip the conversation, needing this to go in a different direction. "What about the neighbor on our other side, like directly beside us? 107. The guy with the bright blue eyes."

A sly grin pulls at her lips. "Ahhh, so you met Dalton Eros?" she muses, a knowing sparkle glistening in her eyes.

"Is that his name?" I question as though I haven't already memorized it, glancing away so she can't see the deception in my stare.

Cara laughs. "Trust me, Dalton Eros is not a name you're going to forget anytime soon, and if you're lucky enough, you'll be screaming it until your throat hurts. That guy fucks like a god."

My brows arch as I glance her way, watching how her cheeks flush. "I take it you know this from your own experience?"

"Damn straight," she laughs, a wide grin across her face. "I think it was the day he moved in . . . maybe the day after, and he was just walking in while I was walking out. I don't even know how it happened. One second I was passing him in the hallway, and the next thing I knew, I was bent over his kitchen counter getting rammed like never before. And that guy . . . goddamn. He's big. Pierced, manscaped, and BIG. I haven't been fucked like that before, like things I didn't know could stretch, were stretching."

"Holy shit."

"Yeah."

"So . . ." I say slowly, catching her eye. "Are you the type of girl who's going to get jealous or pissed off if her new roomie fucked the same guy? Or is he kinda a no-go zone now?"

"Girl, no. Fuck that guy as hard as you can," she tells me. "You see, I'd like to be one of those girls who could stick with the same guy and grow attachments, but let's be real. I'm a whore and love it. I try not to go back for seconds, unless I'm desperate, but also . . . I'm kinda that girl who makes things awkward after sex."

"Huh?" I laugh. "What are you talking about?"

Cara buries her face in her hands, almost embarrassed to be sharing this. "I just . . . I don't know. I can't act like a normal human being after getting dicked down. I get awkward and weird. Getting the guy in bed and stroking his ego . . . and everything else comes so naturally to me, but the second he's finished wiping his cum off my back—awkward."

I laugh and take a sip of my water. "Tell me you're lying."

"Wish I could," she tells me. "Dalton Eros. After fucking him, I told him how pretty his dick was and then awkwardly curtseyed while thanking him for thoroughly rocking my world."

"Oh, well . . . that's not *that* bad."

She gives me a blank stare. "I did it in an old British accent, then spanked my own ass and galloped out of his apartment like a horse."

"Holy shit."

Cara nods. "When I pass him in the hallway now, he averts his eyes so quickly, and just yesterday, I stepped out of my apartment at the same time he did, and I've never seen anyone backtrack so fast. I can still hear the sound of his door slamming closed. It was like an echo sailing down the hall."

I can't hold back my laugh and have to slam my hand over my mouth to muffle the sound.

"It's okay," she tells me. "Laugh all you have to, but just know that the humiliation was worth every second."

Taking another sip of my water, I stand and step back from the counter, more than ready to call it a night. "You know what?" I tell her with a fond smile. "I think you and I are going to get along just fine."

CHAPTER 4

Oakley

My phone buzzes on my bedside table, and I open my eyes to the early afternoon sun streaming through my window. I groan, throwing my arm over my face, trying to block out the sun, but now that I've seen it, it's impossible to ignore.

Letting out a heavy sigh, I reach for my phone, feeling around the table until my hand curls around the cool metal. Tearing it off its charger, I bring the phone over my face and squint into the light as I unlock it. There's a text from Heather, and I quickly open it while wishing she could have allowed me just a few more hours of sleep. I'm a solid twelve-hour-a-night sleeper, and if I don't get in all the z's, I have a tendency of becoming one hell of a cranky bitch.

Heather - Hope you're holding up after last night's shift. The rest of your week looks like this. Let me know if there are any problems. Saturday: 7pm–close, Monday: 5pm–10pm, Wednesday: 5pm–10pm, Friday: 7pm–close.

I quickly start hashing out a response.

Oakley - No problem. I'm good with all of those.

Heather - Perfect. I won't be in tonight, but check in with Hannah. She'll have a set of keys for you. Don't lose them because I'm not getting you another.

Assuming she's not someone who requires a response to every single text, I put my phone down and throw my blankets back before climbing out of my shitty bed. Don't get me wrong, I slept like a baby, but that's only because I was so exhausted after my first shift. Any other night, I would have struggled to sleep on that lumpy mattress. It'll have to do for now though. The second I'm able to save up a bit of cash, once I'm on top of my loans and rent, a new mattress will be my first priority.

I drag my feet as I make my way to my bedroom door, and as my gaze rises and I reach for the handle, I come to a standstill, my eyes widening. A matte black card, the size of a playing card, has been stuck to the back of my door with a small dagger, a glossy black E directly in the center, pierced by the sharp blade.

My heart races, and I find myself just staring at it, unable to move.

I know I was tired when I came home last night, but I'm damn sure that wasn't there. "Cara?" I call out, reaching for the door handle and pulling it open just a fraction, keeping my eyes glued to the black card as if it will disappear at any moment.

I hear her from her bedroom, groaning from being woken. "Oh my God, no. I thought we talked about boundaries."

"I'm not fucking around, girl. Get your ass in here."

She groans a little more, but I hear her throw the blankets back before trudging out of bed. Her door creaks, and I hear her footsteps on the timber floorboards before she finally appears in front of my room. "This better be important."

I clench my jaw, second-guessing everything I learned about this girl yesterday. Reaching out into the hallway, I grip her arm and pull her into my room before closing my door and pointing to the black card stabbed to the back of it. "Did you do this?"

Her eyes bug out of her head and she blinks rapidly, trying to focus. "What the fuck?" she breathes, shaking her head, fear flashing in her eyes. "I . . . no. I swear, I didn't put it there."

"Then how the fuck did it get here?" I question. "I know damn well it wasn't there when I went to bed last night. I would have noticed it. Plus, I locked and deadbolted the door when I came in after my shift. You're the only other person in this apartment."

"Hey, don't be accusing me of something I didn't do," she argues, getting defensive. "When I tell you I didn't do this, I mean it. I went to bed like twenty minutes after you did and didn't leave my room until right now."

I point to the door again, frustration burning me from within. "Then how the hell did this black card get stabbed to the back of my door?"

She shakes her head. The longer she looks at it, the more freaked out she seems to get. "I have no fucking idea. I watched you deadbolt the door," she says, moving closer to the back of my door to get a better look at the silver dagger and what looks to be some kind of calling card . . . but for what? "This shouldn't be possible. Are you sure it wasn't there before you went to bed? You were pretty exhausted. You could have easily missed it."

"There's no way I would have missed that," I mutter. "Besides, you were here all night. You would have seen if someone came in, right? Did anyone come knocking on the door? Or did you leave for a minute?"

"No, nothing. I literally didn't move from the couch all night."

I drag my hands over my face, pushing them up into my hair as I pace my room, my gut telling me what I already know. Our creepy as fuck neighbors did this. There's no other explanation. They were stalking me all night, and now they've somehow managed to slip into my room in the dead of night to put this here.

My hands shake as Cara moves even closer to the back of the door. "E," she murmurs. "What does that even mean?"

"I've got no fucking idea," I tell her. "But I think we've got bigger problems to work out than that. Like how the hell did someone get into our apartment while we slept? And more than that, how was this asshole able to stab a knife through the door with neither of us noticing?"

Cara's whole body shakes as she fumbles back and drops her ass on the edge of my bed. "I don't like this, Oakley," she says, her eyes wide and terrified. "I swear, if you've brought some kind of mess from back home—"

"I haven't," I rush out.

"Swear it to me," she insists. "I read way too many dark romance books to be cool with any of this. It sounds hot in books, but in reality, I don't fucking like it. I can't handle this type of shit. If there's something I need to know or you're mixed up with some questionable dudes, then tell me now because this living arrangement isn't going to work. I'm sorry, but I need to look out for myself."

"I swear," I tell her. "I'm not mixed up with anything."

Cara watches me a second later, as if trying to figure out if she can trust me, and after what feels like a lifetime, she finally nods. "Okay," she says. "So, what do we do? Should we call the police?"

I shrug my shoulders. "I . . . I don't know," I tell her. "I think we should check the apartment first. You know, make sure nothing is missing. Check the door and windows and . . . I don't know. Try and figure out how this happened before we go and make claims to the cops that someone broke in here."

Cara lets out a heavy breath and pushes up from the edge of my bed. "Yeah, you're right," she says, striding across my room to the door. She takes the handle and pulls it wide, peering out into the hallway before thinking better of it. "You know what, you seem braver than me. Maybe you should go first."

My jaw drops. I hadn't even thought about that, but now that I have, the thought is ingrained deep in my brain, sending shockwaves of fear pulsing through my body. I hold my hand out. "Rock, paper, scissors goes first."

She clenches her jaw before finally holding out her hand. "Shit."

Ten seconds later, I creep out of my bedroom first with Cara all but glued to my back. We slink out into the living room, my gaze sweeping from left to right and the moment the front door comes into view, I scan over every single one of the locks, making sure they're exactly how I left them.

"There," Cara says with a gasp, pointing toward the living room window. "The blinds, look. They're not straight. It's like someone's climbed through them."

My brows furrow as we dart across to the kitchen, checking over the window. My hand snaps out and grips the cord for the blinds, and with a ferocious tug, the Venetians rise to the top of the window frame. Reaching for the window, I find the lock has been messed with. "Holy shit," I breathe. "Someone really did break in here."

"Oh God," Cara cries, her hands in her hair as she paces back and forth through the kitchen. "Oh God, oh God, oh God. I can't handle this."

"It's okay. I have plenty of cash from my tips last night. We'll call a locksmith and get the lock replaced before my shift tonight. We'll be okay. This is clearly just someone trying to leave me some kind of message. I just wish I knew what it was. But now the message has been left, they won't come back again."

"How do you know that?" she cries, not trusting my reasoning one bit, and to be completely honest, I don't trust it either. "You can't go to work tonight and leave me here by myself. What if this guy is some kind of messed-up serial killer who gets off on raping college girls and then guts them?"

"Fuck, thanks for that visual," I say, shaking my head, feeling as lost as ever. "Look, I can't cancel work this early. I had to fight for this job and promised that I was trustworthy. I can't risk screwing it up so quickly. But just come with me. Call a few friends and sit in the bar while I work and after I close, we can walk home together."

"Okay," she says, looking nervous. "And until then?"

"Until then . . . we pretend we're not fucking terrified and go about our day as though nothing happened. Whoever this asshole is, he's not going to get the best of us."

Her eyes are wide as she stops pacing and gapes back at me. "Really?" she questions. "Because I don't know about you, but I'm damn sure he's already got the best of me."

"We're going to be okay," I tell her, not trusting it one bit. "Go and have a hot shower and calm down, and while you do that, I'll organize the locksmith."

Cara lets out a heavy breath, her cheeks blowing out in the process, and without another word, she takes off to the bathroom. With Cara occupied, I scurry back to my room, scooping my phone off my bedside table, and as I search for a locksmith, I can't help but glance up at the calling card again.

This really is messed up.

Finding the number for a locksmith, I hit call and wedge the phone between my ear and shoulder before striding back to my door. As the phone rings, I find myself reaching up to the dagger and curling my fingers around the hilt. It's so sleek and cool with intricate designs etched into the blade. It almost looks ancient, as though someone spent way too many hours working on this thing by hand.

I yank it out of the back of my door, gripping the calling card with my other hand as it comes free. I bring the card closer to my face, scanning over every inch of it. The glossy E stands out on the black background, and I hate to admit it, but the card is almost sexy. It's alluring and draws me in, making me wonder what secrets it possesses. What the hell does the E stand for and where did it come from? Who left it here, and why is it important that I received it?

Flipping the card over, I scan the back just to check I'm not missing any important clues, but it's blank, giving absolutely nothing away. The locksmith's voice sounds through the phone, and I discard the card on my bedside table before getting busy booking him. I breathe a sigh of relief when he confirms our appointment for this afternoon, and before I know it, Cara is out of the shower and I'm getting in right after her.

The afternoon drags by as we wait for the locksmith to arrive. We don't mention the card or the dagger, but simply sit in silence, willing this bullshit to just go away. I don't need drama in my life. I had plenty of that in Missouri with my ex, and I was more than happy to leave him behind.

I hear the sound of a motorbike on the street and find myself creeping toward the living room window. The rumble is so loud, I feel the vibrations through the ground and right up into my chest. Peering out the window, a soft smile pulls at the corners of my lips, finding none other than Dalton Eros.

Last night he was covered in shadows as I talked to him in the darkness, but now, in the light of day, I see it all. He's not just gorgeous, he's delicious. Tall, muscled, and holy hell, the smoldering thing is even better than I remember. Dark pants and a black shirt hug his body, and I find myself desperate to tear it off him with my teeth.

Dalton straddles a black Harley, looking like sex on legs, and everything deep in my core clenches.

I'm in trouble.

It's one thing meeting an alluring stranger out in the street but seeing him straddling a bike like that is my weakness. I don't know how he did it, but in one fell swoop, Dalton Eros has found my kryptonite and isn't afraid to use it against me.

My mouth waters, and as if sensing my stare, Dalton glances toward my living room window. A short moment of panic tears at my chest, and I consider running for my goddamn life, but what's the point? He's seen me now. I might as well own it. Besides, a man like that knows what kind of effect he has on women.

Dalton holds my stare, and there's something raw in his eyes, something that has me ready to fuck him right there out in the street. As if he's reading the wicked thoughts ripping through my mind, a sly grin pulls across his lips. He winks and I just about die.

Holy fuck. I'm not just in trouble, I'm as good as dead.

This man will get whatever he wants from me, and I'll give it up willingly before begging for more.

He reaches for the handlebar and pulls back on it, revving the engine and letting the sound rumble recklessly through the quiet street. The sound is deafening, but damn, it's doing something to me I wasn't expecting. I'm dripping wet, and the realization of just how far I'd go to get what I need from this man almost drops me to my knees.

Dalton doesn't take his eyes off me as he puts the Harley into gear, that cocky grin still lingering. He laughs and just like that, he hits the gas, taking off down the street like a bat out of hell, leaving me gasping for air.

The chokehold this man has on me is like nothing I've ever experienced. He's got me right where he wants me, and I wouldn't have it any other way.

Moving back to Faders Bay might have just been the most careless thing I've ever done. Though one thing is for sure, if I'm gonna get screwed, then I hope to God it's by a man like Dalton Eros.

I spend the rest of my afternoon in a mess of thoughts, switching between the card and the dagger, Dalton Eros and the three fucktards who stalked me through the night. Without a doubt, I know those guys must have had something to do with breaking into my apartment. There's no such thing as coincidences. At least, not to me. The likelihood that it was anyone else is slim to none, especially the night after they followed me to work and stalked me straight back home again.

They had something to do with this. They know what this card means, and I'm not going to stop until I get to the bottom of this.

By the time 6:30 p.m. rolls around, Cara is ready to go. We lock up the apartment and make a point of double-checking all the windows, but the locksmith assured us that no one would be able to break through these new locks without physically smashing the glass to make it happen. Though I'm not going to lie, assurances from some stranger don't reassure me at all.

We make our way down to Danny's Bar, and since it's still early, the place is nearly dead. Cara finds a booth to sit in while she waits for her friends, and I leave her to go and clock in for the night. Finding a fresh apron, I wrap it around my waist and make sure to say hi to the kitchen staff.

Since there are still a few minutes before I'm due to start my shift, I do what I can to introduce myself to anyone I didn't meet last night before making my way out to the bar and getting shit sorted. Hannah has been holding down the fort, and there are a few stray glasses left out on the bar. I get busy moving them to the sink and wiping down the counter as Hannah tends to orders.

"Wow, I wasn't sure you'd be down for another shift," she says with a smirk, mixing a few vodka sunrises before sliding them across the bar to a couple of girls who look like they're ready to let loose after a hard week of college classes. "Starting on our busiest night couldn't have been easy."

"Not gonna lie, I slept like the living dead last night, but you can't get rid of me that easily," I tell her, noticing out of the corner of my eye that Cara has met up with her friends and looks a shitload more relaxed than she did in our apartment.

Feeling better about the situation, I get lost in my work and the hours quickly tick by as more customers fly through the doors until it's standing room only. Another two girls join us behind the bar, and I find the night a lot easier to get through than my last shift. There's a good flow, allowing me to spend a little extra time with each customer, making sure to give them the best service possible and ensure they want to hit me up with all the tips they've got.

There's a better mix of people here tonight as well. Last night, the bar was packed with dumbass jocks and men who wished they fit in with the dumbass jocks, but most of those guys are probably still nursing their hangovers. Tonight is all about fresh faces and students who want to let off a bit of steam. There are groups of women and men trying to hit on them, but unlike last night, there's a little more class about the place, and in turn, I'm not left filling up endless schooners of beer. I get to mix drinks. Women order cocktails I've never even heard of, and it's honestly one of the best nights of my life.

Who would have known I'd enjoy this so much?

I'm well into my shift when that same chill sails through my bones that I'd felt last night, and without even looking up, I know they're here again. My gaze discreetly sails across the room, and sure enough, they're right there in the corner, just as they were last night.

My jaw clenches and the happy, chilled vibe I've been feeling all night dissipates into thin air. I try to think back to when I got home last night. Cara said the dude with the snake was Cross and the blonde surfer dude was maybe Sawyer, but the other guy . . . the one who lives directly opposite our apartment, he's the mystery.

Thoughts of that card stabbed against my bedroom door resurface, and a shiver sails down my spine. I find myself staring straight into the eyes of the main douchebag, and without a word spoken between us, I can almost feel him knowing exactly what I'm thinking.

He did it.

It was this asshole who violated my privacy, this asshole who welcomed himself in through my living room window and crept into my bedroom while I slept.

Unease rocks through me and my hands start to shake, even more so when a wicked smirk kicks up the corner of his lips, making him look like the devil. His friends talk quietly among themselves, and I watch as they slowly make their way around the bar, moving closer and closer with each step.

I swallow hard, the thought of them actually approaching me makes me want to hurl.

"Excuse me," a girl calls from in front of me, demanding my attention. "My drink?"

"Shit, sorry," I say, trying to focus on what I'm doing, placing her drink up on the bar and taking her money, though I'm not surprised to find the tip she leaves is piss poor. I deserve it, which makes me want to scold myself for allowing these strangers to get the best of me, again.

Turning to my next customer, I suck in a breath finding Dalton Eros smirking right back at me, those smoldering good looks making me want to die. "Well, hey there, Firefly."

Oh dear God. Be cool, Oakley. Be cool.

"You stalking me, neighbor?" I chime, my lips pulling into a flirty grin.

"That depends," he murmurs, that deep rumbly tone doing wicked things to me. His eyes sparkle, and I prepare myself for whatever's about to come flying out of his mouth. "Does the fear get you hard like it does me?"

I lean forward onto the bar, letting him see the desire in my eyes, and the three disapproving stares from across the room only serve to spur me on. "Did you come here to remind me how much of a manwhore you are, or can I actually get you a drink?"

He shakes his head, his eyes practically dancing with laughter. "I came here to tell you I'm taking you out tonight," he says. "And there's not a damn thing you can do about it."

"Oh really?" I question. "I'm not sure if you've noticed, but I'm kinda working tonight."

"I'm a patient man," he tells me, leaning against the bar and bringing himself dangerously close, his lips so near to mine I can feel his sweet breath brushing against my throat. "I'll pick you up after closing."

"Does that ego of yours ever get you in trouble?"

His grin widens, and it makes the butterflies flutter through my stomach. "Like you'll never know," he tells me before pushing back off the bar and gripping it between his strong fingers. "Don't eat. I'll feed you later."

And with that, he slips away into the crowd, once again leaving me breathless.

CHAPTER 5

Dalton

"**T**he fuck do you think you're doing?" Zade demands, shoving his hands against my chest as I slip out the back of Danny's Bar, Sawyer and Cross in tow. His dark eyes blaze, and for the first time in a long time, I feel like I'm staring down the barrel of a gun. "You're getting too close. You know the fucking mission. She's my sacrifice. In two months, I'll be cutting her beating heart right out of her goddamn chest and you're trying to tell me you want to get attached to the bitch first? Fuck off, man. You're smarter than that."

"Watch yourself," I say, shoving him back. "You might be the fucking heir of Empire, but you're not there yet."

Sawyer scoffs, shaking his head. He's one of my best friends, but

I know exactly where he lies on this. "I warned you this was going to happen. You shouldn't be getting close to this chick. Stop thinking with your dick, man. You're gonna get us all in trouble, and worse, you're gonna get attached. You need to cut it off with this chick."

"What's the big fucking deal?" I say, stepping out into the alley and lighting up a cigarette. "Apart from stalking her last night, have you even had a conversation with the girl?" Zade glances away. He knows I'm damn right. "She's horny as fuck, and don't pretend you haven't noticed. If I'm not laying it down, she'll find it somewhere else. This way, we can keep her close. She won't be out there looking for dick if she's got it right next door."

Cross runs his hand through his hair, letting out a heavy breath before looking at Zade. "Fuck, man. He's got a point. We can't risk her slipping away."

"She won't slip away," Zade argues, leveling Cross with a lethal glare. "There's four of us and one of her. How fucking hard can it be to keep her in our sights? We live right across the hall from her. None of us need to be getting attached. Forty-one fucking days and she'll be dead. Do you really want to get attached to that? Because I won't fucking hesitate to take her out. I don't give a shit if you fall for the bitch. I'm not risking it. If I don't make this sacrifice on the sixtieth moon, I don't claim leadership. I don't need to explain this to you, man. You fucking know how important this is."

I clench my jaw, hating how fucking hard he's going on this. It's been a little over two weeks since he dragged that dagger across his old man's throat, finally taking the bastard out. Everything was cool, he went and performed his rituals just as tradition dictates, but something else happened there . . . something he's not telling us, and whatever it is, it's got him all kinds of fucked up.

"What's this really about, Zade?" I question, stepping up to him. "You've never given a shit how I've gotten my dick wet before. Why start now?"

"Do you not see what position you're putting me in?" he says, the sound of the bar deafening behind us. "You're going to fall for this chick, and I'm going to slaughter her without a second thought. There are thousands of other chicks around here who are willing to suck your dick. Fuck one of them instead. I don't need this to get complicated."

"When have I ever fallen for some random girl?" I question. "Come on, man. You know me better than that. You've been my best friend since we were kids. When I tell you I can handle this, you should be able to trust me."

Zade drags his hand down his face. "I don't fucking trust anyone."

"Yeah, you made that crystal clear," I tell him. "But either way, Oakley's expecting me to pick her up after her shift, and I fully intend to do that. Besides, did you see the way she was watching over her shoulder last night? You three have already fucked with her head. Just because you're going to end her life in forty-one days, doesn't mean you need to make the last two months of her life miserable."

"He's right," Sawyer says. "The Circle specifically stated she had the heart of an innocent. We might not be the kind of guys a father wants his little girl fucking with, but we're not about to spend the next two months torturing her. Besides, if we go too hard, we risk her packing up her shit and taking off. She's already scared and she needs something to keep her grounded. Something that excites her about being in Faders Bay and makes her want to stick around, despite her fear. Dalton can be that reason."

A grin stretches across my face, and I watch from the corner of my eye as Cross shakes his head, knowing I've got Zade right where I want him. The fucker can't argue with that logic.

"Fuck," he grunts, his jaw clenched as his hands ball into tight fists. He steps into me, barely able to control the wild, reckless emotions exploding through his system. "If you fuck this up, it'll be your heart I offer up as a sacrifice. You got that, Eros?"

"I'm not gonna fuck it up. I know what I'm doing."

"I've got a lot of enemies, man," Zade warns, grabbing the back of my head and forcing me in close. "It's one thing for The Circle members to know who she is, but if word gets out to the rest of Empire that she's my sacrifice, there's no telling what could happen. There'll be a target the size of Texas on her fucking head, a target not even we could protect her from. They'll do anything to keep me from getting in power."

"You don't think I know that?" I spit, tearing away from him, not lost on the fact that we have to protect her in order to be the ones to kill her. "I know what's at stake just as much as you do. You don't think we'll all suffer right along with you? You might have the blood of Empire running through your veins, but it's all of our necks on the chopping board. If anybody else gets into power, we're all fucking dead. They'll take us all out."

Zade lets out a heavy breath, visibly trying to calm himself as Cross steps forward. "It's in our best interest to keep her close, man," he mutters. He's usually a man of very few words, but when Easton Cross speaks, you fucking listen.

Zade looks back at me, shoving a finger into my chest. "Take her to the rooftop, nowhere else," he says, knowing damn well we have security cameras already set up all around that building and he'll be able to keep an eye on us. "I don't want her getting familiar with this city. If you're doing this, you're going all the way. I want her dependent on you, reliant, can't go a fucking day without checking in with you. You got it? Make her fall in love with you. Become her whole fucking world."

I look my best friend dead in the eye, a grin pulling at my lips as her gorgeous face flashes in my mind, the very thought of getting to play with this girl getting me hard. Making her fall in love with me might just be the best thing I'll ever do.

"Consider it done," I tell him just moments before watching the three dickheads slink in through the back door of Danny's Bar, more than ready to spend their night watching over our girl, protecting her from the very people we belong to.

Candice rumbles down the street, the purr of her engine almost as good as the feel of my cock sinking into a slick, warm cunt. Exactly what I plan on doing with Oakley tonight. And if she's anything like I've imagined her to be, tonight is going to be one hell of a good night.

It's a little after two in the morning when I pull up out front of Danny's Bar and peer through the old windows. The lights are still on, but from what I can tell, they're just starting to close up. There are still a few people lingering outside, and I can clearly make out Zade, Cross, and Sawyer hidden in the shadows across the road.

I meet Zade's stare, and with a firm nod, the three of them make their way back toward the shitty apartment complex, where I don't doubt they'll use this opportunity to slip into her room and get a feel for her space. She was home last night, and despite my efforts to try and get her out of her apartment, it just wouldn't happen. She may be desperate to spread those pretty thighs for me, but she kept her word. She wasn't about to fuck a perfect stranger she met on the street, despite being her neighbor. They'll get in there tonight though. Cara is all too willing to help out where needed. After all, she's been dropping to her knees for Zade for years.

After waiting ten minutes, Oakley comes out of Danny's Bar with two of the other girls, and as one of them locks up, Oakley glances back over her shoulder, watching me through a curious stare. The corners of my lips kick up into a wicked grin, letting her see the filthy intentions in my eyes. Her cheeks flame the brightest shade of red, and I'm more than ready to see just how red I can make her.

She says goodbye to the other girls and they each go their separate ways, one of them walking in the same direction the boys had gone. And if she knew what kind of men she was walking toward, she'd be smart to run the other way.

Zade DeVil is not a good guy. It's as blunt as that. He takes what he wants, not caring who or what must suffer at his hands to get it. But despite his calculating, lethal ways, he's still my best friend. It's not his fault his father molded him into the perfect soldier. Hell, the asshole didn't need an army when he had Zade, his perfect little pet. He's just that good at what he does. If only the great Lawson DeVil knew what kind of monster he'd created, he wouldn't have been so careless as to allow him to get close enough to slit his throat. He all but handed Zade the keys to his kingdom, though one way or another, Zade was going to take them. Empire has always belonged to him, it's only a matter of making it official.

Oakley turns and makes her way toward me, taking her sweet-ass time, her arms slowly crossing over her chest. She stops short and leans up against the streetlight, watching me with that same curious stare. "Not gonna lie, I wasn't sure if you'd actually show."

Fuck, I love this banter with her. She's not afraid to bring the claws out, and it only makes me that much more excited to start this little dance with her. It's a shame Zade has to end her. I would have liked to keep her smart mouth around.

I arch a brow, feigning offense. "You think I'm the kind of guy to fuck you around?"

"How would I know? You're nothing but a stranger with a pretty face, remember? You could be a serial killer for all I know."

Close. But not quite. The boys and I don't technically qualify for serial killer status. Though that doesn't mean taking a life doesn't get us just as hard. We kill out of requirement, out of defense, or because the order has been handed down by The Circle. It's what we've been trained to do, and damn it, we're fucking good at our jobs. Though, some of us like it a little more than the others.

"If you really thought I was a serial killer, you would have slipped out the back door and taken off before I got here."

"Don't pretend like you know me," she says with a flirty smile. "I could be in the market for a serial killer. How would you know? Perhaps that kind of psychological mind fuck is what I look for in a man."

"Then I suppose you better climb on and find out," I tell her, watching as she pushes off the streetlight and strides toward me.

Oakley doesn't hesitate, stepping in beside Candice and throwing her leg over the back of my bike until she's straddled right behind me, her warm cunt pressed right up against my ass as her hands slip around my waist. "What are you waiting for, Dalton Eros?" she murmurs in my ear, her lips brushing against my skin, saying my name with the kind of purr that has me ready to bend her over this fucking bike and fuck her right here in the street. "You said you'd feed me, and I don't know about you, but I'm starving."

I groan, the sound vibrating through my chest, and without another moment of hesitation, I reach for the handlebars and take off down the street. Oakley squeals, her long blonde hair flying out behind her as she curls her arms tighter around my waist, holding on for dear life.

"Holy fuck," she booms. "This is amazing."

"Just you fucking wait, Firefly."

I hit the gas, taking us faster, and her laugh of glee in my ear does strange things to me. I fucking love it. I've taken plenty of girls on the back of my bike, but not one of them has reacted like this, and I sure as fuck haven't reacted to them like this either.

My hand falls to her thigh as we sail down the road, taking us deeper into the city, and I don't miss the way her fingers slip under the front of my shirt, plastering her hand to my stomach. Her skin is like fire against mine, burning every inch she touches like electricity sizzling between us.

Bringing Candice to a stop outside the best kebab store in the city, and probably the only one still open, Oakley places her hand on my shoulder and uses me to keep her balance as she climbs off. I cut the engine and follow her into the store before ordering for us both and making sure they're packaged up to go.

"Wait," Oakley says as I go to stride back out to my bike. "We're not eating now?"

Glancing around the filthy store, I look back at her, more than ready to break her heart. They might have the best kebabs in the city, but they're also dangerously close to being shut down due to multiple violations, though luckily none of them have anything to do with the way they cook their food. Besides, if I plan on winning this girl over, it's not going to be done here. "Nah, but don't worry. It'll only be another minute and then you can eat."

"Wow, that's bold," she mutters, teasingly. "Starting a first date off by depriving a woman of food after telling her not to eat all night. This better be worth it."

A smirk cuts across my lips as I glance back at her. "Doubting me so soon?"

Oakley rolls her eyes, but I see nothing but intrigue shining through them, and damn do they shine bright. "Where are you taking me anyway?" she asks, narrowing that curious stare on me again.

"You'll have to wait and see," I say, leading her back to Candice. "Now get on so I can thoroughly rock your world."

Oakley laughs as she does exactly as I've asked. "There you go with that misplaced confidence again."

"Trust me," I tell her, starting up Candice and smirking as the vibration rocks through the seat, making Oakley gasp and clench her thighs around me. "I haven't misplaced a damn thing."

Hitting the gas we take off, flying down the road for another ten minutes, though it seems as though time stands still with the way her hand slips beneath my shirt and claims every inch of my torso as her own.

I pull up into the valet parking of The DeVil Hotel and leave Candice running as I offer Oakley my hand. She gets off and stands on the pavement as I hand my keys to the night valet, Joe, who's worked here for as long as I can remember. I'd trust this guy with my life. Hell, there have been times where I've meant that literally. Joe's worked under Empire, specifically under Zade's father, Lawson, for at least the last twenty years, and he's so much more than just a valet. He's been there when we needed a quick exit. At times even been the one to offer lifesaving medical treatment when we've come barreling back here, knocking on death's door. I owe Joe my life, but right now, it's not something Oakley needs to know about.

"Mr. Eros," Joe says with a firm nod, taking my keys.

"Joe," I say with a nod of my own, moving straight past him as I place my hand on Oakley's lower back, leading her into the hotel Zade owns.

"Seriously?" Oakley asks, stepping through to the lobby and glancing up at the impressive high ceilings of the most luxurious hotel in the city. "You brought me to a hotel? What kind of girl do you take me for?"

"First off, you're exactly the type of girl I think you are, don't try to deny that. It's not a bad thing," I tell her, leading her to the private elevator. "And secondly, get your mind out of the gutter. Just because we're in a hotel, doesn't mean I brought you here to fuck. Though that can certainly be arranged."

Oakley laughs as the elevator door opens and I lead her inside it. She walks in front, and I put myself in a position to purposefully have to lean across her to press the button for the rooftop. She sucks in a gasp at just how close I am, though I don't see how this is any different than having her warm cunt pressed right up against me on my bike.

"Rooftop?" she questions, eyeing me with suspicion. "How do you have access to the rooftop?"

"My friend owns the hotel," I explain. "He lets me come up here anytime I need."

"Ahh, sounds like I'm going after the wrong friend," she teases.

I laugh. If only she knew exactly what that friend wanted with her.

The elevator starts to take off, and I know I only have a few seconds to hear that soft gasp, and damn it, there's not a thing I wouldn't do to hear it again. Wanting to see just how far I can push her, I move in front of her, the privacy of the elevator making this moment more intense.

The tension rises as she lifts her gaze to mine, her jaw popping open as a soft exhale of oxygen escapes her plump lips. I step into her and she backs up, but I keep going, getting closer and closer until her back is against the far wall of the elevator, her perfect tits pressed up against my chest.

I see the rapid thrumming of her pulse at the base of her throat, and I will myself not to curl my fingers around it. She's not ready for that yet, but she will be in time. Dipping my head, I bring my lips right next to her ear, not saying a damn word, not even touching her and that's exactly where I stay, letting her feel the brush of my breath against her skin. The rest is up to her.

The silence is deafening, and I lock my hands on the railing on either side of her hips, caging her in as her hand slips up the front of my shirt, her fingers spreading wide over my chest. She starts to tilt her head, opening up her neck for me, silently begging me to kiss her there, but I don't dare. The tension is too thick, and I fucking crave it.

Oakley sucks in a deep breath, her chest rising and falling in quick movements, and I know without a doubt that she'll close the distance, but the elevator dings with our arrival at the rooftop. The second the door slides open, the tension rushes out of the small metal box, and a grin spreads wide across my face.

Realization dawns in her eyes, and I take a step back, all too fucking proud of myself.

"Oh, shit," she breathes, refusing to move, needing a minute to recover. Her eyes remain locked on mine but her rapid breathing doesn't slow. "That was a risky game."

"No, Firefly," I say, blocking the elevator door to keep it from closing between us. "That was just a taste."

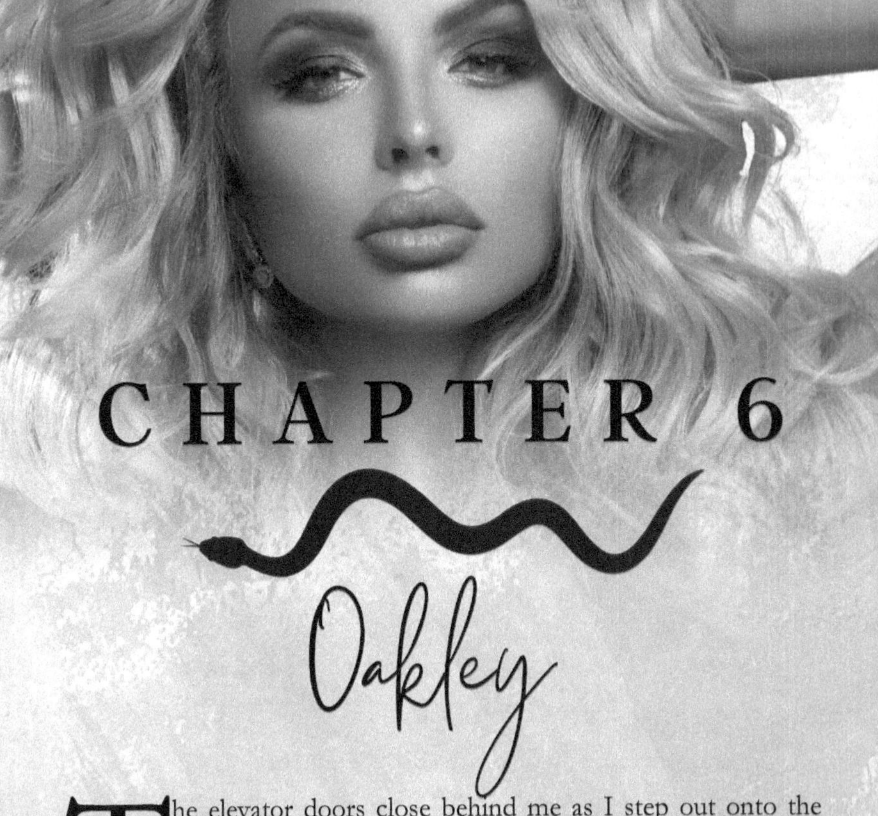

CHAPTER 6

Oakley

The elevator doors close behind me as I step out onto the rooftop of one of the tallest buildings in the city, and I'm instantly struck by the breathtaking view. "Holy shit," I whisper, my voice getting lost in the soft breeze.

I walk right up to the edge, gripping the railing as I peer out at the stunning skyline. It's close to three in the morning, and the city is clouded in darkness, but the soft glow of moonlight combined with the city lights makes for a sight I've never been so lucky to witness before.

A set of strong arms grips the railing on either side of me as I feel Dalton's wide chest press against my back, his warmth completely consuming me. He cages me in, and if he were anyone else, I'd have his balls for how forward he's been with me tonight. Yet there's something about him that has me craving his every touch. I mean, damn, that bullshit in the elevator. He barely touched me, yet I felt like I'd never been so thoroughly fucked in my life.

One thing is for sure. Dalton Eros is not only trouble, he's wicked in all the right ways. He's going to destroy me, and I'm going to drop to my knees and let him.

He stands behind me for a moment, letting me take it all in before his hand falls to my waist, gently squeezing. "Come on," he says. "Let me feed you."

Fuck yes! It's the moment I've been waiting for all night.

My stomach grumbles as I turn to face the rest of the rooftop. My eyes widen, finding a full basketball court and a garden area with sheltered seating. Across the other side of the elevator is a heated pool, steam skimming along the top of the water, barely visible in the night.

My gaze slowly sweeps around the rooftop. It's simply incredible, there's no other way to put it. It was created this way with purpose, like some kind of retreat or escape to get away from the horrors of real life and enjoy the little things the world has to offer.

Dalton starts leading me across the roof, and just when I expect him to lead me toward the garden with the seating, he steps to the right, heading toward the basketball court. "Do you play?" I question, pointing toward the court.

"Something like that," he mutters before indicating for me to take a seat at the edge of the court. He hands me the bag of takeout, his eyes expressing exactly what he's thinking. "Eat up, Firefly. You're gonna need your energy for what I plan to do to you."

I gulp. Fucking gulp.

Dalton doesn't linger on his comment, just tears his gaze away and shuffles down the court as though he'd simply stated what day of the week it was. He scoops up a discarded basketball and starts jogging across the court while dribbling the ball. He shoots from halfway down the court and the ball effortlessly drops right through the hoop, the shot coming so natural to him, it's clear he's been playing all his life.

My stomach grumbles again and not bothering to wait for Dalton to join me, I dig in and eat my kebab as though no one is watching. Though I'd be wrong because, despite not looking my way, I know he's watching every little move I make. "Holy crap," I groan, the kebab going down like a treat. "This is so good."

"Thought you might like it," he murmurs, jogging after the ball, making me wonder how often he comes up here and just fucks around on the court.

"Tell me," I start, following his every move. "Do you bring all the girls up here?"

He shrugs his shoulders. "Not really. Most chicks want to be wined and dined, but that's not really my style, and I figured it wasn't yours either."

"Damn straight," I say, regretting my decision to strike up a conversation as my half-eaten kebab stares back at me, silently begging me to take another bite. "I like this better. It's chilled. There's no forced conversation across a small wobbly table, just two people hanging out."

"What kind of shitty restaurants have your dates been taking you to? Small, wobbly tables? Fuck, Firefly, sounds like you've been screwing around with little boys, not real men."

"Let me guess," I tease. "You're one of these mysterious *real men?*"

"I'll let you be the judge of that," he tells me, glancing back and holding my stare. "But just so we're clear, only a real fucking man can make you come like I'm gonna."

"You're pretty damn sure of yourself."

His lips kick up into a wicked grin, and I see a hint of danger flashing in his eyes that has me ready to kick this party up a notch. I take another bite of my kebab before laying it down on the wrapper and getting up. Making my way across the court, I hold my hands out and he instantly passes the ball.

I start moving across the court, slowly jogging and bouncing the ball as he stands back and watches me through a strange, curious stare. My game sucks. I wasn't a sporty kid and my hand-eye coordination is non-existent, but it's enough to not make me look like a complete idiot. I shoot the ball and it hits the rim of the hoop before thankfully dropping through the basket.

The ball bounces twice before I'm able to catch it, and I turn around, ready to head back up the court toward Dalton. "Alright, Mr. Hotshot, tell me something about yourself," I say, realizing just how comfortable I am up on this roof with him. It's so easy and natural, and I honestly wouldn't have tonight any other way.

"What do you want to know?" he questions, catching the ball as I bounce it back to him. He takes off at a sprint, side-stepping around me like a pro and launching himself into the air before dunking the ball through the hoop. He doesn't even break a sweat.

"Ummm . . . tell me one of those dark thoughts that wander around your mind that's not socially acceptable to say out loud."

Dalton glances back at me, his brow arching as he pauses, the ball locked between his strong hands. "Ooh, that's a dangerous line of questioning," he says, his eyes lighting up, clearly intrigued by the sudden turn our night has taken. "Are you sure you want to introduce yourself to the demons living in my mind so soon?"

"Wow, I'm shocked. You can stand right across from a woman and tell her how you're going to make her scream, yet you hesitate with this. Interesting."

He bounces the ball, the sound flowing with the breeze. "Hey now, I was just trying to save myself from coming across as a douchebag, but if you really want to know, I'm down to share."

"Hit me with it," I tell him. "What naughty little thoughts go through your head that you can't say out loud?"

Dalton smirks and throws the ball from the center of the court, effortlessly dropping it through the hoop. He turns and walks backward toward the hoop, keeping those blazing blue eyes locked on me, not looking the least bit apologetic for what he's about to say. "Depressed girls give the best head because they don't care about breathing anymore."

My jaw drops, and I suck in a gasp. "You did not just say that," I laugh, not sure whether to be appalled, shocked, or simply amused.

"You asked for it," he says, shrugging his shoulders. "But don't think you're off the hook. Hit me with it, Firefly. What nasty little thoughts circle your head that's not socially acceptable to say out loud?"

Sucking my bottom lip between my teeth, I really consider his question, not having thought this through one bit. I was more than ready to ask the same of him, but actually answering it? Well, shit. That's a lot of pressure for one girl.

There's a million nasty little thoughts that fly through my head on a daily basis, but nothing I should be admitting to this guy. "Ummm, okay," I say, grinning so wide I feel the apples of my cheeks squishing up toward my eyes. "Sometimes I find myself wondering what a guy would look like trying to pee if his dick had been cut off. Like . . . is it just gonna spurt everywhere, full on fountain style, or is it going to dribble out all day like a leaking tap? Who knows?"

Dalton stares back at me, horror in his bright blue eyes. "Oh, baby, you're nasty," he tells me while shaking his head. "But this shit ain't real. Tell me something that's buried a little deeper. Don't feed me this surface bullshit."

"Okay," I say, rising to the challenge and taking a few steps toward him. "Getting off with my vibrator is a shitload better than sex with a man."

His whole face drops and there's almost heartbreak in his eyes. "Goddamn, Firefly. All that proves is you really have been fucking around with immature little boys up until now. But don't worry, I got you," he says, stepping right into me and pulling me into his arms, holding me as though my confession truly is the worst thing that could ever happen to anyone. "I'm gonna make this right, okay? There's nothing to worry about."

Rolling my eyes, I shove away from him, realizing all too late that he's just fucking with me. "You're an asshole," I tell him. "But until you've had the McCumster 3000 sucking the life out of your clit at a million miles per hour while ramming yourself with a big, thick silicone cock, then you really don't get a say in the matter. There's nothing quite like it."

Dalton steps straight back into me, his eyes blazing with hunger. "You realize now that you've put the visual in my mind, I won't stop until I've got you spread out before me, showing me exactly how you fuck yourself?" he murmurs, his voice getting deeper by the second. "My eyes locked on your cunt while you slowly push that cock deep inside you. Your tight little pussy stretching around it as the tension in the room gets too high and you can barely breathe. Go ahead. Tell me that fucking yourself alone would be better than anything I could do to you."

I swallow hard. Fuck the tension in that room. The tension on this rooftop is where it's at. "How would I know?" I mutter, keeping my voice low so that he doesn't realize just how dry my mouth has become. "So far all I'm seeing from you is a lot of talk and not a lot of action."

His eyes become hooded, filled with intense desire, and I just know I won't be walking away from tonight without feeling him between my legs. He scoffs, his soft rush of breath brushing across my collar. "Oh, you'll fucking know, baby," he mutters, taking a purposeful step back, putting space between us and allowing me a second to catch my breath. "You can count on that."

Hoooooly fuck. And now I'm wet.

Needing to find just a fraction of control, I try to push the hunger away and get us back into neutral territory. "You're talking yourself up a lot over there, Mr. Eros," I tease, absolutely loving the way his name feels on my tongue, though I know I'll love the feel of his cock more. "What a shame it would be if you couldn't live up to the expectation."

Dalton laughs as though the mere thought of not being able to perform to the best of his abilities is so outrageous that it simply could never happen. "You let me worry about that," he tells me, those bright blue eyes drawing me in as he goes back to bouncing the ball across the court. "What other incriminating thoughts are hidden inside that mind of yours?"

I think it over before shaking my head. "Umm . . . I've got nothing," I say, not able to think of anything that could possibly top the last two. "Hit me with your best pick-up line."

Dalton's lips twist into a wicked grin, and it sends a shiver over my body. He lets the ball go, quickly bouncing across the court until it falls into a soft roll. He turns toward me, slowly making his way back, though the way his eyes lock on mine, it's more like a lethal stalk. "I don't need pick-up lines," he says, moving right into me again, his hands gripping my waist and pulling me in hard against him, the breath whooshing from my lungs. He dips his head, his lips hovering right by my ear and setting off something deep inside of me. His hand slowly moves up my body until his fingers curl around the base of my throat. His voice lowers, his tone deep and raw in my ear. "I'd rather pin you down, than pick you up."

Oooooh fuck.

There's no going back for me now.

Raising my chin, the hand at the base of my throat circles to the back of my neck, gripping it tighter and taking full control as though I had offered it to him on a silver platter. His warm lips come crushing down on mine, and he kisses me with all the force of his desire. It's intoxicating and my knees go weak, but he's right there, holding me up.

Dalton's tongue plunges into my mouth, claiming every inch, and I'm left solely at his mercy. A soft moan rumbles through my chest, and I can almost feel the approval radiating out of him. He's liking this just as much as I am. He craves it, needs it, he's drunk on the fucking power, and I'm going to keep giving it to him because, without a doubt, this man is about to rock my fucking world.

Cara was right. He's barely even touched me and already, I know that what happens up on this roof is going to destroy me for every other man who dares touch me. Nothing will compare to this.

The tension builds between us. We both know exactly where this is heading.

I feel the pulse throbbing deep in my core and I'm desperate to have him take me, but he doesn't dare. He leaves me wanting, letting my anticipation build until the point of insanity.

I feel the cool breeze whooshing across the rooftop as he clutches the back of my neck tighter and pulls me back, breaking our kiss. He hovers over me; those usual bright blue eyes almost pitch black and flooded with intense hunger. "Get on your knees," he rumbles, his voice thick and filled with the kind of authority I can't deny.

Raising my chin in defiance, I let him see the brat deep inside me, wanting to hear the words on his lips, telling me exactly what he wants me to do. How fast? How deep? How fucking hard? My tongue rolls over my bottom lip and I watch how he zones in on the movement, feeling as though I'm claiming back just a fraction of my power. "Why?"

Those already dark eyes flame like molten lava and the deep, raw rumble of his voice makes my knees shake. "Because I'm your fucking god now."

CHAPTER 7

Oakley

The burning hunger that assaults my body is like nothing I've ever felt, and without a damn word, I drop right to my knees, every last bit of feminism flying right off the edge of this damn rooftop. My thighs spread and my pussy aches to be touched, but I keep my stare locked on his, desperate to please him.

I've never felt like this before. Never bent to someone's will, and I sure as fuck never enjoyed it like I do now. I don't care if this man wants to throw me around like a ragdoll and fuck me until I can no longer walk. Whatever he wants, he gets.

Dalton Eros has me in a fucking choke hold. My will, my power, my body . . . they're his to do as he pleases. All I hope is that when he walks away at the end of the night, he leaves me with at least a shred of dignity so I can face the world knowing nothing I do will ever compare to this moment.

I don't even care that he's taking from me first. He's not pretending to be anything he's not. Dalton Eros is no gentleman, and he's not afraid to own it. Though, something tells me he's going to more than repay the favor.

He watches me on my knees, and the throbbing between my legs is getting out of control. I feel myself soaking through my underwear, but all I can think about is the way he grips the front of his pants, slowly lowering his fly.

Dalton reaches inside as my mouth waters, the anticipation of seeing what he's working with almost too much for me to handle. I see the way he grips his cock beneath the fabric of his pants, and I've never been so damn jealous. When he finally frees himself, he releases his cock and lets it stand free like a soldier ready for battle.

My jaw drops.

Hooooly fuck. Cara wasn't lying. I'm going to need both hands and a fucking army to get this pierced monster off.

He's more than ready for me, painfully hard and girthy. I won't even be able to close my fingers around him, let alone my mouth. I rise up higher on my knees, positioning myself right in front of him as he grips the base of his cock, those angry veins only protruding more.

He's so big, the excitement almost knocks me out, and I wet my lips, more than ready to show him just what I can do. He clenches his jaw as I hunger for the bead of moisture forming on the tip of his cock. "Fucking take it," he demands, that raw desire in his tone almost enough to make me come right here and now.

Oh, God. Yes, sir.

Reaching up, I place my hand just below and groan at just how velvety smooth his skin feels beneath my touch. I slowly move my hand up his length as I open my mouth and close it over his tip, his cool piercing rubbing against the roof of my mouth. My tongue rolls over the bead of moisture, greedily claiming it for myself. He's so fucking delicious, my eyes roll with satisfaction.

I take him deeper as I reach up with my other hand, needing to grip him with both hands as I feel him in the back of my throat, that piercing so foreign in my mouth. My tongue rolls around, feeling those angry veins and teasing him as I move up and down, giving him my absolute best work.

"That's right," he rumbles, his thick tone almost lost in the breeze. "Take it all."

I work him up and down as he groans, my name a whisper on his lips. My gaze remains locked on his, and I watch as he takes me in, my mouth never so full in my life.

Everything throbs and the desperation to feel him slamming deep inside of me consumes my every thought. My pussy aches, but I don't dare stop.

Dalton's hand weaves into the back of my hair, curling around my ponytail and taking control, moving me back and forth, his grip tightening with every thrust. I moan around him and his grunt of approval is everything I never knew I needed.

My tongue becomes his bitch, working him like a damn pro, and as he starts to move me faster, I know he's right on the edge. One hand grips the base of his cock, squeezing tighter as the other moves up and down, reaching the parts of him I just simply can't with my mouth.

"Fucking hell," he grunts, his whole body jolting, that low groan only making me crave him more. I take him harder, forcing him deeper until I'm almost gagging on his cock and, not a moment later, he roars as he comes hard, spilling his hot seed down my throat.

I swallow everything he's got to offer, not daring to stop until I take every last drop, and only then do I release the death grip I have on his overwhelming cock. He lets out a heavy breath, staring down at me in astonishment. "Where the fuck did you learn how to do that?"

"I can't spill all my secrets now, can I?" I murmur, making a show of wiping my thumb across my bottom lip.

His eyes blaze and he grips his shirt, yanking it over his head and showing off his glorious, toned body. His pecs are defined and those shoulders and arms . . . holy shit. This guy really is the whole package. "I hope you're fucking ready," he mutters darkly, gripping me by the arms and pulling me to my feet. "Because I have a few secrets of my own to share."

Oh my.

He backs me up, almost flying across the court, and I have to scramble to keep up with him, but my need is too strong and he has to hold me up. At least, until my back slams against the pole of the hoop.

Dalton grips my shirt and tears the fabric right down the center, putting my body on display as I gasp at just how quickly it's all happening. His eyes feast over my body, taking in every inch of me as

I allow the torn fabric to fall down my arms.

He catches the ruined shirt before it drops to the ground and grips my waist, quickly spinning me so that my tits press right up against the cold pole. Dalton unhooks my bra, letting it fall and without warning, reaches around me and ties my wrists around the pole, my ruined shirt the perfect bind.

He brushes my hair off my shoulder and brings his lips down over my skin as his fingers continue trailing down my body. "So fucking gorgeous, Firefly," he mutters, sounding in awe of what he's about to claim.

I groan as his lips roam over my skin, moving up my neck to the sensitive skin below my ear. "You know," he continues, his hands curving around my waist and dropping to the front of my jeans, toying with the button as his wide chest presses against my back. "I thought I was going to ease you into it, let you get used to me first. But after sucking me off like that, I wouldn't dare insult you by holding back."

Glancing over my shoulder, I push my ass back into him, grinding against that massive cock, so unbelievably ready to feel that piercing moving deep inside of me. I meet his starved stare and almost crumble. "I wouldn't expect anything less."

With that, Dalton pushes my jeans down past my hips, taking my thong right along with it. The moment I can, I step out of them, kicking them aside.

He doesn't make me wait, curling his arm around my waist and trailing down between my legs. His foot hits my ankle, kicking my legs apart, and I do exactly what he wants, widening my stance and allowing him the access he demands.

Dalton's fingers are right there, pushing through my folds and skimming over my sensitive clit. My whole body jolts, electricity pulsing through my veins. "Oh, God." I groan, only getting louder as he pushes right up into my pussy with two thick fingers.

"You're fucking soaking for me," he says, pulling his fingers out and pressing them to my lips. He trails them over my bottom lip before pushing them inside. "Suck," he demands in that same authoritative tone that got me in this position to start with.

I open wide, rolling my tongue over his fingers and tasting my arousal, and the moment he pulls them free, he grips my chin, forcing my face back to his. He kisses me deeply, his tongue lapping up what's left on my lips. "So sweet," he croons, his touch roaming back down my body.

He pushes his fingers straight back into me, only this time, they're there to stay. They move in and out, circling and massaging deep inside me, my walls pulsating and throbbing around him. I need so much more and damn it, he knows. I'm at his mercy, my body his to use as he pleases.

"Oh fuck, Dalton," I say with a breathy moan. "More. I need you inside me."

"Be patient," he tells me. "You'll get exactly what you deserve."

I'm just moments from screaming that I've been a good girl who deserves everything he's got when his thumb moves to my clit, pressing down and rubbing small, tight circles. I cry out, my head tipping back to his shoulder. His soft, satisfied chuckle is everything, and I push my ass back against his hard cock again, coaxing him to get this show on the road.

My plan works like a treat, and he groans loudly in my ear, his cock flinching against my ass, unable to resist sinking deep inside of me. And while I'm here wondering how the hell he's going to fit and just how delicious the feeling of being stretched by him will be, he's probably wondering just how warm I'll be, just how tight I'll fit around him, and more so, if I can handle him in the first place.

Fuck, I hope he's ready because I have every intention of taking all of him.

Dalton pulls his fingers free, and I almost cry out at the loss, but he takes my hips and pulls me back, one hand pressing against my back and bending me over, offering me up like a slick, warm platter. I spread my legs wide, feeling the cool breeze against my pussy, and I'm only now just realizing that I'm standing on top of the world, naked as the day I was born, every inch of me on display. There's no doubt this rooftop has surveillance cameras, and I don't doubt that every security guard this hotel has is currently sitting back, ready to watch the show. And yet, I haven't got a single fuck to give.

I feel his piercing right at my entrance, and I let out a shaky breath, relaxing every inch of my core, knowing this is going to be snug. He takes my hips again, holding me still, and the anticipation is too much. I start pushing back against him, feeling his tip enter me.

He's already stretching me wide, and I close my eyes, the pure satisfaction and pleasure knowing no bounds. Dalton groans and takes me further, his fingers digging into my hips. "Fucking hell," he mutters through a clenched jaw. "You good?"

"God, yes," I say with a pant. "Take me deeper."

He does just that, not stopping until he's fully seated inside of me, and I let out a gasp, my pussy already pulsating around him. I mean, fuck, I can practically feel him in my throat, and he hasn't even started fucking me yet. But as if on cue, he draws back until his tip is just inside me, and with a delicious thrust, he slams right back into me.

"Goddamn," he grunts and I cry out for more.

"Again."

He continues to fuck me, thrusting in and out as my clit screams for attention. I pull against my binds, needing to be touched, but he's right there, releasing my hips, one hand on my ass, the other curling over my hip and dropping between my legs.

He rubs his fingers over my clit in small, firm circles and my eyes roll to the back of my head, even more so as his other hand starts exploring. I feel him moving around, his fingers plunging into my pussy right along with his cock, stretching me even wider before gliding up to my ass and pushing them inside.

"Holy shit," I curse, every inch of my body drowning in his unbelievable pleasure. He was right. Up until this moment, I've been fucked by nothing but immature boys who knew nothing about a woman's body, but Dalton Eros—goddamn. He knows exactly what he's doing, how to touch me, how to fuck me, and how to make me scream. This is the pure, honest-to-God meaning of being fucked by a real man.

He takes me faster, my body right on the edge when he starts to rock his hips, his piercing rubbing me just the right way, hitting that spot over and over again. I grip the pole, needing to dig my fingers into something, needing a release for this undeniable pleasure.

My body is wound so tight, every inch of me screaming out of desperation, and with one final thrust, I come harder than I've ever come before. "Oh fuck, Dalton," I cry out as my orgasm tears through my body, my pussy convulsing around him. Electricity pulses through my veins, through my arms, into my fingers, and back down to my core. I clench my eyes, my toes curling with satisfaction, and as Dalton keeps working my ass, cunt, and clit, the high just keeps coming.

It's like fireworks being let off inside my body, my pussy spasms like never before, but as he keeps fucking me, keeps thrusting in and out, my world continues to be blown.

Moments pass, and as I finally start coming down, every inch of my skin becomes sensitive to his touch, and as if reading my body, he eases up, releasing me from his sweet torture. His fingers drop away from my clit and return to my hip, his fingers digging in as those desperate groans and grunts start getting louder.

I clench around him, knowing he's close and wanting to feel him come undone inside of me, I push back, taking him deeper. It takes only two more thrusts until he's right there with me, coming hard and shooting his warm load into me all over again.

His fingers relax on my hip as he lets out a heavy pant. "Fuck, Firefly. That's gotta be the sweetest pussy I've ever sunk into." I nod, barely able to form a single word as he remains seated deep inside of me. He pushes against me, forcing me to step into the pole so I can straighten up, but he keeps his hand on my bare ass. "Just so you know, I plan on claiming that too."

I drop my head back against his shoulder, barely able to keep myself up as he slowly pushes in and out of my pussy like a soft, seductive massage. "There's no way in hell that monster will fit in my ass. You'll tear me apart."

Dalton laughs, his breath brushing across my skin as he brings his hand up to cup my tit, his thumb circling my nipple and watching as it pebbles beneath his touch. "Wanna fucking bet?" he challenges. "You can handle it."

I roll my eyes and laugh. There's just no way, but I like that he thinks so highly of me.

A moment passes as we each catch our breath and before I know it, his other hand slides back down my body. He keeps moving in and out of me, lazy, pleasurable strokes, and I let out a satisfied sigh as his fingers find my clit. He rubs slow circles, and despite just how hard I came, he works my body up again.

Dalton continues teasing my nipple, playing with it as though it were the most intriguing thing he's ever seen. Then just like that, I come again, my whole world completely blinded by unadulterated pleasure.

Letting me come down from my high, Dalton pulls free of me and steps back, giving me a moment to find myself before he moves around the pole and takes my wrists. He unties my ruined shirt while keeping his sharp, skillful gaze locked on mine. Not a single word passes between us, but each of our thoughts are loud and clear—that was simply amazing.

"I've fucked around with plenty of chicks," he tells me. "But none of them feel as fucking good as you do."

"Wow," I say with a stupid smirk. "Smart man. Boasting about all the chicks he's been with just seconds after fucking me bareback. Remind me to go and get tested tomorrow."

Dalton laughs as my hands fall free, and he steps in toward me. "I wasn't trying to boast about the fact I've been a fucking whore. I was trying to explain how that sweet little cunt of yours fit around me like a fucking glove and that I plan on sinking into it every damn chance I get. Morning, noon, or fucking night, I'm gonna be right there, spreading those pretty thighs, and you better be ready for me because I won't be holding back. You and me, we're about to make magic."

Holding his stare, I soften my gaze, letting him see just how ready I am. "You've got yourself a deal," I tell him. "But if I get even a hint that you're getting attached, I'll cut you off cold turkey. I'm not interested in becoming someone's girlfriend. I'm happy to fuck around, but that's as far as we go."

"Same rules apply for you," he says, that same stupid smirk reflected on his face. "I'm not one to talk myself up, but I'm a pretty fucking awesome guy. You're the one at risk of falling in love with me."

I scoff, reaching for my pants and quickly stepping into them. "Oh, you're not one to talk yourself up?" I question, both of us knowing damn well that's all he's been doing since the moment I met him, though for once, a guy actually followed through with his promises and I wasn't left disappointed. "Could have fooled me."

Dalton laughs and strides past me, finding his shirt and tossing it to me before grabbing his pants. I hook my bra and pull his shirt over my head, his heavenly scent wrapping around me. We cut back across the court and he grabs the ball, shooting one last hoop before chasing after it and putting it back where he found it.

I stand over my discarded kebab, my heart breaking as it stares back at me. "Do you think it's still good to eat?"

"It's your funeral," he tells me. "Personally, I'd still eat it. But I want it stated, if it goes right through you and you start shitting yourself, I'm ditching you on the side of the road. I didn't sign up for that, and Candice sure as fuck didn't either."

My brows furrow as I glance up at him. "Candice?"

"Ahh, and here I was thinking you weren't the jealous type."

"I'm not, but when you mention a name I don't know, it's only human to be curious."

A grin widens across his face. "Candice Swanepoel, Victoria's Secret supermodel. I named my bike after her."

A booming laugh tears from deep in my chest. "Why am I not surprised?" I ask just as his phone chimes from deep in his pocket.

Dalton lets out a heavy sigh, almost sounding irritated at having our night interrupted, and reluctantly fishes his phone out of his pocket. He swipes his thumb across the screen and quickly glances over a text before sighing again. He goes to put his phone away when another text comes through just a second later, this one making his lips press into a hard line, his gaze becoming stony and cold.

"Everything okay?" I ask.

"Yeah," he says, dropping his phone into his pocket and glancing back at me, his eyes still sparkling in the moonlight, trying to shake it off. "But we better get going. It's getting late."

I nod, scooping up my half-eaten kebab and dumping it in the trash as Dalton presses a hand to my lower back. He leads me toward the elevator and we don't have to wait for the doors to open. We sail back down just as fast as we came up, and I find myself glancing over at him.

"What?" he questions, not missing a damn thing.

"Why do you call me Firefly?"

A soft smile settles over his face, not smirky or wicked like I usually get from him. This one is sincere and makes his eyes soften, stealing the breath right out of my lungs. "You really want to know?" he asks.

"Would I ask if I didn't?"

The elevator dings our arrival on the ground floor and we step out together, walking out to the valet parking. Dalton doesn't respond, just simply nods toward the valet who hastily retrieves the keys to his bike and hurries off to get it.

We stand in a strange silence for a few moments, and I start to wonder if everything he said to me up on the roof was all bullshit just to get me to spread my legs for him, but when the familiar rumble of his bike sounds through the underground garage and finally arrives at our feet, he dazzles me with a wide smile. "After you," he says, offering me his hand.

I take it greedily and he helps me onto the back of his bike, and not a moment later, we're taking off, heading out of the city and back toward our apartment complex. He pushes his bike to its limits and we fly through the unfamiliar streets until we pass by Danny's Bar and then finally pull to a stop in the parking lot behind our building.

Pressing my hand to his shoulder, I balance myself as I climb off, and as I go to step back and give him space, he captures my hand and pulls me in closer. "The reason I call you Firefly," he murmurs, his voice so soft I can barely hear him, "is because when I first saw you walking through the darkness, you lit up the night like a fucking firefly."

Warmth spreads through my body, and I don't know how to respond, but he doesn't give me a chance before he's moving off his bike and nodding toward our building. "Come on, maybe tonight you'll even let me walk you to your door."

I laugh and roll my eyes. "Don't think you're going to get lucky again," I tell him as he slips his key into the main door of the building. "I'll have you know, I'm a lady."

We step in through the door and let it fall closed behind us, and not a moment later, my back is up against the wall. "You're anything but a lady," he growls, his lips brushing against my throat as he presses his body up against mine, setting me off once again.

Hunger blasts through me. "Okay, I changed my mind. You can definitely get lucky again."

His soft chuckle is like music to my ears as he steps back, putting space between us and offering me a chance to catch my breath. That twisted smirk returns, and I roll my eyes, enjoying his company far more than any girl should. I'm in dangerous territory, but I stand by what I said on that rooftop. I don't want anyone falling in love with me, and I sure as hell won't be returning the favor. I've got college to get through and rent to make. Casual, hot, steamy sex with dangerously wicked men is where it's at.

We start making our way down to my apartment, and I fish my key out of my pocket as he patiently leans up against the wall. Though, if we were smart, we'd take this to his apartment. As far as I know, he lives by himself. He hasn't mentioned anything about a roommate, and I know Cara is cool, but I'm not so sure how she'd feel about listening to me ride this asshole until the sun comes up. Though to be honest, she's probably the type to listen through the wall and get off with us like some kind of messed-up threesome.

The door unlocks, and just as I glance toward Dalton, I hear the soft click of a door behind me. Knowing exactly who lives across from me, my heart kicks into gear, a gasp of fear sailing through my lips.

I whip around, but I'm too late. He's already here, towering over me. A scream tears from between my lips, and like lightning, his hand shoots out, capturing me behind my neck as his other slams up over my face, a cloth wedged between us, muffling my screams.

I fight for breath, inhaling the strange scent on the cloth, my mind instantly going fuzzy as I desperately try to fight for my freedom, searching around, but Dalton is nowhere to be seen.

Fear like I've never known consumes me, and as I look up at this terrifying stranger towering over me, I know this is the end. My body goes limp, my eyes close, and just like that, I fall into his strong arms as my world turns black.

CHAPTER 8

Oakley

My body slams against a hard wall, my head foggy and disoriented. I hear scuffles and roars of protest around me, but I can't open my eyes, can't scream for help. I try to pull myself from the fog, but it's impossible. My body feels too heavy to even attempt to fight.

What did he do to me? Where has he brought me?

My hands are yanked behind me and roughly bound, and my shoulders scream in agony just moments before something sticky covers my mouth.

"Oakley," I hear a familiar tone calling through the fog. "Firefly, come on. Wake up."

I groan, the sound piercing against my skull, the ache like nothing

I've ever known.

A door slams in the distance and my body jolts with the shock as I fight against my heavy eyelids, desperately needing to regain control of my body. Laughter sounds in the background mixed with the rough familiar grunts and groans of someone in despair.

Dalton? Is that him?

"Oakley. Fuck. Come on, wake up," grunt, "we have to get out of here."

I fight against the fog, and it slowly begins to clear, but I'm a long way from feeling like myself. Lead pulses through my veins, weighing me down, and I struggle to hold my head up, but Dalton's labored voice keeps me awake.

My heavy lids finally begin to ease, and I peer into the brightness. As reality comes back to me, I'm struck with the horrors of this new nightmare. I'm locked in what looks like a basement, my back against a concrete wall with my hands bound too tight behind my back.

I sit on the cold floor, my ankles bound and my knees pulled up toward my chest, and as I hear Dalton's familiar grunts, my gaze snaps across the cold room, finding him sprawled on the ground, beaten and bloodied. A metal cuff is locked around his wrist and connected to some kind of lock protruding from the concrete wall.

I try to call for him, my words muffled and inaudible against the tape on my mouth, but I keep trying until he finally lifts his head off the ground. Every part of my soul breaks, seeing the defeat in his once bright eyes. "Firefly," he breathes, relief thick in his broken tone. "Thank God, are you okay? We have to get out of here."

I shake my head and realize my face is wet from tears, panic searing through my chest. I look around, trying to search for some kind of escape, trying to put together some kind of plan, but there's nothing, not even a visible door in this small concrete box.

Dalton pulls up to his knees and does what he can to crawl closer toward me, but only gets a foot before the chains on his wrist pull taut. "I . . . I can't get any closer," he says, agony thick in his tone. "Can you move? Can you get to me? If I could just free your arms and legs . . . then maybe."

Dalton lets out a heavy sigh as he lets his thoughts trail off, almost as though already giving up, but I won't dare let him. I don't know what this bastard wants with me, but whatever it is, Dalton isn't going to go down because of it.

I try to move, but whatever my twisted neighbor used to knock me out is still wreaking havoc over my body. I'm able to straighten out my legs, flopping them to the side, and I try to stretch out toward him, his other hand reaching out and barely brushing past my ankle.

"Fuck, Oakley. Come on, baby. You need to shake off whatever they gave you."

They? How many of them are there? I thought it was just the neighbor directly opposite me.

The tears stream down my face, but I try to hold myself together. These assholes aren't going to get the best of me. Pulling my legs back in, I struggle to get my knees back to my chest, but the second I do, I lower my face to my jeans, using the coarse material to try and get the tape off my mouth.

"Yes, good girl," Dalton says as the movement has my body aching that much more. "Keep going."

I don't dare give up, moving my head across my knees as tears drop from my face, soaking into my pants.

The time it takes to release the tape gives my body just that little bit more energy as it slowly works off whatever was on that cloth, and the fog begins to fade. The tape eventually comes free, and I let out a heavy gasp, finally able to take a decent breath.

"Fuck," I say, my voice foreign to my own ears. "Are you okay?"

"Don't worry about me, Firefly, I'll be fine. We just have to get out of here."

"How?" I cry. "There's no way out. You're cuffed to the fucking wall of a goddamn concrete box."

"You can't think about that," he urges. "Just one thing at a time, and right now, all you need to concentrate on is getting to me so I can free your wrists."

I swallow hard, my throat never so dry. "Okay," I say, my voice breaking, trying to find the courage to fight this.

Using the wall, I press my back against it and plant my feet on the ground before raising my hips and shuffling them over. I do it again, moving toward Dalton inch by inch. "Good," he encourages, getting himself into a better position to be able to help me. "Keep going. You're almost here."

I curse with every movement, the pain like nothing I've ever known, but the closer I get to him, the stronger my determination becomes. I'm painfully aware of just how long this is taking, and after what feels like a lifetime, Dalton is finally able to reach out to me, his hand coming straight to my face.

He pulls on my chin, forcing my stare up to him, and I try to meet his eye without falling apart. "We're going to be okay," he promises. "I'm gonna get us out of here."

I nod, barely able to breathe as I try to turn away from him, offering my wrists as best I can. He grips them and attempts to lift the tape, scratching at it with his nails. "Fuck, it's not lifting," he says with a pained curse, trying to adjust himself to get better access.

A loud bang sounds from outside the concrete prison and my whole body shakes, silent tears streaming down my face. "What do they want?" I murmur.

"I don't fucking know," he tells me. "But whatever it is, they're not going to get it. I swear, Firefly, I'll get you out of here."

Defeat pounds through my chest, knowing it's not going to happen. I don't know how I managed to offend this asshole, but whatever it was, it's my greatest regret.

How could he do this? Who does shit like this?

Moving to Faders Bay was supposed to be my new beginning. It was my fresh start to put the past behind me and discover who I really am on my own, but this is so far from what I had in mind. It's barely been two days, and I've already got myself kidnapped by some messed-up psychopath and his friends. They're probably going to kill me. I'm a goner and Dalton is going to be nothing but collateral damage.

"Who the hell are these guys?"

Dalton shakes his head, still working tirelessly on the tape. "No fucking clue," he mutters. "They moved into the building a little after I did, right at the start of the school term, but I don't think they attend classes. I never see them on campus, just in the halls. They watch everything. They know what times people leave their apartments, who they talk to, and who they don't. It's fucked up, Oakley. These assholes are bad news. Tell me you're not involved with them."

"I swear," I say, the terror claiming every inch of me. "I've never met them in my life. All I know is that since the minute I got here, they've been following me. They came to Danny's Bar while I was working and just sat there and watched. After my first shift when I met you outside, they were lurking in the shadows. I couldn't see them, but I knew they were following me home. It's like some kind of sick game to them, and I just . . . I don't know what they want with me."

Dalton doesn't respond, probably making a plan to never get involved with me again. I mean, fuck, not even awesome rooftop sex is worth this shit. I wouldn't blame him if he left Faders Bay and never looked back.

"Do you . . . do you know anything about them?"

"Not really," he murmurs. "The blonde guy lives across from me. I spoke to him once, right when he was moving in. I think his name is Sawyer or some shit like that. He seemed cool, but there was something off about him. I've kept my distance since then."

"And the other two?"

"Don't know," he says. "From what I can tell, they're both the silent type. They have a lot of parties, but they never actually mingle with the people who come over, just keep to themselves. The bastard across from you, his name is Zade. He's a real fucking asshole, but that's the extent of what I know about him. From what I can tell, the three of them are tight, almost like brothers, but there's something more there, something fucked up. I don't want anything to do with it."

Zade. His name is Zade.

I swallow hard, my throat getting drier by the second. I'm in real fucking trouble here.

"I . . . I think they broke into my apartment last night."

"What?" he rushes out, his hands pausing at my wrists for a minute. "Why didn't you say anything?"

I shake my head, feeling like a fucking idiot. "I wasn't sure if it was them or not."

"Fuck, Oakley," he says, clenching his jaw. "You were about to let me drop you home, knowing damn well those assholes broke into your apartment. What the fuck were you thinking?"

"I . . . I don't know," I cry. "I had the locks changed. I thought it was going to be fine. I didn't know they would take things this far."

"Clearly it's not fucking fine."

Anger blooms through my chest, and if I could pull away from him, I would. "Stop acting like this is my fault," I demand, the irrational rage making me act out against the only person who can actually help me right now. "How the hell was I supposed to know this Zade asshole is a fucking psychopath? It's not like I went and knocked on his door and was like, *Hey, I've noticed you've been stalking me and I've got some nasty kinks. Would it be a hassle if you could violently kidnap me in the middle of the night, and if it's not too much to ask, could you possibly leave me gagged and bound in a fucking concrete prison? Mmkay, thanks.' ''*

"I'm not—fuck," he cuts himself off, and a roar of frustration tears from deep in his chest. "I wasn't trying to blame you, okay? I just wish you had told me so I knew to look out for it, or I could have taken you somewhere else. For fuck's sake, we were in a damn hotel. We could have stayed there for the night and been fine, but we're not. I'm fucking stuck here, getting beat simply because I spent my night fucking you."

Guilt like I've never known sails through my chest and buries itself there. "I'm sorry," I whisper, a lump forming in my throat and making it hard to breathe. "I bet you've never regretted screwing a girl more than you regret me."

Dalton's hand pauses on my wrist, his thumb gently brushing against my skin. "Don't say that," he murmurs. "I don't regret you one fucking bit. I just wish things could have turned out . . . differently."

"Oh really?" I mutter darkly, the sarcasm coming out at the worst possible time. "For a minute, I thought maybe this is exactly what you wanted."

"Really? These fucking psychopaths are probably out there plotting how they're going to gut us and you wanna bring out the jokes?"

"No," I spit, the two of us clearly not vibing as well as we did up on that rooftop. "All I want to do is get the fuck out of here and never have to see them again."

The tape finally starts to lift and Dalton does what he can to release my wrists, this small ray of hope pushing him to go faster. He grunts with the quicker movements, in more pain than I could imagine, which only has the guilt getting that much worse.

My hands come free, and just as I go to reach for the tape around my ankles, there's another loud noise from outside our prison.

Dalton and I both freeze, our heads whipping around and following the sound as my heart races erratically, the fear completely crippling me. Last time, the noise stopped, only this time, it keeps going, sounding as though someone is standing right on the other side of the wall with heavy chains.

There's a loud clang followed by the sound of scraping metal, and I shake my head, my eyes wide. "No, no, no, no, no," I chant, knowing whatever it is they've brought me here for, this is it. This goes down now.

Will I be raped? Beat? Slaughtered like cattle?

I can't handle this, can't take the fear.

The wall falls back, and I realize it's a hidden door. Had my mind not been so foggy, I might have seen the narrow lines framing the door. It looks heavy and thick, made solely for the purpose of not being able to hear the person inside scream, but it's the last thing on my mind the moment my three neighbors step into the room.

Zade.

Cross.

Sawyer.

They're so tall, the intimidation immediately washes over me. They're dressed all in black, their sharp eyes not missing a damn thing. Zade stands back, keeping his distance, his arms crossed over his chest and those dead eyes locked on me, yet somehow I can tell he's the ringleader of this bullshit. Cross and Sawyer are just along for the ride.

They're terrifying. Their ability to control a room is like nothing I've ever seen before.

I shrink back against the wall, willing myself to disappear, but I'm frozen. I look between the three of them, my breath catching in my throat. It's clear that Zade isn't enjoying this. He's not getting a thrill or any kind of rush . . . no, this is a necessity for him. He's simply doing what he must, leaving all sense of emotion at the door. But from what I can tell, this man doesn't have the ability to feel. The others though, Sawyer and Cross, there's a sick hint of pleasure in their eyes. They look ready to jerk off at the thought of having me locked up, theirs to do whatever they please.

Sawyer crouches down, a sick smirk playing on his lips. "Well, well," he says, his gaze flicking toward my hands that are no longer bound. He's barely said a thing, yet with each word, he commands the room, and I find myself physically unable to look away. "It seems we've got ourselves a little problem."

Cross takes a step toward me, and the fear that already consumes me only gets stronger. I shake my head, my eyes wide. "No, no," I panic, terrified they'll come any closer. "Don't touch me."

Cross doesn't hesitate, stepping right in front of me and crouching down. His forceful fingers grip my chin, and he tears it up, forcing my stare to his. "Then you shouldn't have been such a naughty girl," he rumbles, his tone oddly delicious yet stony, cold, and terrifying at the same damn time.

I try to pull my chin free, but his grip is impenetrable, holding me hostage until he decides otherwise. His lips twitch, and like lightning, he rises, gripping my arms and pulling me up with him. He spins me, slamming my chest against the concrete wall as a raw scream tears from deep in my throat. I turn my head, my eyes locked on Dalton's stare. His eyes are so wide, terrified of what's about to happen.

Cross's body presses against mine, and the dread rests heavily in my gut.

This is it. He's going to rape me.

He dips his face, his lips right by my ear as he grips both of my wrists, his skin so chilling against mine. I try to pull them free, but he's so damn big. Having his body pinned against mine is like having a concrete block pressed against me. "Don't fight it," he murmurs in my ear, his every word turning my blood to lead as he tries to wrangle my wrists back together.

I scream as he pulls against me, not shy about using force. "Don't fucking touch her," Dalton roars, fighting against his chains. "Leave her alone."

Sawyer laughs and steps into Dalton's side before his heavy boot kicks out, slamming into Dalton's ribs, the blast sending him crashing against the wall and dropping back to the ground. Dalton groans in agony, and I try to hold myself together, my bottom lip quivering.

"Come on, now, Dalton. Surely you know better by now. If you hadn't touched what's ours in the first place, none of this would have happened." A wicked grin pulls at the corner of Sawyer's lips, his dead, chilling eyes sweeping toward me as he crouches down in front of Dalton, taunting him. "She sure is pretty, isn't she? I bet you enjoyed her," he says. "Tell me, just how sweet does she taste?"

Bile rises in my throat, but before I can voice my opinion, Dalton's pained grunt tears through the concrete prison. "Don't fucking touch her," he spits through a clenched jaw as Cross finishes rebinding my wrists. Only this time it feels different. It's not the same tape that was on me before. This feels cold and heavy, like some kind of metal cuff.

Sawyer laughs, and the sound makes my stomach clench. "Oh, I'm gonna do more than just touch her. But don't worry, you'll be able to watch."

"No," I breathe, the terror reaching right through to my chest and squeezing with a vice-like grip.

Sawyer rolls his tongue over his bottom lip, his eyes taking me in like the worst kind of predator, imagining all the disgusting things he's going to do to me. I'm just about ready to try and fight my way out of here when Cross tugs against my bound wrists, dragging me backward. He's so damn strong that I have no choice but to move with him, and when he shoves me hard to the ground and hooks my wrists around a metal lock embedded in the wall, all sense of survival begins to plummet.

After making sure I'm secured with absolutely nowhere to go, Cross backs up, positioning himself just slightly to Zade's left, almost as though he's flanking him. Sawyer laughs and straightens up, almost looking bored of the situation before moving to Zade's right, the three of them like some kind of lethal force to be reckoned with.

My gaze sweeps over the three of them before locking onto Zade's. He's clearly the leader of this little performance. "What do you want with me?" I spit. "I've done nothing to you."

Zade doesn't move, doesn't flinch, doesn't even blink. It's as though I didn't say a damn word, and it's clear this man is void of all emotion. He's dead inside, and nothing in this world could possibly be more dangerous. This is the kind of man nightmares are made of, the kind you see splashed across wanted signs with the warning *do not approach for your own safety.*

He just stares at me, and it's so damn intense, my hands shake with fear. The corner of his lips flinch with the slightest smirk, and it changes everything. His whole demeanor shifts for the worse, and a chill sails right down my spine. This asshole is psychotic.

Zade nods toward Dalton, and as though releasing his hounds, Cross and Sawyer move to Dalton, and just like that, I watch as they beat him senseless. Dalton grunts in agony, and I scream, tearing against my cuffs until my wrists bleed. "STOP IT," I wail. "OH GOD, PLEASE STOP."

It goes on for another minute before Zade's powerful tone rips through the cell. "Enough." And like good little henchmen, Sawyer and Cross immediately stop, stepping away from Dalton before silently making their way out the door.

Zade remains, not even bothering to look at Dalton, just keeping his deadly gaze locked on mine. The seconds tick by as he watches me fall apart, watches the blood from my wrist trail down my arm. Then without another word, he turns and walks away, pulling the big concrete door closed behind him.

CHAPTER 9

Zade

My penthouse suite at The DeVil Hotel has a panoramic view of the city below, and I sit quietly looking over the moon-soaked streets as Sawyer and Cross talk shit. This has been my home for the past three years, and every inch of this building has been designed and created by me. Most people think it was my father's building, think I was handed it like some spoiled rich kid who grew up with a silver spoon in his mouth. But the truth is, I fought for this.

At sixteen, I had this dream fully funded. At eighteen, I bought the real estate. At nineteen, my contractors moved in. At twenty-one, the DeVil Hotel was complete and considered one of the most luxurious hotels in the world. And now, at twenty-four, this is my home.

Everything that happens in this hotel is run by me. The staff, the guests, the fucking thread count of the bedding in each room. I know every square inch of this building better than I know myself. Staying away from it these past few weeks has been a challenge, but if it means ensuring Oakley Quinn remains in my custody, protected from those who want to see me fail, then I'll do it.

No one will touch that girl apart from me. The day I carve her heart out of her chest and offer it as my sacrifice is the day my life truly begins. The power of Empire will be mine and nothing will stand in my way.

The distant clanging of metal sounds through my apartment, and I sit up on the couch, my gaze flicking toward the door. From the outside, the containment cell looks like any other room, but looking closer, the automatic locking system gives away my little secret. Once through that door and into the harsh reality of my world, there's the real entrance of the containment cell. A heavy-duty door with a steel locking system. A little barbaric and over the top, sure, but it's just the way I like it. Unless you know the cell like I do, there's no breaking out of there.

Dalton, on the other hand, is one of the few exceptions.

I hear the familiar creak of the heavy-duty door opening and closing before the subtle beep from the keypad. There's a soft click of the automatic locking system releasing, and before I know it, Dalton Eros is standing in my living room, a guilty smirk stretched wide across his face.

He stretches out, having been balled up in that cell for close to twenty four hours. "Really, asshole?" he questions, his calculated stare locked on Sawyer. "You just had to go for the ribs. You know I broke those last month."

Sawyer stands, grinning like the fucking Cheshire cat. "Had to look real, brother." He strides over to Dalton and claps him on the back, no hard feelings between them. "You good though? We didn't hit you too hard, did we? I know you can be a little bitch sometimes, but I figured you would have manned up a bit more in front of your little girlfriend."

Dalton just stares at him, wiping blood off his top lip as Sawyer strides to the kitchen, helping himself to my fridge. But the truth is, Dalton gets off on the pain. The fucker was probably rocking a semi the whole way through that beating, and we all fucking know it. "She's not my fucking girlfriend," he mutters under his breath, leaving both me and Cross to roll our eyes.

Dalton walks through to my living room, dropping down on my couch. "Come on, man," I grumble. "You're getting blood all over my couch."

He scoffs, wiping the back of his arm across his face. Dalton broke his nose a lot as a kid, and now snapping it is as easy as a quick flick of the wrist. That thing never did heal properly. "Chill out. It's black leather. It'll wipe right off. Besides, it's nowhere near as bad as what you've done to this thing."

My lips pull just a fraction, and for a minute I was worried the fucker might have made me smile. "How is she?" I ask, nodding toward the cell he just came out of.

"Funny, I thought you didn't give a shit," he says as Sawyer walks back and tosses an ice pack into Dalton's lap. He takes it gratefully and slaps it across his ribs, trying not to cringe. Though he's been through worse—a shitload worse. Hell, we all have. Only for Dalton, it was at the hands of his father.

"I don't," I tell him firmly, making sure he hears me loud and clear. "But if she gets even a hint that you're not who you say you are, we're fucked."

Dalton lets out a heavy sigh. "It's fine. She passed out an hour ago and after coming off the hard shit, she'll probably need to sleep it off for a while."

I nod. "Either way, you can't be out here long."

"I know," he mutters, a distant look in his eyes. He glances back up at Sawyer across the room. "Did you really have to make her think you were about to rape her? Bit far, don't you think?"

"What's your fucking problem?" Sawyer argues, his brows furrowed as he watches his friend. "You know I wasn't gonna touch her. I was just fucking around with her, having a little fun."

"She doesn't know that," Dalton argues. "She was in there almost breaking her fucking wrist thinking you were going to rape her."

I watch Dalton closer, my gaze narrowed to slits when it hits me. Anger and frustration tear through my chest, and I notice Cross tensing across the room, seeing exactly what's coming. "I fucking told you not to get attached."

"I'm not," Dalton argues. "I just . . . she's a cool chick and if you just gave it a fucking chance, you'll see that."

"She'll be dead in a little over a month," Sawyer says. "What does it matter?"

Dalton glares at Sawyer again, and if the asshole isn't careful, Dalton won't hesitate to put him in his place. None of us are known for having patience, and right now, Sawyer is testing Dalton's like never before.

Not letting this get out of control, I demand Dalton's attention. "You telling me you didn't fuck her up on my roof? Or are you trying to tell me you did and you fucking plan on doing it again?"

He looks away, not answering my question, but he doesn't need to. I see it right there in his eyes. He fucked her, alright. He fucked her until he couldn't see straight, and what's more, that little cunt of hers has got a choke hold on his dick.

I stand, my hands pushing through my hair. "Fuck, Dalton. What am I supposed to do now?" I demand.

"Nothing. The plan stays the same."

"And when I carve her heart out of her fucking chest? What then? Are you gonna try and take a shot at me?" He clenches his jaw and looks away again. "FUCK."

Dalton stands, getting in my face. "I can handle it," he tells me, rage burning through his eyes. "The. Plan. Stays. The. Same. I'm not getting attached."

Cross scoffs from his position near my window, his arm braced over his head as he stares out at the darkening city below. Venom slithers down his arm and weaves through his fingers, the sleek black snake more than just a pet to him. They share some kind of bond, something I'll never understand. All I know is that snake is a little bitch. If anyone apart from Cross touches her, she'll sink those fangs into their throat without a second thought. "Keep telling yourself that," he mutters, not even bothering to look our way.

Dalton balls his hands into fists. "Just tell me what you found."

I watch him a moment, each of us locked in the other's stare, and the longer I hold it, the harder it becomes for him to keep control. He breaks, glancing away, knowing damn well who holds the power here. Slipping my hand into my pocket, I pull out my phone and bring up the image of Oakley's bedside table. I flip it around to show him and he curses, seeing the black calling card of Empire and the dagger discarded beside it. "While you were busy fucking your new girlfriend on my roof, we were in her apartment finding this."

"Fuck," he spits, running his hand over his face, knowing damn well what that means. After all, we've been the ones to leave the exact same message a million times before. "Someone's put a hit out on her head."

I nod, glancing at the image as he hands it back to me. Empire is full of old traditions and rituals, but on top of that, they believe in a fair fight. Whoever broke into her apartment and left this message right under our fucking noses, they were leaving a warning. Oakley Quinn is going to die.

"You know who left it?" he asks.

Sawyer shakes his head, striding toward us. "No fucking idea. That's why we brought her here. You know how these things work—"

"Twenty-four hours," Dalton states, knowing it all too well. When you leave a warning, you follow through and make it quick. It's a sick game really. The majority of people these warnings are left for have no fucking clue what it means. "You know what this means, right? One of The Circle members gave up her name. They betrayed you."

I nod, remembering the second I saw the calling card in Oakley's apartment and coming to the same conclusion. "And the only reason someone would want her name is because they want to take her out and challenge me for leadership."

"It'll never work," Cross says. "You're too strong, and you're the rightful heir. The blood of Empire runs through your veins. They can try all they want, but they can't take Empire. It'll never happen."

"No," I agree, "But they'll fucking die trying, even if it means putting a bullet between my eyes in the process."

Dalton starts to pace. "So what do we do?"

"For now, all we can do is wait," I tell him, letting him in on the plan. "Assuming she got the calling card some time in the early hours of Saturday morning and it's now Sunday night, we have to make our move now. So, you're gonna take your ass back into that cell and put on the fucking show of a lifetime. Make her believe you're on her side. Sawyer's going to stay here in case you need anything while Cross and I head back to the apartment block to take this fucker out."

Dalton nods, knowing there's no other choice, and as if making a point, Cross strides across the room and picks up his gun off my pool table before checking over his silencer. Tonight we plan on making this game a quick one. No lingering. We'll be in and out, and when this hitman arrives expecting to find Oakley hidden away in her apartment, it's me he'll find, my gun pressed right up against his temple.

He'll never see it coming.

Cross checks his bullets, though he won't be needing them. I fully intend to take out this hitman myself. Tonight, this is personal. An attempt on Oakley's life is a direct attack against me, and I don't take this shit lightly. When I rise to power in forty moons, everybody will know what I stand for. They will fear me, but unlike my father, they will respect me.

I join Cross at the pool table, collecting everything I need and slipping my dagger into position on my belt, preparing myself to take this motherfucker's life as effortlessly as though I was selecting what to have for dinner.

The sun disappeared below the horizon an hour ago and we're quickly running out of time. This hitman won't show up until late in the night, but I fully intend to be there, ready and waiting for when he finally arrives. What can I say? I'm a calculated motherfucker. I don't take a single move without knowing what will come from it. Which is exactly how I knew damn well that allowing Dalton to get close to Oakley was going to be a mistake, but it's not my mistake to learn from. He understood the consequences and still insisted, and because of that, he's going to get hurt.

Catching movement across my penthouse, I glance up from the pool table to see both Dalton and Sawyer in the kitchen. Dalton holds a glass of water, slowly sipping, while Sawyer mutters something to him, probably reminding him to keep his head up. Not a moment later, Dalton lets out a heavy sigh and puts his glass down, making his way back to the cell with Sawyer hot on his heels to chain him back up and make sure the door locks securely behind him. The tension between them is long gone.

Venom slithers over my hand on the pool table, bringing my attention back to what I was doing, and with Cross ready to go, we don't prolong this another second. He scoops Venom off the table and the snake weaves through his fingers, settling comfortably in his hand.

Within the space of fifteen minutes, we're pulling to a stop outside the apartment complex, my Escalade parked right beside Dalton's Harley. We slip out into the night, moving around the back of the building and slipping in through Sawyer's bedroom window, making sure we're not seen by anyone on the street.

Peering through the peephole in his front door, we find the hallway clear and slip out of the small one-bedroom apartment. It takes barely ten steps to reach Oakley and Cara's door, and before I even have the chance to knock, the door opens and we slip inside.

Cara looks up at me with big eyes as I scan the room, making sure we're not too late. I know exactly what she wants, but that won't be happening tonight. Hell, any other night. I lost interest a long time ago. The only reason I've allowed her into my bed is simply out of convenience. Besides, she's Sawyer's twin sister, and that shit just gets complicated.

"Here," I say, handing her a set of keys. "You're sleeping in Sawyer's apartment tonight. Don't come back here until I say you can. Got it?"

Disappointment flares in her eyes as she flicks her gaze toward Oakley's bedroom. "Is this about the calling card we found on the back of her door?"

"You know damn well it is," Cross says, striding right by her, the two of them unable to see eye to eye, though who the fuck knows why. She's never liked him and simply out of principle, he refuses to like her.

I meet her stare. "You should have told me," I tell her. "I shouldn't have found out after breaking in here last night. We put her here because I thought I could trust your judgment. Do I need to reconsider who I keep in my corner?"

Cara swallows hard and shakes her head. "Don't be an ass," she says. "You know you can trust me. I thought you left the card."

"I didn't."

Her eyes widen, understanding exactly what that means. "But then—"

"Yep."

"Shit."

Getting bored of her line of questioning, I pull the door back open. "Are you going to get out of here, or would you prefer to hang out and wait for the hitman to come and confuse you for Oakley?"

Her eyes widen, and within the span of two seconds, she dashes into her room, grabs a set of pajamas, her Kindle, and her vibrator then makes a break for it down the hall. I don't close the door until I hear Sawyer's front door closing behind her, then wait a moment later, listening for the soft click of the lock and deadbolts.

"Alright," I say to Cross, closing the door behind me and flicking each of the locks. "Let's do this."

Knowing any trained hitman would be watching the apartment

from a distance, we make a show of turning on the TV and sporadically flicking a few lights. Then wanting to get this show on the road, we turn them all off. Anybody looking in from the outside would assume the occupants of the apartment have gone to bed.

Whoever this guy is, he clearly knows which bedroom belongs to Oakley, so Cross and I slip into her room, leaving her door cracked and the window unlocked, almost making it too easy for the bastard.

We wait a little over twenty minutes before finally hearing a scratching noise from the living room, and a sick enjoyment fills my veins. I move into position behind the door, covered in shadows as Cross readies himself by the window, covering all our bases.

The room is pitch black, darkness clouding every corner, without even a hint of moonlight streaming through the window. It's perfect. Just how I like it.

There's a soft whir of the window being opened before an even softer thud as the hitman lands on the living room floor. He moves around the apartment, checking the coast is clear while leaving the window open for an easy getaway.

Excitement thrums through my veins, and I reach for my gun before thinking better of it. A gun is too easy, too forgiving. This is an attack on me, so I'm gonna make it count. I'm going to use this to send a message. Anyone who tries to fuck with me will suffer at my hands.

My palm closes around the hilt of my dagger, and the cool iron feels like victory in my hand, the anticipation sending a wave of adrenaline pulsing through my veins. It's addictive, a fucking rush, and I wouldn't have it any other way.

The bedroom door creaks open so slowly that the wait to end his life is almost painful.

The hitman takes a step and then another, and my hand flexes around the hilt of the dagger. He moves past me just enough that I step in behind him, his eyes locked on Oakley's bed. He doesn't hear me behind him, and he sure as fuck doesn't see Cross by the window. We were trained better than that—better than him, apparently.

I move with him as he takes a closer look at Oakley's bed, realizing something isn't right. Her bed is empty. I can also feel the panic firing through his veins. His body straightens, and just as he's about to bail, my arms snap out.

One curls around his forehead, gripping his hair and yanking his head back in a death grip while the other shoots to the base of his throat, my blade resting against his skin. The need to interrogate him is strong, but with his gun firmly clutched in his hand, I'm not taking any chances. Just because I've got the advantage, doesn't mean he can't free himself of this.

There are other ways for me to get the answers I'm looking for, and this isn't it.

Cross steps out of the shadows, and without even a hint of hesitation, I let my blade fly free, slitting his throat as effortlessly as carving a Thanksgiving turkey.

The hitman falls to the ground, and the familiar gurgling of blood is like music to my ears. I meet Cross's stare, and just like that, he nods before pulling out his phone and ordering the clean-up crew. He steps around the body, and as he moves out of the room, I realize just how far I would go for this.

Nobody is going to stand in my way. Not The Circle, not the members of Empire, and definitely not Oakley Quinn.

Come the night of the sixtieth moon, I will carve her beating heart out of her chest, and her sweet screams of agony will be the greatest reward I'll ever receive.

CHAPTER 10

Oakley

A soft metal thud sounds through the cell, and my eyes fly open, my heart racing like never before. I was asleep. How fucking stupid could I have been to allow myself to fall asleep? Fuck.

Fear overwhelms me, and I quickly glance around the cell, my eyes snapping from side to side.

Dalton is gone, his cuff dangling against the wall. How could that be? What have they done to him?

The heavy door begins to open as fear paralyzes me, and instead of trying to fight back, I close my eyes, pretending to sleep as I listen to every last sound around me. I hear two people walk in, and despite my closed eyes, I can feel their intense stares locked on my face. "Fuck, is she still sleeping?" Dalton's voice murmurs through the cell.

An irritated scoff sounds through the cement prison, and I try to figure out who it belongs to. "For your own sake, you better hope she is," the voice responds. Maybe Sawyer? I don't know. I haven't been around them enough to recognize their voices. All I know is that it's definitely not Zade. "Otherwise, you're fucked."

"Tell me about it."

What. The. Actual. Fuck?

A body drops to the ground across the prison, and my curiosity gets the best of me. Peering through my eyelashes—trying to remain as still as possible—I find Dalton as free as a bird, a filthy smirk pasted across his face as he reaches for his cuff and locks himself back into it.

He curses with his movements, and Sawyer crouches down, quickly glancing toward me before determining that I'm still asleep. "This is so fucked up, man," he says, reaching out and scuffing up his hair, making him look more disheveled than he is. "But just say the word and I'll happily break another rib. I know how you get off on that shit."

Dalton chuckles, testing his wrist on the cuffs, making sure it's not too tight. "Fuck off, bro. You've been pulling your punches all day. Your sister could hit me harder than that. You're just lucky I know how to make it look convincing."

"Keep running your mouth like that, and I'll happily beat you over and over again. You forget, Dalt, you've been my best friend since we were kids. I know when something really fucks you up, and right now, that rib is fucking killing you."

Best fucking friend? What in the fresh hell is going on here?

He's one of them. This is all a fucking game to him. He got me alone, fucked me, and gained my trust just long enough to screw me over. This must have been all part of their twisted plan since the beginning. He kept separate from them, was lingering outside the apartment complex when I walked home after my first shift, then last night he got that text and immediately said it was time to go.

I'm such a fucking idiot.

Dalton played a part in this. He set it up, made it possible for his friends to capture me, and now, he's sitting here beside me, acting as though his world is about to implode, making promises to get me out of here.

Who the hell is this guy? He told me he didn't know them, barely even knew their names, but he was lying. He knows exactly who they are, and he played me like a fool, allowing me to walk right into this trap.

Dalton grins up at Sawyer. "Look who's running his mouth now," he says before discreetly glancing at me, narrowing his gaze, and I try not to give myself away. "Alright, man, get out of here. She'll wake up soon, and I don't want her catching you in here. The longer she thinks I'm on her side, the better."

Sawyer nods, glancing my way as well. "If she wakes up, try and get some information out of her. There's a reason why she was chosen. The Circle wouldn't have offered her up if she didn't know something they wanted to keep quiet. These bastards would take every advantage they could get, and his sacrifice is the perfect opportunity. Two birds, one stone."

The Circle? Who the fuck is The Circle?

Dalton nods. "My thoughts exactly."

With that, Sawyer walks out of the concrete prison, pulling the door closed behind him, and the second the soft thud sounds through the room, I close my eyes, determined not to say a damn word.

Hours pass before I hear the sound of the door again, and this time, I can't resist opening my eyes. All three of my captors walk in, just as intimidating as the first time I saw them.

They crowd near the door, assessing the room as I lift my head, locking my gaze onto Zade's. His eyes are like lasers zeroing in on me, and I can't help but notice small splatters of blood across his arms and clothes.

He takes a stride toward me and my whole body tenses, fear blasting through me as Cross and Sawyer remain situated by the door. I try to crawl away, yanking hard against my cuffs as Dalton's roar rockets through the room. "Don't fucking touch her," he demands. "I swear, I'll fucking kill you."

His words mean nothing, and I violently shake my head, tears falling onto my cheeks. Blood drips from my wrists as I pull against my binding, and I watch as Zade's sharp gaze takes it in, not missing a damn thing. "No," I breathe as he crouches down before me, a twisted smirk settling onto his lips. I swallow hard, certain that this is it for me.

Tonight, I die.

"Please, I swear, I didn't do anything," I cry, desperately trying to pull away from him. "I'll give you whatever you want, just please—"

His hand shoots out, the same cloth he used outside my apartment clutched in his palm. I try to scream and turn my head, but he's too strong, and within seconds, my world fades into darkness.

CHAPTER 11

Oakley

onsciousness comes back to me, and I open my eyes to the brightness of my apartment, the early morning sun streaming through the window.

I glance around, disoriented and confused as I find myself sprawled across the couch in the middle of the living room, my aching wrists now perfectly bandaged.

How the hell did I get back here? Was it all some kind of dream?

My head pounds and the same brain fog I experienced in the cement prison rears its ugly head once again, leaving me desperate to slip back into a peaceful state of unconsciousness. I feel like I'm coming off a night of excessive drinking and partying way too hard. God, I just wish I had some answers, but the only one I've got is that

Dalton Eros is not who he says he is. Hell, that's probably not even his real name.

My whole body hurts, and I try to piece together everything that's happened over the last . . . shit, I don't even know how long it has been. Was I trapped there one night? Two? I have no fucking idea.

I need to sleep this off but knowing those three assholes could be right across the hall messes with my head. I lay awake, staring at the ceiling, unable to figure out what the hell they wanted with me. I just don't get it. Why kidnap someone, lock her up in your creepy as fuck cement prison, then let her go so soon?

They didn't hurt me. Didn't touch me. Barely said a damn word.

Don't get me wrong, I've never been so happy to wake up in my own apartment feeling as though I'd been roofied, but what was the point? Why kidnap someone and hold them captive, only to set them free? It doesn't make sense.

A noise at the door sends me into a blind panic, and I shoot up from the couch with wide eyes as I grip the side of the couch, ready to launch myself up at a moment's notice. I try to remember exactly where the knives are in the kitchen when I hear the familiar sound of a key slipping into the lock.

Oh, hell no. This is not happening again.

I dart through the small apartment on shaky legs, every slight movement making my head spin. I will not be caught off guard by these pricks again. This time I'll be ready.

My hand curls around the biggest kitchen knife we've got just as the door swings open. Clutching the knife tighter in anticipation, I position myself ready to fight.

Cara strides through the door, her stare locked on her Kindle, only glancing up as she hears the loud sigh of relief escaping from my lips. "HOLY FUCK," I breathe, letting the knife clatter to the kitchen counter. "You scared the shit out of me."

She gapes at me, her Kindle falling down by her side. "I . . . me?" she demands, her voice hitching up higher. "Where the fuck have you been? I thought you were laying in a ditch somewhere. I was about ready to call the cops. I mean, damn girl. I'm all down for getting so fucked up you can't remember your name, but if you're going to go out on a bender and not come home all weekend, the least you could do is let me know so I'm not worried about you."

I shake my head, bracing my hands against the counter and giving myself a moment to just breathe. My heart continues to race, but with every slow exhale, I finally start to find some peace. "What day is it?"

"It's Monday," Cara laughs, kicking the door closed behind her and moving across our small apartment. "Just how big was that bender?"

"God, I wish it was a bender."

"Huh?" she says, pausing by the counter to glance back at me. "What do you mean? If it wasn't a bender, then where the hell have you—" Her eyes open wide, a grin stretching across her face. "Oh my God, you little hussy. You were with a guy."

My night with Dalton flashes back to me, and I can't deny just how good it was. My wrists tied around the pole, his authoritative demands making me wet, the way he had me on my knees. Good God, it was everything . . . right up until his gut-wrenching betrayal.

"Oh, I was shacked up with a guy, alright," I mutter. "But it's really not what you think."

"Eh," she grunts, her lips twisting with disappointment. "You better not be holding out on me. I just spent all night reading the dirtiest filth I've ever gotten my hands on with no way to scratch that itch."

"What?" I say, glancing up at her, the realization that it's barely seven in the morning and she was only just walking through the door. "What do you mean no way to scratch that itch? Where were you last night?"

"Oh, umm . . . I had a family thing and stayed at my brother's apartment downtown, and I wasn't about to pet the kitty in his spare bed, you know what I mean? But," she says, "it sounds a lot like you're trying to change the topic. Who's this guy you're talking about?"

"Not *guy*," I grumble. "*Guys.*"

Her jaw drops and she looks at me as though I've just lived her raunchiest, wildest dreams. "Oh, hell yeah, girl. Fuck me. You really are a little hussy, aren't you?" She pulls up a chair, looking at me with wide eyes. "Tell me everything, every last juicy detail."

"What the hell have you been smoking?" I say with a scoff. "I didn't get railed by four psychopaths, I got kidnapped and held hostage in a fucked-up little cement prison."

Her brows furrow as she stares back at me. "Okay, now who's been smoking?" Without a word, I hold up both of my hands to show my bandaged wrists and watch as her face falls. "You're . . . you're not making this up."

"Trust me. I really wish I was. One minute, I was standing in the hallway unlocking our door after working Saturday night," I tell her, skipping over the rooftop fuckfest, "the next I know, I was knocked out and thrown in a cell."

"Shit," she breathes, wide eyed. "What happened? Who did this to you?"

"Who do you think?" I tell her. "Our creepy as fuck neighbor and his turd-tastic friends."

"Zade?" she questions, shaking her head. "No, he's intense, but surely he wouldn't do something like this. Are you sure—"

I straighten from the counter, my gaze narrowing on my roommate, suspicion pulsing through my veins. "You told me you didn't know his name."

Her gaze falls away, dropping to her hands. "Oh, umm . . . yeah. When you didn't come home yesterday, I asked around the neighbors. Someone mentioned his name. Clearly we're not the only ones who have noticed something . . . different about him."

I watch her a moment longer, unease laying rigid in the pit of my stomach. I want to be able to trust my roommate, but I can't help feeling as though she's hiding something. She hasn't given me any reason not to trust her yet, so I feel as though I should give her the benefit of the doubt. It doesn't sit right with me though.

"Right," I say slowly, not wanting to let on just how suspicious I am.

"So, you're sure? It really was Zade?"

"Positive," I tell her. "I was just coming home, had the door unlocked and everything when he came out of his apartment. I looked him dead in the eye and screamed while he knocked me out. Next thing I knew, I was locked up in some kind of cement prison."

She gapes at me. "Holy shit. That's fucked up. We need to call the police."

I shake my head. "No. No way," I rush out. "These guys aren't screwing around. Calling the cops and trying to make a report isn't going to get me justice. The only proof I have of this happening is my torn-up wrists, and who's to say I didn't do it myself? I can't tell them where they were keeping me or why they did it. It's not enough. They'll get questioned and then it'll get dropped, and I'll be the one to face the consequences."

"Are you serious?" she questions, almost looking disgusted with my decision. "So, you're just going to let them get away with it and do nothing?"

"I'm not going to do nothing," I argue. "And they sure as hell aren't going to get away with it. I just need to figure out what they want with me. As soon as I've got that, the ball will be right back in my court, and the second it is, those assholes better watch out."

Cara shakes her head. "This sounds like a dangerous game, Oakley. Maybe you should just let it go. Keep your head down, go to class, and try to forget it. Move on. If they're willing to take you like that, what else are they capable of? Maybe you shouldn't be trying to screw with them."

She's right. This is a dangerous game, and I know without a doubt, what they did to me isn't even scratching the surface. There's something wicked there, something evil and cruel. I see it every time I look into Zade's eyes. And sure, call me stupid, but it's not in my nature to let this go. I need to see this through. I need to know what they want with me.

"I—"

A knock sounds at the door, cutting me off, and my back stiffens as a chill sails down my spine. I stare at it, my eyes wide as my pulse beats erratically in my ears. My hands shake, and I back up until my ass hits the kitchen cabinets.

"Ugh," Cara mutters, sliding off her chair. "Hold that thought."

Panic tears at my chest, realizing she's about to answer the door, but before I can even attempt to object, she's already there with her hand curling around the handle. She pulls the door open to find Dalton standing out in the hallway, his gaze already locked on mine. "Oh, thank fuck," he breathes, gripping the doorframe and making a show of barely being able to hold himself up, still looking beaten and bruised. "You're okay. They knocked me out, and when I woke up in my apartment, you weren't there . . . I thought—"

"You thought what?" I growl, rage blasting through my body. I storm around the kitchen counter and through the small apartment, his sharp stare tracking my every movement. "You thought this bitch is so fucking daft that she wouldn't realize what the fuck was going on?"

Cara glances between us, confusion marring her pretty face. "Umm . . . maybe I should go."

"Good idea," Dalton snaps, his stare unwavering, a nasty tone in his voice for someone pretending to be on my side.

Without sparing me one more glance, Cara ducks and runs,

taking off toward her room and leaving me with the traitor. I hear her bedroom door slam, but I don't doubt the little weasel is listening through the walls.

"What the fuck are you talking about?" Dalton says, his tone now soft and pleading, the realization of being alone with him now setting off alarms inside my head. He goes to step over the threshold, but I hold up a hand, stopping him from coming any closer. Instead, I move toward him, listening as he tries to plead his case. "Did they . . . did they do something to you? Because I swear to God, Firefly, if they touched you, I'll fucking end them."

A scoff tears from the back of my throat, and I step right into his arms, my hands clutching his shoulders. Then, just as those strong arms go to close around me in a warm hug, I bring my knee up as hard as possible, nailing him right in the balls. The fucker drops to the ground so damn fast, I don't even have time to pat myself on the back. "Ahh, fuck," he spits, clutching onto his junk as he curls into a ball on the ground. "What the hell was that for?"

"Do you honestly think I'm that fucking stupid?" I roar, my jaw clenched as I allow the anger and frustration to fly free. "You're a goddamn snake. I heard every fucking word, asshole. I know you're one of them."

"What . . . what are you talking about?" he spits. "One of who?"

As if right on cue, Zade's door opens, and I instinctively take a step back into my apartment as he assesses the situation out in the hall. His laser-sharp stare makes me want to throw up. "One of them," I say, narrowing my stare on Zade while discreetly holding my door, more than ready to slam it shut and lock the bastard out if he even thinks about inching toward me.

Dalton looks up as if only now just realizing Zade is here, and I have to give it to him, the asshole is a good actor. He blanches as he takes in Zade and almost tries to scurry away. He gets to his feet, his ferocious stare locked onto Zade. "Get the fuck away from her, you piece of shit."

I laugh. "Wow, laying it on thick, huh?" I say.

He whips around with wide eyes, and honestly, that's a dead giveaway right there. Who turns their back on their kidnapper? "What . . . what are you talking about?" he says through a clenched jaw, those startling blue eyes suddenly not doing anything for me.

"Cut the shit, Dalton. I heard every fucking word in that cell. I watched you walk back in and cuff yourself to the wall, listened to you joking around with Sawyer, heard your little plan to try and get information out of me. Surprise, asshole, I wasn't asleep."

I laugh, shaking my head as I watch his demeanor shift. The carefree, fun guy I'd met out on the street suddenly morphs into a cold, calculating asshole, just like his friends. "You're imagining things, Firefly," he says, his words now turning my blood cold.

Pulling on the door, I narrow the opening, feeling the sharp bite of Zade's stare still heavily locked on me. He's clearly the mastermind of this whole thing, but I keep my attention focused on Dalton. After all, Zade was clear in his intentions from the start. I knew to be wary of him, but Dalton? He's a snake in sheep's clothing. He deceived me, used my body, and then showed his real colors. "You almost had me fooled. Honestly, it was a good little act, getting me alone on that rooftop, making me crave your touch and fucking me until I couldn't breathe, but now I'm done. You can go and play your twisted little games with someone else because I'm through with you."

A hint of anger flashes in his eyes, but I've only stabbed the knife through his chest. I haven't yet had a chance to twist it. "Hear me now, snake. If you even think about screwing with me again, I will make you wish you'd never met me."

"Okay, you got me," he says, stepping into the doorway, his foot positioned just right to keep me from being able to shut the door. He reaches up and grips the doorframe, looking like the fucking god I remember from the rooftop. "But be honest with yourself, you know there's something between us. You felt it up on the roof, I know you did. And yeah, I might have told a little white lie, but don't fuck this thing between us because of that."

"Little white lie, huh?" I demand, a smirk settling onto my lips, and then without warning, I shoot my fist out, jabbing him right in the ribs where Sawyer had kicked him. He goes down like a sack of shit, falling out of my doorway and slamming into the wall on the opposite side of the hall, clutching his ribs. "You set me up to be kidnapped by your fucking psychopathic friends. You're the worst of them all, a fucking snake. So yeah, there might have been something real up there on the roof, but let me be clear now. Any shred of feelings I might have had for you died in that fucking cell."

Snapping my gaze back to Zade, I let him see the full extent of my rage. "You better watch your fucking back," I warn him. "Nobody screws me over and gets away with it." And with that, I slam the door between us, knowing without a doubt that I can't possibly back down now.

CHAPTER 12

Oakley

My hands shake as I stand out on the street in front of my apartment complex on Wednesday night. I've just finished a long shift at Danny's Bar, and as expected for a Wednesday, my tips were shit. Though at least I didn't have four sets of eyes watching me all night like the rest of the week. Standing out here in the cold, I now know why.

There's one hell of a party going on inside, and I'd bet every dollar of my shitty tips that the four assholes responsible are the very same assholes who've been making my time in Faders Bay a living hell.

College students spill out into the street, and the noise is insane. But hell, these are our college years, right? It's all about parties, sex, and rock and roll. If it weren't, these prime years of our lives would be considered nothing but a failure . . . you know, excluding the degree we're all tirelessly working toward.

I've spent the past few days doing everything in my power to try and avoid running into any of my neighbors. I stalk the hallway on a regular basis, always checking when the coast is clear before needing to slip out. I've seen Dalton once, standing at the end of the hallway, just watching me as I left for classes. He didn't say a word, and I sure as fuck didn't either. But I felt the heaviness of those bright blue eyes tracking my every step.

The other three are a little different.

Zade has shown up at the bar, silently sitting in the corner, watching me like the creep he is, while Sawyer just happens to be taking the same classes. Cross seems . . . different. He hasn't openly stalked me in the same way his friends have, but I still feel him watching—him and that little black snake of his.

Tonight feels like a trap.

I'm probably thinking too much into this. Cara warned me my first day that the neighbors like to throw parties, and I'm sure this is probably just like the rest of them. Only the thought of walking in there and making my way down the hall scares the shit out of me. They could be hiding in any of the open apartments, ready to jump out at me and drag me back into the crowd. No one would even notice.

My hands shake as I try to peer through the bodies, looking out for . . . everything. I want to know exactly where they are, just how many bodies I need to get through before reaching my apartment, where Cara is, and just how loud I'll have to scream before someone might hear me.

I should have stayed at the bar and offered to close for Heather, but she insisted she had it under control and sent me home. I'll never agree to that shit again.

For a moment, I consider breaking in through my bedroom window, but the more I think about it, the more ridiculous it sounds. So instead, I find the balls I clearly dropped and hold my head high. It's now or never, and there's no way in hell I'm about to let these assholes get the best of me. Besides, it's just a party. What could really go wrong?

Pushing through the bodies, I make my way inside the main door and into the hallway, and in this confined space, the music seems so much louder. People barge past me, random guys shouting about how fucked up they're getting while high-pitched laughter comes from the girls. I've barely taken a step before I'm drenched with someone's drink, and I realize that breaking in through my bedroom window was probably one of my better ideas tonight.

My eyes remain wide, constantly searching for the faces from my nightmares, and when I get halfway down the hall, I start to wonder if they're even here at all. Passing by Cross's apartment first, I find myself stopping to peer in. There are bodies scattered everywhere and my curiosity gets the best of me. I slip into his apartment and see the layout is exactly the same as mine, only there's barely anything in here. An empty snake enclosure and a couch. No TV, no rug, no pictures, nothing at all that indicates what kind of man lives here.

It's as though he doesn't really live here . . . and maybe he doesn't.

Making my way deeper into his apartment, I find his bedroom and slowly reach for the handle. The door is locked and something inside my chest tightens. What the hell am I thinking trying to get into his bedroom? This is ridiculous. This man had a hand in kidnapping me. He was the one who fastened cuffs around my wrists, slammed me up against the wall, and ensured any chance of my escape was forfeited.

Getting out of there and squeezing my way back into the hall, I find myself wondering about that snake enclosure. It was huge and very clearly looked after, but it was empty. Surely if he wasn't here, the snake would be back in its home, safe and sound. That could only mean they're still in the building, still waiting for me to make my biggest mistake yet.

A shiver trails down my spine as I finally reach my apartment and whip my key out of my pocket, more than ready to slip inside and lock the door behind me, but I find myself glancing over my shoulder at Zade's apartment.

The door is wide open, and it's like a beacon welcoming me in.

I pause, shivers sailing down my spine. I shouldn't. It's asking for trouble, but I can't stop thinking about getting in there and discovering anything about this stranger that could help me, or at the very least, answer some of the burning questions that have plagued me since the moment I moved in.

Shit.

This is insane.

I should open this damn door, get inside, and lock the bastard out behind me. Am I an idiot for even considering this? Hell, I know I am.

Fuck.

Without another thought, I slip across the hall, trying to keep myself hidden between the bodies. The moment I step over the threshold into Zade's apartment, my stomach starts to crawl. I'm going to be sick, and come first thing tomorrow, I need to book myself an appointment with a therapist to figure out how I could willingly do something so stupid. But I'm here now and I'm not going to waste an opportunity like this.

There's not a lot to see in his small apartment. It's just like Cross's. There's a couch and flatscreen TV, but for some reason, I don't think he uses it. The layout of his apartment is different, with the kitchen and living room at one end and the bedroom and bathroom at the other.

I don't bother walking into the kitchen since I can see everything from where I am. Instead, I find myself wandering to the bedroom. I look left and right before curling my hand around the handle and testing my luck. The latch releases, and I suck in a breath, my eyes widening with the realization of what's about to happen.

I should run. I should shove this reckless curiosity back down where it belongs and take off before this shit turns sour. And yet, instead of making a break for it and having my best interests in mind, I discreetly slip inside the bedroom of my kidnapper.

Closing the door behind me, I step into an empty room, my gaze immediately scanning the space around me. There's a queen-sized bed up against the side wall with a small bedside table next to it and no windows. The room smells just like him, and it's almost overwhelming, making me feel as though he's in the room with me. There's no denying it though, it smells damn good. It's intoxicating, similar to that wicked stare of his.

Not wanting to be here any longer than necessary, I start searching, looking for any clue that will tell me who he is or what he wants with me. I start with his wardrobe, finding a whole lot of nothing. His clothes are neat, almost with military-style perfection. Not a damn thing's out of place. Shoes are in a straight line, a few shirts and pants, but not nearly enough for someone who's supposedly living here full time.

Suspicion gnaws at me, and I close his closet before turning back to the rest of his room, and honestly, there's not much to look at. Making my way across to his bedside table, I plonk my ass on the edge of his bed and feeling that this is somehow too intimate, I get right up again.

Pulling open the top drawer, I find an envelope, and despite my better judgment telling me I don't want to know what's in it, I reach in, my curiosity knowing no bounds. As my fingers curl around the smooth envelope, I feel something cold and hard beneath it and quickly pull my hand away.

A gasp of terror flies from my lips as I stare at the gun tucked into the drawer.

A fucking gun.

I'm no prude. I wasn't expecting to find this place the picture-perfect home with flowers and teacups, but I sure as fuck wasn't expecting this. Though, I shouldn't be surprised. The asshole kidnapped me and locked me up in a fucking cell. I should expect someone like him to have a gun. Hell, after what they put me through, I should have a gun.

My brow arches, the thought already rooted in my brain, and without even a shred of hesitation, I reach for the gun and tuck it into the back of my jeans. Hell, Zade was probably planning on using this thing on me anyway, so rather than considering this theft, it's simply a lifesaving move. Consider it forward thinking with a side of self-preservation.

Making a mental note to google how to use this thing, I bring my attention back to the envelope. It hasn't been sealed and I flip it over for easy access, much like the way Dalton had me up on that roof. Opening the top, I tip it up and discard its contents onto Zade's bed, and my world goes cold once again.

A handful of black calling cards—like the one I'd found stabbed to the back of my bedroom door—fall from the envelope and scatter over his bed. I suck in a gasp, reaching for one and skimming my thumb over the glossy E on the front. I knew it was that bastard. I fucking knew it.

Seeing another bit of paper camouflaged within the calling cards, I reach for it, pinching the corner and pulling it up. The scattered cards fall off the bed and I stare down at a photograph of me. Turning it over, I find my full name, the address of this apartment complex with my unit number, my phone number, and my social security number.

Why am I not surprised?

Feeling my world closing in on me, I slip both the photograph and one of the calling cards into the back pocket of my jeans. I can't help but feel as though there's so much more going on than just coincidentally living next to four psychopaths. They must have known who I was before I moved in here, knew where to find me, and had all these personal details. I've been targeted by them. The only question is, why?

Knowing I need to get out of here now more than ever, I grab the cards and shove them into the top drawer, not bothering to slide them back inside the envelope.

Spinning around, I go to race out of Zade's room when I come face to face with all four of the assholes with the door closed behind them. I immediately fall back, fear paralyzing me to the point I can't even scream. How did they get in here without me noticing?

All I know is that I'm alone with my kidnappers. The one place in this world I can't be.

Zade steps toward me and my knees almost crumble under me. He steps again, and I find myself backing up until there's nowhere left for me to go. "It seems we have ourselves a little situation," he rumbles, his thick, deep tone vibrating through my chest as he takes that final step, moving directly in front of me.

Those dark, dreary eyes lock onto mine, and I find it almost impossible to breathe. "I'd suggest you back the fuck up," I warn him, finding my voice.

The corners of his lips pull into a twisted smirk and he looks at me like some kind of bunny that's unknowingly wandered into the lion's den. "Or what?"

My hand moves faster than lightning, gripping the gun at my back and whipping it out, pressing the barrel right up against his chest. "Or I'll fucking put you down."

His grin only widens, not even glancing at the gun. Hell, it's like he doesn't even see it. "You want to play with the big boys, baby?" he questions. The way he calls me *baby* does wicked things to me. "Go ahead, pull the fucking trigger."

Unease blasts through my chest as he presses into the gun, daring me to take the shot. Zade's eyes blaze with excitement, the power struggle getting him off, and I quickly realize this is a challenge. One he knows I can't win.

A hint of disappointment flares through his eyes as my hand shakes, and I can't help but wonder if he wants me to pull the trigger. His hand moves at my side, and before I know it, my chest slams against the wall, my hand shoved hard behind my back.

Zade presses in, while somehow still managing to keep his distance, his body just barely a breath away from mine. His hand curls over mine on the gun, his lips hovering by my ear. "Release it."

Swallowing over the lump of fear blocking my throat, I hesitate, not wanting to give up the only leverage I have. But his hand tightens, squeezing mine until I physically can't hold on to it a second longer. A pained squeak pulls from deep in my throat, and Zade takes the gun and hands it to Sawyer. Assuming that's it, I go to push away from the wall, but Zade's hand is right there, shoving me back again. "Not so fast," he growls, this time his whole body presses up against mine, his breath brushing against the curve of my neck. "You've got something that belongs to me."

I shake my head, more than ready to deny it until I'm blue in the face, but he doesn't wait for my response and simply slips his hand straight into the back pocket of my jeans. Zade's fingers curl around the photograph and calling card, slowly dragging them back out before tossing them carelessly on the bed.

Knowing he's got exactly what he wants, I shove back against him, and he takes a step back. Though something tells me if he wanted to keep playing this wicked game of cat and mouse, he could have easily done so.

I spin around, not liking him having the advantage, though any step I take in this room, I'm severely outnumbered. No matter what I do or say, I'm at the mercy of their hands.

"What's that card?" I demand. "What kind of bullshit are you involved in?"

"It seems you're lost," Zade tells me, ignoring my question as Dalton's sharp gaze flicks between me and Zade with a strange mix of curiosity and fear.

"Lost?" I question. "You'll have to forgive me. I thought breaking into people's apartments is just what we did around here. Consider it a debt now paid."

"You don't know who the fuck you're talking to."

"And you do?" I challenge, pointing toward my picture on his bed. "You've been fucking with me since the second I got here, and clearly whoever gave you that picture thinks I'm someone else because I didn't sign up for any of this shit. I don't know you, or your friends, and I sure as hell don't owe you a damn thing, so either tell me what you want with me or leave me the fuck alone."

His eyes sparkle, a strange excitement flashing deep inside of them, and I back up toward the wall again. "I know exactly who you are, Oakley Quinn, and you're wrong. You owe me more than you could ever understand."

I watch him for a moment, my gaze narrowing further with every word that comes out of his mouth. "Oh my God, that's it," I breathe, realization dawning. I may not be callous, cold, and cruel like he is, but one thing's for sure. Without intending to, he's shown me a weakness.

His brows furrow, clearly having no fucking clue what I'm talking about. "That's what?"

"You have some kind of rape fetish, don't you?" I question. "I can see it in your eyes. Every time I argue or put up a fight, something comes alive in your eyes. You want me to run and scream just so you can pin me down and assert your power over me. Or is that it? You have a power kink and like to be the big boss in charge, but something like that only comes from being a scared little boy with daddy issues. Tell me, did your daddy beat you as a kid?"

Anger flares through his eyes as Dalton discreetly moves closer. He curls his hands into fists at his side, while the rest of his body remains impossibly still. Getting under his skin is the best rush I've ever felt . . . only second to what Dalton did to me on the roof.

Feeling braver than I should, I step back into Zade, my tits brushing across his chest. I lower my voice to a soft whisper. "Tell me, does locking your hand around a woman's throat get you hard? Squeezing tighter and tighter until she's gasping for air, your fingers bruising her porcelain skin? You love it don't you? You crave power, and when you don't have it . . . well, that's just something you can't handle."

"You don't know what the fuck you're talking about," he growls.

"Oakley," Dalton warns, creeping in closer. "Back the fuck off before you do something you can't come back from."

I scoff, raising my chin just a little higher, looking Zade dead in the eye. "Have you ever taken it too far? Got carried away fucking her tight little pussy while gripping her throat and then realized she was already dead?" Something flashes in his eyes and I scoff, realizing I'm onto something here. "I'm right, aren't I?"

"Watch yourself," he says, seeming in complete control despite the rage burning through his stare. "Or would you prefer to find out exactly how hard taking your life is going to get me?"

A shiver sails down my spine, and I watch him through a curious stare. I know damn well he has the means to follow through on that promise, but something tells me that he won't. When I pushed him, Dalton stepped in, worried about letting this get too far, and if they really didn't care what happened to me, he would have finished me right then . . . yet here I am, still breathing, still free to say what needs to be said.

A smirk pulls at the corners of my lips, and I look up at him with a pitying stare, but only for the purpose of bruising his ego. "Why'd you let me go?"

"What?"

"On the weekend. You kidnapped me and held me hostage in your little bullshit prison, went as far as letting that asshole insinuate he was going to rape me," I say, pointing toward Sawyer. "Yet not a single one of you touched me. Why's that? What's the point? Why exert the effort of taking me and holding me captive, only to let me go?"

Zade clenches his jaw, refusing to answer, but it's fine. I'm more than happy to offer an answer of my own. Feeling the confidence soaring through my veins, I lock my stare onto his and let him have the cold, hard truth. The conviction in my tone seems to make him uneasy. "It's because you're not man enough to follow through. You can talk the talk, but when it comes to taking that final shot, you don't have the fucking balls."

I'm violently thrown up against the wall, Zade holding me up off the ground with nothing but his hand locked around my throat. I try to scream, but not a damn sound comes out, my airway blocked, leaving me desperate for air. "Is that something you're willing to bet your life on?" he questions, a fierce determination in his eyes.

My hands shoot up, clutching at his fingers, desperately trying to pull them back. I fight against him, my shallow gasps getting smaller by the second. I'm running out of time, running out of oxygen, and I quickly realize just how wrong I am. He does have the balls to do it, and what's more, he fucking lives for it.

Dark spots start to appear in my vision, and as he stares back at me, I see relentless cruelty in his eyes. He's not going to kill me, at least not yet, but he's sure as fuck going to keep playing his twisted little games.

"Zade," Dalton warns, a scary, low pitch in his tone, his warning clear as day. "We still need her."

Zade doesn't even flinch, and it's as though he doesn't hear him.

"Come on, man," Cross says, the snake weaving between his fingers.

The darkness swallows me, consuming my body and sending ice shooting through my veins like venom, and yet he doesn't relent, his fingers only tightening around my throat.

My hands go limp, falling to my sides, and the fight dies inside me as my lungs burn and ache. The desperation is overwhelming, and I see my whole life flashing before my eyes. I never should have come in here, never should have challenged him.

Then just like that, as I start to fall into unconsciousness, Zade releases me. I fall heavily to the ground, desperately gasping for air, and without a single word, my four captors turn on their heels and walk out the door, leaving me as I slip into a world full of darkness.

CHAPTER 13

Cross

"**Y**ou took it too fucking far," Dalton mutters as we make our way through the old train tunnels, our footsteps echoing through the darkness as Venom twists her way up my arm. Dalton shakes his head, fury rippling through him. He's been like this since we left the apartment complex, and honestly, I'm about ready to throttle him.

Dalton said he wouldn't get attached, and the little bitch is practically drooling over the girl already. He's putting Zade in a fucked-up position, and in the end, we're the ones who are going to suffer. Dalton should know that. There's no way in hell Zade isn't going to go through with this. He's worked too hard to get where he is. Come the night of the sixtieth moon, she will die, and Dalton better be ready.

Zade walks up ahead, not wanting to hear what any of us have to say. Tonight rattled him. Oakley might have been way off on her judgment, but something about her delivery got under his skin. Perhaps it was the fire in her eyes. She challenged him like no other woman has, and he didn't fucking like it.

Zade DeVil has always lived in black and white, but Oakley Quinn has gray written all over her.

I'm not going to lie, the little she-devil has a spark to her, something that has me wanting to know more. I'm curious to see what makes her break, just how far she can be pushed. Not even with Zade's hand around her throat did she crumble.

She was fucking petrified, but she sure as shit didn't break.

Making our way deeper through the old train tunnel, we find the door on the right, and Zade steps up toward it, slipping the old brass key into the lock. It looks just like every other maintenance door in here, only this one is different. So fucking different.

Zade turns the key and we all listen for the familiar sound of the intricate locking system within the wall. We have many entrances to our underground compound, but this has to be my favorite. Parking lots of high-rise buildings, church basements, there's even one below the city prison, but this right here . . . this one was the first.

Empire is the most exclusive society this country has ever seen, home to those who boast power and wealth. Politicians, law enforcement, judges, and CEOs of multi-billion-dollar corporations. How else would we get things done? We're a system, a partnership, and we have each other's back.

Being a member of the most exclusive society gets you whatever you could possibly need. Want a college degree without the bullshit? Consider it done. Need to fake your own death? Easy. Accidentally put a bullet through your wife's fuck boy? Not a problem, it'll be dealt with before you've had your breakfast.

Empire is a well-oiled machine, everybody pitching in where needed, and because of that we've thrived for generations, each of us benefiting from a system that rewards power. I wouldn't have it any other way.

Walking through the old door, we each stop at the security checkpoint. I place my hand on the palm scanner while also leaning in toward the retinal scanner, watching as a blue light flashes behind it and scans my eyes. My face appears on the screen with my name and Empire member details. "Welcome Easton Cross," the robotic voice says. "Please enjoy your stay."

"Oh, I will," I tell it, letting Venom slither in through my shirt sleeve and up over the back of my neck where she likes to stay. I don't know what it is about these tunnels, but she doesn't like them. She gets agitated down here and usually, I try not to bring her. But with the party at the apartment complex, there was no way in hell I was about to leave her behind.

Bringing my hand up, I brush my fingers over her body, letting her know she's safe before sailing down the steps, sending me deeper underground.

Sawyer trails behind me, and as we hit the bottom of the narrow stairs, he reaches ahead to the gold-plated, wrought iron gate—the main entrance of Empire's greatest compound. Sawyer unhooks the heavy chains before pushing another key through the lock and giving it a firm twist. He pushes the heavy gate open and we trail in as he holds it for us. Once inside, Sawyer pulls the gate shut and locks it again, our security one of our greatest assets.

There's another set of stairs, and the further we get, the more at home I feel. We go farther down, deeper into the darkness, then finally, we push through a third door and Empire stares me in the face. A cloud of the most expensive Cuban cigar smoke hits me before I even get a glimpse of the rich mahogany bars that line the room.

Welcome to the most exclusive gentlemen's club this world has to offer.

The country's most powerful men linger around with cigars hanging from their fingers, boasting about their achievements as dancers grind on their laps. Every room I walk through tonight will look just like this.

The city of Faders Bay was built on the backs of the men of Empire after our compound was completed all those years ago. Faders Bay quickly became a home for our families, schools for our children, workplaces, hospitals, and stores, and has since grown into something incredible.

We make our way into the compound, my feet skimming the dark Italian marble, and with every step we take, I feel their curious stares fall toward us. It's always a fucking party down here, always alive and thrumming with dancers and booze. But since Lawson DeVil, Zade's father, was found dead in his home, there's been a strange tension in the air. We're in this mourning period, a transitional time for Empire, and it puts everyone on edge. There's no telling what could happen. Everyone has always been curious about Zade. He was the leader's only son, the heir who would one day reign, but now that curiosity is almost overwhelming. He has the attention of every last man in the room, whether he's looking this way or not.

Everybody is wondering what will happen. Whether Zade is ready to lead our people and if he has what it takes. Just one sign of weakness will have the foundation of Empire crumbling. We may be a society built on blood and trust, but the kind of men we surround ourselves with can smell weakness. If Zade can't fulfill the role left by his father, it'll be a fucking blood bath.

They won't stop until Empire is theirs, even if they have to burn it down to get it. That much was clear the second a hit was put out on Oakley, which is the very reason we're here.

Someone betrayed Zade, and it starts with The Circle, our highest members. I suppose it somewhat works like a board of directors for a big company. They all think they hold the reins, when in fact, they're nothing but glorified pencil pushers for Zade . . . or at least, they will be by the sixtieth moon. The Circle answers to the blood, and since Zade is the only remaining heir, the only living member with the blood of Empire pulsing through his veins, that makes him a big fucking deal around here. Which is exactly why we need to figure out who the fuck ordered that hit.

Sawyer's father, Nikolai Thorne, steps out of a side room, his sharp gaze locked on his son. "Sawyer," he demands, his tone low and full of authority.

Sawyer nods and takes off to meet his father, and I watch with a sharp eye. Down here within the walls of Empire, Nikolai is a straight-to-business kind of guy. He's one of our twelve Circle members, and when the time comes for him to pass, Sawyer will take that position. Nikolai's been training him his whole life, pushing him to be the best, and it's paid off. Sawyer is more than ready to walk in his father's shoes. Despite Sawyer having absolutely no interest in taking over the position from his father, that won't stop him honoring the tradition and duties expected of him. It was what he was raised to do.

Me? Not so much. My father was a piece of shit, and the day he died was the best day of my life.

With Sawyer occupied, Zade looks at me. "Know what you're doing?" he questions, flicking his gaze to Dalton, and despite being on different pages when it comes to Oakley, I know Dalton will always have his back.

I nod, my stare sweeping the room—a room full of suspects. "We'll find this fucker," I promise him. "The asshole was as good as dead the second he decided to step out against us."

"Keep your eyes open," Dalton says, reaching out and taking a glass of whiskey from the waitress getting around in nothing but black lingerie, fishnet stockings, and a pair of black heels that make her ass look good enough to bite. He lifts the glass to his lips and finishes every last drop in one swig. "Whoever this bastard is, he'll be here tonight trying to cover his tracks. After his hit went south, he'll be desperate and will eventually slip up."

Zade nods, his sharp gaze out at the mingling crowd. "Good. Find this bastard and bring him to me," he says, his tone chilling and cold. "In the meantime, I'm going to have a nice little chat with my Circle members."

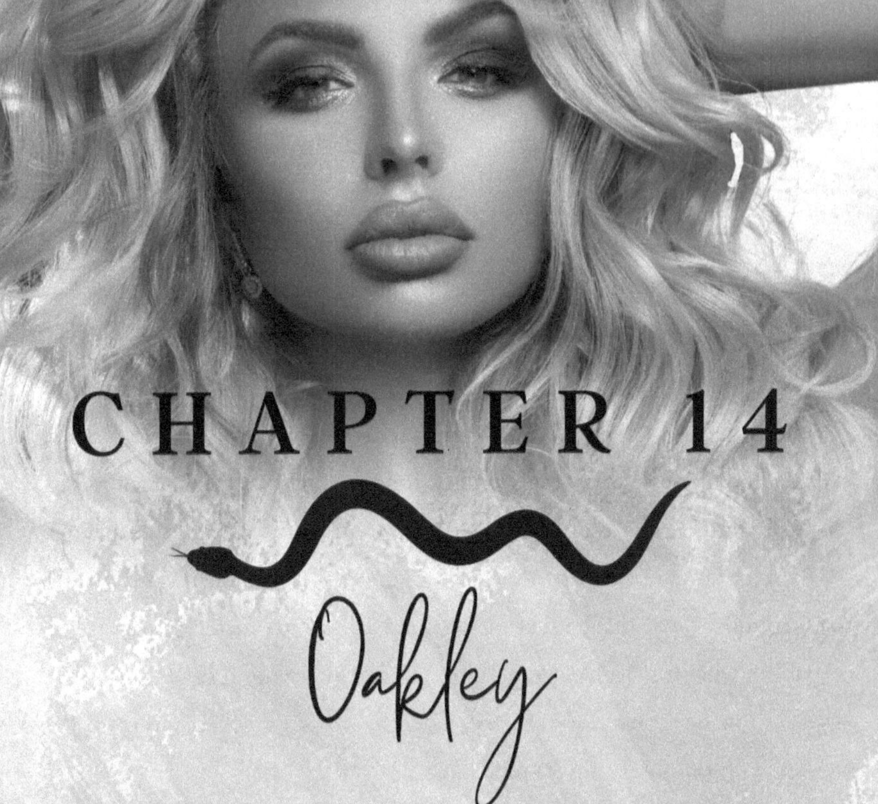

CHAPTER 14

Oakley

My eyes are wide as I stare at Cara's small TV, listening to all the sordid details about the DeAngelis brothers in the latest True Crime serial killer documentary. I hoist my blanket up, covering my mouth and nose while my eyes peek out over the top, unable to look away despite knowing the three psychopathic brothers are going to make frequent visits in my dreams, and it won't be the good kind of dreams.

They're ruggedly sexy, but there's something in their eyes, something that reminds me of Zade and Cross, and I don't like it one bit.

Chills sweep over my body, listening to the descriptions of exactly what these brothers have done and I tug my blanket right up. "I don't know how the hell you watch this shit," I say to Cara, my throat straining with every word.

"Isn't it awesome?" She beams and reaches forward to grab my bottle of water before double-checking how much I've drank. "You sound like shit, girl. What did I tell you about drinking water? If you don't keep it up, it'll never get better."

I groan and grab it from her, hating that we're talking about this again. Wednesday night was one of the worst nights of my life, and I'm still a little foggy on the details. One second, Zade's hand was around my throat, and the next thing I know, I might have been dead on the ground . . . or maybe just passed out. I have no fucking idea, but if that's what it feels like to die, I don't want anything to do with it.

I've never been so terrified. The way my lungs ached and my body gave up on me . . . it was terrifying.

I remained on Zade's bedroom floor for nearly two hours, not having the strength to get up and cross the hall to my apartment. But the moment I did, I fell through the door and right into Cara's arms. She nursed me back to health as I sat with tears streaming down my face, then she climbed into my bed with me and told me everything was going to be okay. I feel like shit for being suspicious of her before.

Cara has been a great friend, even going out and finding me a new concealer to mask the bruises Zade left on my skin. Though, to be honest, I think it's easier to go for the whole turtleneck look, despite how much I loathe anything touching my neck right now. Either way, I have work tonight, and there's no way in hell I'm about to walk into Danny's Bar sporting my new temporary necklace—courtesy of Zade.

"You know," Cara says as the documentary flashes to a still shot of a beautiful woman looking back over her shoulder, an image that looks as though it must have been taken by the feds. "That chick there, Shayne something. Apparently she's with all three of the brothers."

My face scrunches as I glance back at her. "Huh? What do you mean with them all?"

"Like, she's all of their girlfriend. You know, sharing is caring and all of that juicy shit."

I gape at her, in no way believing this at all. I mean, damn, it sounds like a dream come true, but there's just no way. "How the hell is that supposed to work?" I question. "They're leaders of a mafia house, and I don't know how many of those you've met before, so correct me if I'm wrong, but I doubt someone who runs a billion-dollar empire is down for sharing his toys."

Cara laughs. "You never know with these types of guys. Maybe group activities are their thing."

"Wait." I blanch. "You think they're all doing her at the same time?"

We both glance back at the screen, taking in the three ruggedly sexy men staring back at us, and that tiny woman. "Nah," Cara says slowly. "She can't fit all three of them in there at the same time. Look at her, she'd break. But then . . ."

As she trails off, I know exactly where her mind has gone because mine is right there with hers. "Not gonna lie," I say. "Getting with all three of them at the same time sounds like—"

"Every single one of my filthiest dreams come true?" she finishes for me. "I bet guys like that come with some pretty messed-up kinks. Like chains and guns and—"

"Guns?" I question. "What the fuck are they doing with guns?"

Cara just stares at me, her brow slowly arching, willing me to figure it out on my own. The moment I do, I suck in a gasp. "Noooooo," I breathe. "Really? Up there?"

"Uh-huh." She grins, her eyes sparkling with silent laughter.

"No, there's no way that shit really happens," I tell her, convinced she reads too many books because damn, that wild imagination of hers is going to get her into a world of trouble.

Cara laughs. "Girl, okay. Tell me this. Would you do it? Three guys at once?"

I think it over and give an easy nod. "Yeah, I'm not going to say no, but all the guys have to be packing some serious heat. I mean, if I'm getting railed like that, it's gotta be worth my while. Oh, and obviously no one-pump chumps. It's gotta be all night long." I burst into a coughing fit and she hands me my drink again, her brows furrowed as she watches me sip my water. "What about you?" I try to ask without dying.

"Girl, do you even have to ask?" she questions, giving me a knowing look, her lips twitching as she tries to keep a straight face. "What about four?"

"Four guys?" I ask, my brows shooting up. "Oooh, shit. That's a lot of dick."

"Uh-huh," she agrees with a nod. "That's like . . . dick central right there."

I nod right back. "Cock mania."

Cara all but drools down her chin. "Okay, risky question," she warns me, putting me right on the edge. "You know these four asshole neighbors of ours. If they came knocking on our door and said they were here to clean out your pipes, would you throw it back for them?"

I stare at her as though she's just lost her mind. "Are you insane? They kidnapped me and then almost killed me two nights ago. Hell no, they can go and clean out some other bitch's pipes."

Cara laughs. "No, no . . . I mean . . . personalities aside. Based on looks alone. If they were totally acceptable, honest, hard-working guys who just happened to stumble upon this apartment and you were all alone and needy."

My face flames as I really consider what she's asking me. All four of them are the perfect example of man candy. Those intense stares, the strong arms, the authoritative tones, and fuck me, those bodies. They're all tall and god-like in their own way, and damn it, if Dalton hadn't done what he did, I'd already be on my knees for him again. "Damn it," I say, this question frustrating the crap out of me. "Okay, if they were four regular guys that just happened to stumble across this apartment and were trapped in our asshole neighbors' bodies, then yes, absolutely yes. I'd do my stretching, drink plenty of water, and a quick google on how that's actually supposed to work. I mean, I've only got three useful holes, and I don't want someone stuck with a lousy handy while his friend is getting the good shit. I'd have to figure something out. Also, like . . . where do they all stand? Or do half of us stand and the other half lay down?"

"Huh," she breathes, her brows furrowed, deep in thought, and then just like that, her phone is in her hands and we're squished together on the couch, working out exactly how this insane little fuck fest is supposed to go down.

We're barely even scratching the surface of our research when my head snaps up and I catch sight of the time, my eyes widening in raw panic. "Ahh, shit," I say, noticing the time. "I have to start getting ready for work. I'm gonna be late."

Cara's eyes bug out of her head, gaping at me as though I just told her I'd prefer one dick over four. "What? Work? Are you insane?" she shrieks. "You can't go to work like that. You can barely talk. Besides, you can't just bail on me with this. We have a lot of content to get through before either one of us can be considered thoroughly educated."

"I'll be fine," I throw back, tossing my blanket off and getting to my feet. "And somehow, I think you'll be just fine with researching on your own. Besides, it's so loud on a Friday night that I don't even need to talk. No one can hear me anyway. I just pour beers and take money."

"I want it stated for the record that I don't like this," she says, throwing her blanket off and marching to the kitchen for a bottle of wine. "Though, if you're planning on working, I'm not going to say no to getting a little fucked up and seeing if Josh up on the third level has any friends."

I laugh and shake my head as I trudge down to my room, pushing through the door and quickly getting ready. I do what I can to cover up the bruises on my neck, and before I know it, I'm flying back out the door.

"Don't forget your water," Cara calls after me, making me double back and toss all our blankets around before finding the bottle halfway under the couch.

I get back to my feet and glance up at Cara, already well and truly through that bottle of wine. "Don't get too fucked up," I tell her, though there's really no point. She'll be annihilated before I even get to the bar. "And if you happen to screw Josh and a bunch of his friends, try and remember every nasty detail because I'll need them all." And with that, I take off out the door, hoping to God I don't run into any assholes on the way.

Reaching the bar with two minutes to spare, I hurry to the back while waving to Heather and Hannah on my way. It was a miracle I made it here unscathed, but now I have to somehow get through the rest of my night. I don't doubt that at some point they'll show up here. Three of them with cold, hard stares while the fourth just looks at me with guilt.

I go to clock in for the night and as my gaze lifts to the small tablet, I pause, finding a sealed black envelope stuck to the screen with my name written in fancy calligraphy across the front. My blood runs cold, and I quickly scoop it up before anyone sees it. As I flip it over, I find that same glossy E stamped on the back.

Every nerve and cell in my body screams at me to burn it, but the curiosity is just too great. Clutching the envelope tighter, I finish clocking in, and the second I can, I race to the bathroom and slam the door behind me.

There could be anything inside this envelope, and my gut tells me it's from one of the boys. My hand shakes as I flip it over and slip my finger under the seal to break it open. A million thoughts fly through my head. It could be a note. A warning. An apology.

I almost start laughing at the absurdity of that last one. There's no way in hell it would be an apology. Hell, I don't think a single one of those guys has ever muttered the words *I'm sorry* in their lives.

With my shift starting any second, I slip my hand inside the envelope and pull out the paper hidden within. My brows furrow as I glance over the elegant design.

It's an invitation.

Starting from the top, I scan over it again, making sure I'm reading it properly.

Dear Miss Oakley Quinn,

You are cordially invited to attend the 145th annual Empire ball, celebrating the birth of our great institution and the sacrifices made by the honorable men before us.

What. The. Actual. Fuck?

A ball?

Hell, I thought this envelope was going to include instructions on how to build a bomb just so one of them could have the luxury of making it explode in my face, but a ball? A freaking ball? What the hell is going on here? That was the last thing I expected.

The invitation goes on to give details about the time and date, venue, and dress requirements, and as I try to wrap my head around all of this, I find myself already wondering what I might wear.

I must be insane for considering this, but already in this one little invitation, I've received so many answers. The biggest of all—Empire.

I don't know what it is or what they stand for, but it's a starting point. All I know is that for some reason, those four assholes want me at that ball, and I'll be damned if I show up with them. No, I'll be going alright, but I'll be going on my own terms. And this time, I'll be the one with the upper hand.

CHAPTER 15

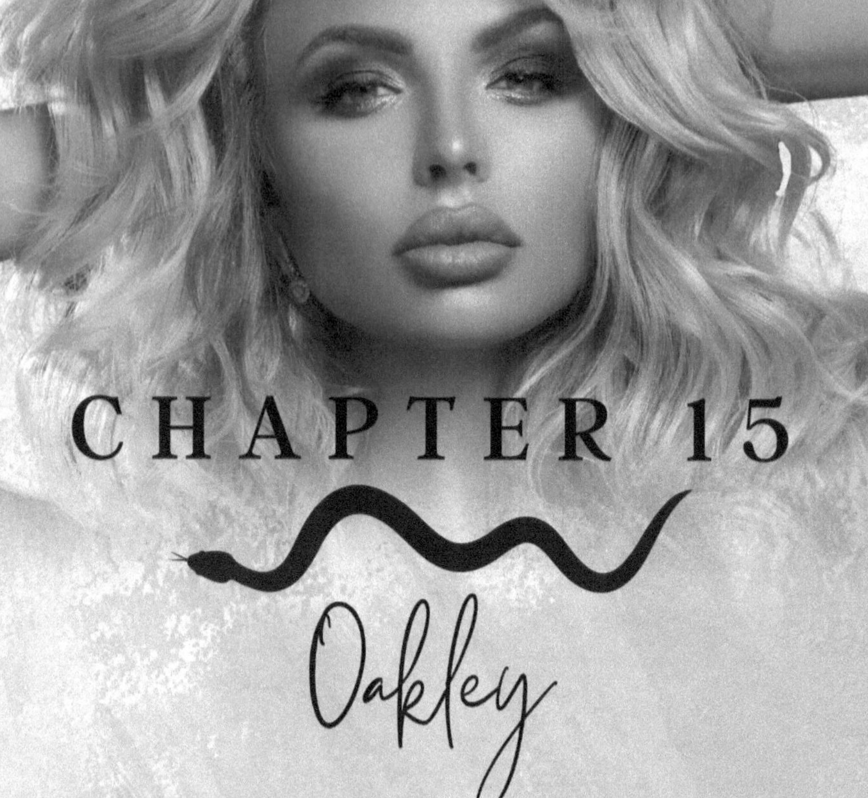

Oakley

The floor-length golden gown makes me feel as though I'm the most beautiful girl in the world, so it's a shame my hair has got me looking like a drowned rat. What was I thinking when I decided to get ready in my car? This is ridiculous. I almost broke the gown just trying to get into it, but I refused to get ready anywhere near that apartment.

No one can know I'm going to this, not even Cara. She'd kill me if she knew I received a fancy little invitation to a grand ball from our neighbors and didn't burn it right away. I had to tell her my aunt was in town for a dinner date and to check I'd settled into my apartment okay. She had no reason not to trust me and even helped me conceal my bruises on my way out the door.

So here I am in a cheap rental gown that's absolutely stunning, trying to fix my hair in the shitty little sun visor mirror with absolutely no way to get my hands on either a straightener or curler. I have to somehow manage to tame this bird's nest with nothing but a brush and my quickly fading will. Not to mention, my makeup is up next, and this shitty little mirror is not offering the best light.

After twenty minutes of nothing but flat-out struggling, I slip my feet into a pair of heels and let out a shaky breath. This is it. I'm ready . . . At least, I hope I am. The last two encounters I've had with these guys haven't been great. Kidnapping and almost murder. Is that what this Empire thing is all about? God, I wish there were some way to know what I was about to walk into, but something tells me a quick Google search isn't going to give me the answers I need.

Why do I have to be such an idiot? Fuck. My father would be rolling in his grave right now.

Double-checking the invitation, I find the venue information and hit the gas. My hands shake the whole way there, but there's no backing out now. It's a ten-minute drive, and I quickly find a parking space before climbing out of my car. People linger outside, women in gorgeous gowns that look as though they're worth more than I could make in a lifetime, their partners dressed in fancy five-piece suits, looking absolutely flawless.

Glancing down at my cheap rental gown, I've never felt more out of place, but I'm not here to fit in. Hell, I'm hoping I can slip through the door, find out what I need to know, then get out of there before anyone starts asking questions. If I happen to get out of there before any of my twisted neighbors see me, even better.

Gaping up at the magnificent building, my jaw drops. I've only driven through the city once and didn't get a chance to see much, but this . . . this is incredible. I feel like I've been transported back in time. The architecture looks as though it was pulled out of a Jane Austen movie and it has me ready to play out my wildest *Pride and Prejudice* fantasies. If only I actually believed any of the men inside this building were anything like Darcy.

Wanting to get this over and done with, I gather my confidence and try to remember that I have a set of steel balls, bigger than anyone who could show up here tonight. Okay, that might be a stretch. I have an attitude problem and a mouth that just seems to run no matter how bad the situation.

I make my way toward the grand entrance and keep my head down while clutching the invitation in my hand. There's a security checkpoint, and I fall in line behind the other guests, nerves blasting through my system. I wasn't expecting this. I was hoping I could just stride right through the front door and get lost among the other guests.

Security surrounds the building, and I wonder who the hell has been invited to this thing when I reach the front of the line. "Name," the security guard asks.

"Oakley Quinn."

His head shoots up, his brows furrowed as he looks me over, a strange curiosity in his eyes. "Quinn?" he questions.

I nod and he watches me a second longer before looking down at his clipboard, scanning through the list of names. "I'm not seeing your name on the list, Miss Quinn. Please move aside."

He goes to look over my shoulder, preparing for the next guest, but I hold my ground. They're not kicking me out that easily, not after all the effort I went through to get my hair to cooperate. I hold out the invitation, clearly with my name scrawled across the front. "I have a personal invitation," I tell the guard before letting out a frustrated sigh. "Look, I don't want to be here any more than you probably do, but someone inside that building wants me here tonight. I'm not leaving until I figure out why."

The guard looks at me with a blank stare. "You're the type to cause a scene if you get refused, aren't you?"

A wide grin stretches across my face. I don't need to respond; he knows damn well that I will.

Letting out a heavy breath, he waves me in and my grin turns into a genuine smile. "Thank you. It was a pleasure doing business with you," I tell him, only to receive nothing but a blank stare in return, clearly lacking in the sarcasm department.

Hurrying in before he changes his mind, I come to a startling halt, finding a breathtaking ballroom before me. I stand up on the top level, a grand staircase leading down to the stunning ballroom below. It's absolutely everything, fit for a queen on the most important nights of her life. The top level circles the whole room with arched balconies overlooking the ballroom below.

Chandeliers hang from the roof, filling the room with the brightest lights—a perfect contrast to the dark, intricate designs across the marble floor. High-arched windows line the walls, showcasing gorgeous gardens decorated with breathtaking fairy lights with the cityscape in the background, and I realize that despite everything, tonight might just be one of those magical nights I'll never have the luxury to experience again.

Despite my desperation to have my grand Cinderella entrance moment, I slip straight past the elaborate staircase and around the top level of the ballroom, overlooking the crowd below. There are people everywhere, and as I scan over the faces of the guests below, I realize there are more than just a few familiar ones.

Politicians, council workers, and the chief of police. Hell, even the local hospital administrator has a champagne glass in hand as he mingles with the crowd. Many of these faces I've seen splashed over the front of magazines and newspapers, boasting about their accomplishments in the community. Most of them have pockets lined with gold and silver, more cash than they know what to do with, and I can't help but feel this isn't a good thing. These are prominent figures of the Faders Bay community, the type of men who shouldn't have anything to do with the likes of Zade and his friends.

As if on cue, my gaze sails over the four boys, and my stomach all but drops out of my ass.

Good Lord, take the wheel.

These men. Holy shit. It was one thing seeing them in my apartment complex, stalking me like the creepy fucktards they are, but in their five-piece suits, looking sharper than ever before . . . I'm a goner. They're channeling David Beckham at the royal wedding, only in different shades, their jaws nearly as sharp as their suits.

My knees shake and my core clenches. This isn't fair. How am I supposed to concentrate on getting answers when they look like that? The only thing keeping me from making a fool of myself is the knowledge that these aren't the kind of guys I should be screwing with. Only then, Dalton turns around—holy fuck. Why does he have to be such an asshole? The way he looks tonight, damn. I'm ready for round two, though I will never give him the satisfaction.

I wonder if I could somehow trick him into taking a mold of his dick . . . you know, for scientific reasons of course.

Wanting to get this over and done with, I make my way around the top level before discreetly skimming down the far stairs and moving into the crowd. I keep my head down, but as I make my way through the ballroom, I can't help but feel the stares of the people around me.

I glance up and meet their curious gazes, some looking at me as though there's something familiar about me, something they can't put their finger on, while others watch me with sneers of disgust, knowing I don't belong. Either way, I don't like it.

Shuffling past them, I keep my eye on the prize. The boys are over toward the far corner, near one of the many bars, and wanting to be as discreet about this as possible, I slip deeper into the crowd, doing what I can to keep my head down.

Moving toward the edge of the room, I try to listen in on as many conversations as I can, but for the most part, it's just old men boasting about what kind of pull they have or the sneaky, under-the-table deals they were able to push through. Nothing jumps out at me, though one thing is clear. These upstanding men of the community, the very men who are supposed to look out for the health and wellbeing of the people around them, are nothing but frauds. It's all a front, a room full of powerful people who are able to make things happen for those around them.

Trying not to let the disgust show on my face, I finally reach the boys, doing what I can to keep my distance. I turn my back as I shuffle toward the bar and scoop a glass of champagne off the waitress' tray before she takes off with it.

Lifting the glass to my lips, I sip on what can only be described as pure liquid gold as I discreetly turn my head, listening to the boys' conversation behind me.

"This is our fucking chance," Zade seethes, his voice shifting as though he's scanning the room. "Keep your eyes open. Every conversation that goes down tonight, I want to know about. We got nothing at the compound, and I'm not about to let these fuckers get away with it again."

My brows furrow. Who's getting away with what?

There's a short silence before I hear Sawyer's familiar tone, the sound of it sending a chill down my spine, remembering exactly what he said to me in that concrete prison. "One of us should have stayed behind. She's left unprotected."

"No," Zade responds. "It's too fucking easy. Whoever is behind this is here keeping an eye on us. They want to know what we know. They won't be making another move until they're confident we don't have a name. Besides, she's out tonight."

What the fuck is going on here? Who the hell is this *she* they keep referring to? Is it me?

"That won't stop the bastard sending out another hit," Dalton says, his tone deep and full of concern.

"I don't think so," Cross says. "He knows he needs to up his game. That hitman was a fucking joke. If he wants to get to her, he's gotta get through us first, and anyone around here knows that's a fucking suicide mission. Only someone with the right connections could pull this off."

There's another short silence before Zade finally speaks again. "Put out feelers tonight. Talk to the wives and daughters. They'll tell you just about anything you want to know if they think they're about to get fucked by one of you bastards. I'll hit up—"

A loud gasp tears from my throat as something cool slithers over my hand on the bar, and I realize it's Cross's snake. I'm about ready to make a run for it, but a hand closes around the back of my neck, whipping me around with such force that I can't even scream.

The guys crowd me, my back pushed up against the bar. "What the fuck do you think you're doing here?" Zade demands, his tone loud enough to grab the attention of the guests around us, their curious stares flashing our way.

"What the hell is wrong with you?" I spit, shoving his hand off me, though something tells me he only obliges because we're in a very public space. "You invite a girl to a fucking ball and then forget about it?"

"I didn't invite you to shit," he says.

Still holding my invitation, I slam it up against his wide chest and he tears the paper out of my hand. "Well, it had to have been one of you," I say. "I'm not fucking stupid. The glossy E on the envelope was the same one on that stupid calling card you left in my room."

Each of them look clueless and my brows furrow, glancing toward Dalton. "You didn't send me this?"

He shakes his head as unease flashes in all of their eyes. They glance between themselves as though they just figured something out and are having some kind of silent conversation between themselves. Zade though? He just looks pissed. "They lured her out," he tells the boys. "And we fucking missed it."

"They're trying to make a fucking scene in front of the whole company," Sawyer says. "Trying to make you look weak."

A raw panic starts to pulse through my veins, and despite how much I hate these assholes, I find myself wanting to stick to them like glue. "What the hell is going on?" I demand, "Who sent me that invitation?"

All four of them ignore my question, and as if on cue, they each turn to scan the room, looking high and low until Cross nods toward the farthest corner of the room. "Sniper. Northeast corner. It's a fucking hit."

"Shit," Zade spits, grabbing me and shoving me hard into Dalton's chest, his steel grip closing around my arms. "The three of you go hide her. Don't let her out of your fucking sight, got it? I'm going to end this now."

They nod, and before I know it, Zade disappears into the crowd like a fucking ghost, but I don't get a chance to linger on it as Dalton drags me away with Sawyer and Cross hot on our heels. They move like lightning, and as I struggle to keep up, Dalton's grip on my arm is the only thing keeping me on my feet.

We push through to a private storeroom and Sawyer locks it behind us before shoving a hardback chair under the handle. I'm knocked aside as the boys immediately start to pace. This must be the room the caterers are using for extra storage. "How did we fucking miss this?" Dalton roars. "A hit in front of the whole fucking society. That's the kind of betrayal you don't come back from."

"They want him to look weak," Sawyer says, his eyes wild. "They're going to turn the whole society against him, making them think he can't handle it."

I throw myself back toward them, the anger blasting through my chest, not even caring that they're suddenly talking openly in front of me and are probably on the verge of answering some of those darker questions I'm probably not ready for. Right now, I have my own set of questions, and I won't stop until I get what I'm looking for. "One of you assholes better tell me what the fuck is going on right now or I—"

"Or you'll what?" Cross demands, stepping in front of me, just as lethal as Zade.

Without even taking a second to think it over, I curl my hand into a tight fist and nail him with the hardest uppercut I can possibly manage, watching as he sucks in a sharp breath. "I'm not fucking scared of you," I lie. "Now answer my fucking question before I tear your balls out through your throat."

Cross's jaw clenches and Dalton shoves between us, pushing us apart. "Enough of the bullshit," he says. "Both of you sit your fucking asses down. We've got bigger problems than this."

"Then go right ahead and enlighten me, asshole," I demand, refusing to back down. "Who sent me that invitation?"

Dalton shakes his head, the frustration in his eyes making it clear he's not going to answer.

"Just great," I scoff. "After what you did to me, you fucking owe me. Now tell me what I need to know."

Sawyer whips around. "We don't fucking know, alright? It's probably the same prick who left that calling card in your room."

I fall back a step, gaping at him. "Wait, that wasn't you?" I question, my voice shaking at the thought of there being someone else after me. "I thought it was Zade."

Sawyer's face scrunches with confusion. "Why the fuck would Zade leave you a calling card when he doesn't want you to know shit about any of this?" He lets out a breath and goes back to pacing in front of the door. "Look, just sit down and shut up, and we'll all be out of here soon."

"I—" I shake my head, the unease and wariness making me feel sick. Not knowing what else to do, I walk across the room and crack open a wooden carton before peering in with a smile. My hand curls around the neck of a bottle, and I pull it out, glancing over the label and not understanding a word of it. Though it's definitely French, so it must be good.

Popping the top, I bring the bottle right to my lips. If I'm going to suffer in here with two assholes and a backstabber, then the best I can do is make sure I don't remember it.

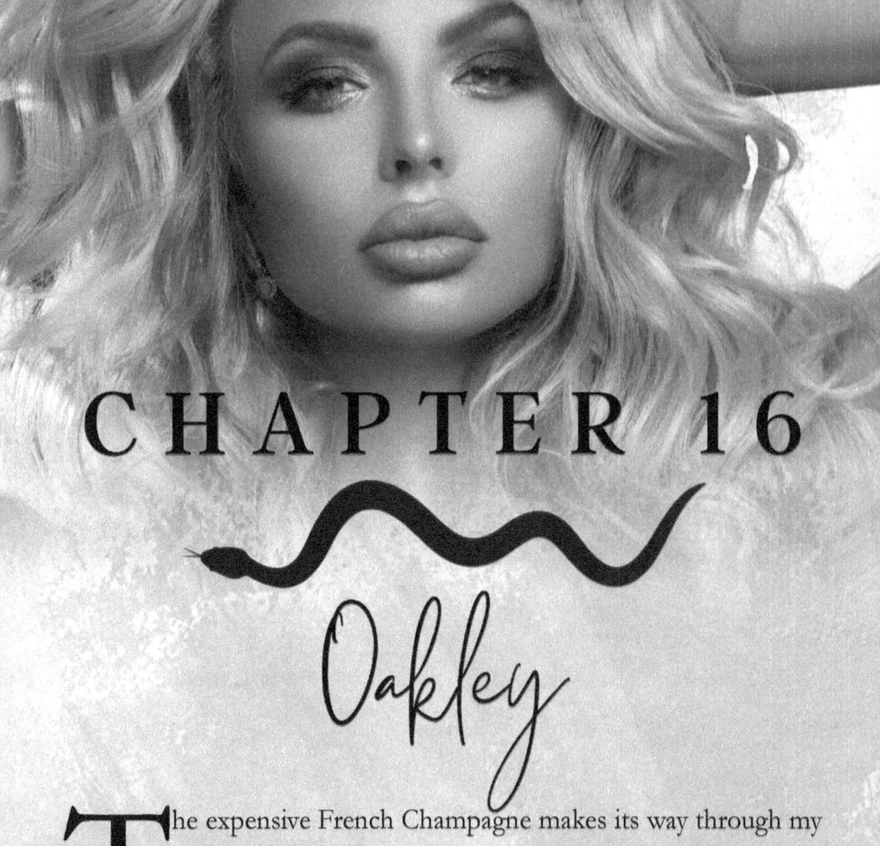

CHAPTER 16

Oakley

The expensive French Champagne makes its way through my body, taking away the unease and fear of being locked in this room, and suddenly making me feel much braver than I actually am. The bottle is just about empty as I shuffle around the room, watching the way my golden gown swishes with my movements.

I'm a princess. A horny princess. All I need is a pretty tiara, a castle, and a strapping young man packing a lot of heat. I'd be the happiest girl in the world.

The thought of ever being able to accomplish something like that has an unladylike chuckle forcing its way through my lips, and the sound has Dalton's head pulling up. He watches me with desire, and I like it so much, but I'll be damned if I let him touch me again. Though that doesn't mean I can't make him hurt.

I lock my eyes onto his as I keep my body moving through the room. My fingers brush over my collarbone and I watch as his attention drops to my hand. I slowly skim it down my body, between the plunging neckline of my gown, and let a seductive smile fly free across my face.

I have both Sawyer's and Cross's attention too, but I keep my eyes locked on Dalton, watching the way his cock thickens in his pants. So fucking delicious.

This is going to be fun.

Striding toward Dalton, I keep my eyes locked on his, making sure there's just enough sway in my hips to hold every last ounce of his attention. I walk right up to him, my finger brushing up his strong arm as he sits before me. I trail it over his wide shoulder as I make my way behind him and then lean down, my lips right at his ear. My tongue pokes out and I roll it up the side of his neck before capturing his earlobe between my teeth.

Dalton groans and adjusts his monster cock in his pants, the outline of his piercing staring back at me. "Just so you know," I tell him, my voice so low he turns his head just to hear me. "I'm going to fuck your friends."

Glancing up, I peer over at Cross who watches the way Dalton's face falls. "I think I'll start with him," I tell Dalton. "Good God, he's big. I bet he's even bigger than you. I won't lie though, that cock of yours was delicious. It's a shame I'm going to fuck your friends so hard it'll erase any memory of you ever being there."

I roll my tongue over my bottom lip, letting him see the hunger in my eyes. His jaw clenches as he realizes just how far I'm willing to take this. "I bet a man like that likes to go in bare. He'll fuck me until I scream, and once he's done and his warm cum is trailing down my thigh, I'll fuck Sawyer, and it'll be his name on my lips."

"Be my guest, Firefly," he says, swallowing hard. "You know no one will be able to fuck you like I did, but if you want to whore yourself out, that's your business."

I moan his name in his ear, and his whole body tightens. "I changed my mind," I whisper, and a ray of hope briefly sparks in his eyes, but I'm not the one, and today is not the day. I'm more than happy to shut him down all over again. "I'm gonna fuck them together. Cross in my tight little cunt, while Sawyer claims my ass, and all you'll be able to do is watch."

Dalton scoffs. "Whatever you say. They won't fucking touch you."

"No?" I question, brushing my hand under his chin and forcing him to glance back at his friend. "Look how they're watching me. See the hunger in their eyes? They want to taste me, fuck me, feel me squeezing their cocks. They wanna know how warm it is, how tight it is. They wanna know everything that you do. Don't try to deny it, Dalton. You're the one who put the thoughts in their heads. You're the one who left them wondering what's so fucking good about me. Why's this bitch got Dalton Eros in such a fucking bind?"

Dalton tears his chin out of my grasp, and I see the frustration clouding his eyes. Without waiting for whatever insult is coming my way, I stride across the room, taking another swig of Champagne. I don't know how this is going to go or who's going to end up where, all I know is that I'm down for whatever's coming my way. Whether Dalton can find the balls to demand I get on my knees or not.

I reach the door, raise my hand to the small dimmer by the frame, and give it a subtle turn, letting the room darken around us. I leave just enough light for Dalton to witness every last thing I plan to do to his friends, and as I turn back to them, I find all three of their heated stares locked on me.

None of them make a move, leaving the ball in my court, and I take full advantage. Glancing between Sawyer and Cross, I know without a doubt that Sawyer would be the easiest to crack, but I'm not interested in easy. I like a fucking challenge, and something tells me that getting Dalton's friends to worship at my feet is going to be the best kind of revenge.

Reaching up my back, my fingers curl around the small zipper, and I slowly drag it down as I move closer to Cross. His eyes lock onto my body, watching as the fabric loosens around me. I trail my fingers up to my shoulder and he follows the movement just as I knew he would. I push the thin strap off my shoulder and the dress bunches around the top of my breast, the low lighting creating a soft glow across my skin.

His dark eyes become hooded, and I step right between his legs, reaching down to his hand and bringing it up to touch my body, gently pressing it against the curve of my breast. My hand overlaps his and I apply more pressure, letting him know just how badly I crave his touch. His thumb stretches out, brushing over my nipple, and I suck in a breath as it hardens beneath his touch.

I release my hand, leaving him to explore, and he doesn't hesitate, brushing his fingers across my chest to my other shoulder and pushing the flimsy strap down my arm. The dress falls to the ground and I step out of it, making a point to remain in my heels.

His heavy gaze sails down my body, examining every inch of skin as I stand before him in nothing but a black thong. Cross trails his fingers down my waist and over my hip, and just before he slides them lower between my legs, he stands, crowding over me.

My gaze lifts to his, and it's only then I realize just how heavy I'm breathing. "You don't know what you're asking for," he mutters, that thick, rich tone making my pussy weep.

The tension rises between us, and knowing damn well what I want, I reach toward him, tugging his dress shirt out of his pants before gripping his belt buckle and tugging him into me. "I think you and I both know I'm fully aware of what I'm asking for. Just as we both know exactly how hard you're going to give it to me."

His gaze hardens, watching me as his hand grips my waist, his snake peeping out of the neckline of his shirt. "Here's what's going to happen," I tell him, adopting that same authoritative tone Dalton used with me on the roof, telling him exactly what I want and how he's going to do it. "You and Sawyer are going to man the fuck up and rail me until I scream, and we're going to do it right here until Dalton can't possibly take it anymore. He's going to watch, and he'll have no choice but to fuck himself right there in that chair. Are we clear?"

"I don't take orders from the likes of you," he says, looking at me as though I'm beneath him, and right now, I'm more than okay with that. The less attachment there is, the harder he'll be willing to fuck. "I'll fuck you how I want, where I want, and you're going to take it like a good little whore."

I raise my chin, letting him see the defiance in my eyes. "Welcome to the party."

Holding my stare, he reaches down between us and grips the lacy fabric of my thong before tearing it clean off my body. He doesn't dare look away, letting his intentions be known. If we're doing this, we're making it count.

Taking my waist, he lifts me off the ground and puts me on the table in the center of the room. He's not gentle, and I like that about him. Still holding my gaze, he tugs at his suit, pulling the pieces off one by one before standing before me in nothing but his pants, his belt buckle undone.

Tattoos cover his torso, and my gaze drops to his body, taking in the sharp ridges of his abs and the intricate designs covering his skin. His tattoos aren't like the ones I've seen before. There's something . . . cruel about them, something purposefully cold. The lines are bold, harsh, chilling, and I can't help but wonder if this design has anything to do with the people out in that ballroom.

My gaze continues down his body and I see his cock straining through his pants, making me crave him so much more. I was right. He's fucking huge.

Cross takes my thighs and spreads them wide before stepping into me. His gaze drops down my body again, his tongue rolling over his bottom lip. I bet he can smell my arousal, smell my desperation. His eyes flash back to mine and, in an instant, my back hits the top of the cool table.

I suck in a breath, but before I get a word out, Cross reaches up to the snake around his neck. It immediately twists around his hand, and before I know what the fuck is going on, he lowers the snake to my waist.

My heart starts to race, and I glance up at him, nervousness consuming me. I don't do snakes or any other kind of animal that could turn me into a fucking corpse. I'm more than ready to say something when Cross's thick tone sounds through the room. "Bitching out already?" he questions. "I knew you couldn't take the fucking heat."

Oh, hell no.

The snake starts slithering up my body and I do what I can not to panic while also trying to remain impassive. After all, there's no way in hell this motherfucker is about to know just how fucked up that one little move has got me. "For someone who talks a big fucking game, it's taking you a while to get on your knees," I tell him. "What's the matter? Not sure what you're doing?"

His eyes flame, and a low growl tears from the back of his throat. He takes my thighs and drags me to the very edge of the table, and I suck in a gasp, the anticipation destroying me. His hand comes down over my pussy as his fiery gaze remains locked on mine.

His fingers push down between my folds, slowly teasing and taunting me with what's to come, skimming over my clit and making me squirm as his snake trails across my body. He applies just enough pressure to my clit to make me groan, and just when I think I'm right on the edge, he pushes those same thick fingers deep into my pussy.

"Oh, God," I groan, tipping my head back. He's barely even gotten started, and I'm already on the edge.

His fingers move in and out before he takes them away, and I look back up at him, watching as he lifts his fingers to his lips. He opens wide and sucks them clean, his eyes blazing like never before. His fingers fall away and the way his tongue rolls over his bottom lip has got me in a fucking chokehold, but it's got nothing on the satisfied groan that tears from the back of his throat. "Eros was right," he mutters, that dark tone doing wicked things to me. "You've got the sweetest fucking cunt I've ever tasted."

Before another second passes, he drops to his knees, his mouth closing over my clit.

I cry out, the overwhelming pleasure too much for me to handle. He works me with his tongue as I push up onto my elbows, needing to watch the way his tongue rolls over my clit and destroys everything I ever thought I knew about having my pussy eaten. He sucks, nips, and teases, pushing me right to my limits. Then he slides those two fingers deep inside me again, curving them just right and massaging me from within. My eyes roll to the back of my head, and I'm about ready to explode when I see Sawyer stand from the corner of my eye.

I glance across at him, locking onto his stare as he strides toward us, slowly peeling off his suit jacket. It falls to the ground and he gets started on the rest of his attire, probably regretting the choice to wear such an intricate suit.

By the time he reaches me, his shirt is gone and I stare up at that gorgeous body. He's perfection, a fucking Adonis, but what's more are those piercing green eyes scanning over my body. He releases his belt buckle just as Cross flicks his tongue over my clit, and I cry out with undeniable pleasure.

Sawyer releases his cock and it's everything. Long and thick with angry veins, just the way I like it. He's not pierced like Dalton, but there's something about Sawyer's cock that has me desperate to taste.

He reaches out to me, gripping my chin as his thumb runs along my bottom lip, almost daring me to back down. But I won't fucking dare. Ever since Cara mentioned it in our apartment, this is all I've been able to think about.

Hearing a pained curse from across the room, my gaze snaps to Dalton's, and I grin wide seeing the irritation and jealousy flashing in his stare. This is exactly what you get when you stab a knife right through my back. He pulls against his pants, adjusting that monster cock, and I don't doubt he's feeling the pain.

Pulling against his grip on my chin, Sawyer forces my stare back to his. "When you fuck me, your eyes stay on me," he says, a tone in his voice that has my pussy clenching around Cross's fingers, making it impossible to look away.

I let him see the desire in my eyes, let him know just how hard I'll work for this, but at the same time, I'm not about to make it easy on him. "Prove you're worth fucking and I won't need to look away."

Goddamn, I must have a death wish.

Sawyer's thumb returns to my lips and he forces it inside my mouth, pulling down on my jaw until my mouth opens wide, though just like Dalton's, it's not going to fit. "I don't need to prove shit," he tells me. "So why don't you fucking take it and I'll let you know if you're worth fucking when I'm done?"

Oh, apparently Sawyer has a nasty streak after all, and I fucking love it.

A grin pulls at my lips, but I'm done talking. It won't be long until Cross has me coming on his fingers and when that happens, I fully intend to have Sawyer's cum hitting the back of my throat. He wants me to impress him, wants to understand what Dalton saw in me on the roof, and damn it, I plan on giving him my best work.

Opening wider, I reach for his cock, and he moves in enough for me to close my mouth over him. A small bead of moisture rests on his tip, and I greedily lap it up, rolling my tongue over his head and watching the way his face morphs from being this dominant asshole to a guy who just saw his whole life flash before his eyes. And it takes me even less time to realize just how easy this is going to be.

Sawyer's hand weaves into the back of my hair as Cross's snake settles high on my chest, the very end of its tail curving around my tit, but it's almost as though it's not even there, my attention far too focused on the boys. I work my mouth up and down Sawyer's impressive cock, my tongue working its magic as my grip tightens around his base.

He groans, his hand tightening in my hair, and I resist the urge to smirk. "Fuck, Doll," he says through a clenched jaw, his eyes glued to mine. I work him faster and harder, pushing him right to the edge as Cross does the same to me.

My pussy clenches, and as Cross sucks my clit into his mouth, his tongue flicking the sensitive bud, my world comes undone. I come hard, my orgasm blasting through me with a ferocity I wasn't prepared for. It sails through my body, electrifying every last nerve and bringing me to life.

My pussy spasms, convulsing around Cross's fingers as a low groan tears from the back of my throat, the sound muffled on Sawyer's cock. My high rocks through my body, and I feel like a junkie taking a hit of the purest heroin right through the bloodstream. Nothing less than euphoria.

My tongue rolls over Sawyer's cock, and just when I think he needs a little more, his hand tightens in my hair and he holds me still as he thrusts deep into the back of my throat, hot, delicious cum spurting into my mouth.

I swallow him down, not wasting a damn drop as his whole body jolts with satisfaction. His hand relaxes in my hair and the undeniable pleasure across his face is the sweetest thing I've ever seen.

Coming down from my high, Sawyer pulls free of my mouth, and I roll my tongue over my bottom lip as I try to catch my breath. But as Cross stands, his hungry stare locked on mine, I realize this is far from over.

His cock strains against the front of his pants with the need to slam straight back into me again. I hear Dalton across the room, sense him going to town on himself, but I don't dare look his way. I'm completely consumed by Cross's stare alone.

He reaches for me, removes his snake from my chest, and pulls me off the table. "Turn around," he demands, and damn it, I do exactly as he asks. Spinning on my heel, I barely get a chance to find my bearings before Cross pushes me to my knees. He comes down with me as a shiver of anticipation trails down my spine, and just as I get a glance at Dalton's mouth-watering cock across the room, my chest is shoved down to the ground and my knees spread wide.

Cross's cock hovers at my entrance, and just as he takes my hips, his fingers digging into my skin to hold me still, he thrusts deep into my cunt. I cry out, not being able to see just how big he is, but damn, I can more than feel it. He stretches me wide as he sinks lower, taking me deep and rough.

My eyes roll, pleasure rocking through my body, and before I know it, he's pulling back again. I groan at the way his cock moves inside me, and I can't help but slip my hand beneath me and feel him there. His cock is coated in my arousal, and it's one of the best feelings in the world.

He moves in and out of me and I lower my hand just an inch, my fingers brushing over my clit and rubbing tight circles as he rocks into me, thrusting again and again. I hear his desperate grunts as his fingers dig deeper into my hips and I push back against him, taking him deeper.

"Fuck, Cross," I pant, barely able to take another second as my body gets closer and closer to the edge. "God yes. Don't stop."

He's relentless, ferocious, and fucking godly as he fucks me, and it's everything I didn't know I needed. Dalton moves closer, and I look up, watching as he stands before me, his heavy, thick cock in his hand. He moves it up and down, working himself as he watches his best friend fuck me.

In. Out. In. Out. It's fucking magical.

Dalton gets faster and I recognize that intense, wild hunger in his eyes. He's going to come and it spurs me on. I press harder against my clit, the tight circles becoming erratic and desperate. My body jolts as Cross groans, and with one more thrust of his thick cock, my world detonates.

I come hard and fast, my eyes locked on Dalton's as his body stiffens, the best kind of pleasure rocking through as I watch him come. His eyes are glazed over with pleasure, but it's nothing compared to how he came on that rooftop. That was fire, and this right here is ice.

Pleasure overwhelms my body as Cross relentlessly fucks me, and just as it becomes too much for me to handle, he lets out a satisfied roar, shooting hot spurts of cum deep inside my pussy. He doesn't stop, doesn't release me until he's completely emptied himself, each movement making my high only that much stronger.

My pussy convulses around him, and after a moment passes, I finally come back to earth. I drop my face to the ground, pure exhaustion claiming my body as I try to catch my breath.

Cross releases my hips and doesn't say a word as he pulls out of me, but I watch the way Dalton meets his stare, something passing between them.

Knowing Zade is bound to come back at any moment, I reluctantly get to my feet, scooping my gown off the ground and stepping into it. "Here," Sawyer says, moving into me and taking my waist. He gently spins me and my back stiffens, waiting for that same asshole to return, but he simply takes the flimsy zipper and helps me back into my dress.

I brush my hair back over my shoulder as I feel Cross starting to leak out of me, making me feel like some kind of sex goddess. "Thank you," I whisper, meeting his green, blazing stare.

Sawyer simply nods before stepping away, and just as Cross finishes dressing, a sharp knock sounds at the door. "Yo, it's me," Zade says from the other side.

Dalton quickly crosses to the door and removes the chair wedged under the handle. He pulls it wide and Zade comes in, his knuckles covered in blood. He takes a step deeper into the room, and I watch as his deadly expression morphs into something a little more sinister.

He inhales deeply, his narrowed gaze locking onto mine before glancing at his friends, and without a fucking word, he knows exactly what went down in this room. "Get your fucking shit," he says, clearly not happy with this turn of events. "We're leaving."

"What happened?" Cross questions, finding my torn thong on the ground and kicking it toward me. "You get the bastard?"

Zade shakes his head. "The sniper took off the second we clocked him, but I caught up with him trying to escape through the basement." His eyes darken as he pulls the expensive pocket square from his suit jacket and starts cleaning off the blood staining his hands. "The fucker wouldn't break."

"Wouldn't break?" Dalton questions, his brows furrowed as though the mere thought of Zade not being able to break someone is simply unheard of.

Zade shakes his head and Sawyer meets his stare. "They're gonna keep coming."

Cross presses his lips into a harsh line. "Where does that leave us?"

Zade lets out a heavy sigh before lifting his cold gaze back to me, that usual calculating stare somehow even more terrifying. "Bring her with us," he states, his tone chilling and cruel. "Then we'll figure out exactly what we're going to do with her."

And just like that, Sawyer's tight grip curls around my arm, the soft touch from before now long gone. "Lucky you," he tells me, shoving me hard toward the door. "Looks like you're going to get some answers after all."

CHAPTER 17

Oakley

Waking up in the most luxurious silk sheets is definitely something I could get used to, as opposed to the sandpaper I sleep in back in my apartment. Which reminds me, that's exactly not where I'm waking up right now, despite my relentless objections.

Last night, Zade demanded they take me back to his place, and at first, I was confused, assuming he meant the apartment across the hall from mine. Only when we arrived at the DeVil Hotel and found ourselves in the penthouse suite, everything became crystal clear.

I was right. Zade doesn't live in that shitty apartment across from me. His life is here, and after having a quick glance around, it's clear this is more than just a home to him. This place is his whole life. He has a connection to it. Every inch of the apartment looks as though it fits him perfectly. The sharp lines, the cold marble, hell, even the ridiculous security measures he had to take to get up here.

The only problem is, I don't want to be here.

They haven't exactly kidnapped me. I have free rein to walk around, but when it comes to striding right out the door, that's where they draw the line. I have to admit, it's a huge step up from their usual tactics of locking me in a cement cell.

When we got in, Cross muttered something about a spare bedroom and thrust a towel into my hands, offering me a shower. Though it felt like more of a demand, and it was one I was more than happy to refuse out of sheer pride. But the moment I walked into the bathroom, I couldn't resist.

I figured Zade was loaded when I realized he owned the penthouse in one of the most luxurious hotels in the country, but it didn't really occur to me just how rich he must be until I walked into that bathroom. It was stunning, and after flicking the lock on the door, I bypassed the massive shower and went straight for the bath.

It wasn't until I was fully submerged in the hot water that the question hit me—Why the hell are the boys renting cheap-as-shit college apartments when Zade has a home like this? I can't pretend to know anything about the other three's financial situations, but assuming they have anything to do with whatever last night's ball was about, I could make a solid argument that their pockets are just as deep as Zade's.

After I'd soaked in the bath for over an hour, I wrapped my towel around me and left the bathroom in search of something to sleep in. The boys were sitting out on the balcony, their sharp gazes locked on me through the window, and it was almost as though the second I walked out, their conversation died. They must have been trying to figure out what the hell to do with me. But I couldn't care less because I was captivated by the stunning panoramic view of the city.

The city lights glittered and danced on the horizon, and I found myself pausing in the middle of Zade's ridiculously impressive home, my hair dripping over the floor just so I could take it all in.

Realizing that I was standing in nothing but a towel, I quickly scurried around the apartment until I found Zade's master suite. I welcomed myself in as though I had nothing to lose, quickly bypassing his massive bed before strolling right into his walk-in closet. Tearing open drawers and scanning through his clothes, I found a pair of sweatpants and a white tee and hastily pulled them on.

Coming back to the here and now, I stare out the window into the busy Monday morning, watching as the world passes me by, a sense of restlessness consuming me.

Enough is enough. I can't keep going like this. I need answers and I need them now.

Throwing my silk sheets back, I scramble out of bed and pad toward the door. I have no idea what time it is, but from the silence on the other side of the door, I can only assume it's early. My heart starts to race, not knowing what I'll find. These guys are so unpredictable. One minute I'm kidnapped, and the next I'm a guest in a luxury apartment.

They can flip in a matter of seconds, but what choice do I have?

I'm not about to spend my day locked up in here when I could be out there, figuring out what the hell is going on. Besides, I have work tonight, and I have absolutely no intention of getting locked up here indefinitely.

My fingers curl around the handle, and I slowly inch it open, peering out into the apartment to find Sawyer passed out on the couch. There's no sign of the others, and I bite my lip, wondering how this is going to go.

Slipping out of my room, I tiptoe across the penthouse. Pausing halfway toward the kitchen, I glance down the hall, making sure Zade, Cross, and Dalton aren't about to jump out at me with the twisted idea that they can start hunting me through the apartment like the psychopaths they are.

With the coast clear, I move closer to the couch, my gaze settling over Sawyer as he sleeps soundlessly, his arm propped behind his head. Like this, it's almost possible to imagine him as a nice guy, someone who'll come to my door with a bouquet of flowers, a cocky little grin, and a promise to give me the night of my life. But then I go ahead and remind myself that he's nothing but a cold, calculating asshole, just like his friend. His only redeeming quality being that cock between his legs.

I go to slip past him when I notice his phone left on the end of the couch, and my brow arches. Now is probably the only chance I'll get to make a run for it. I could slip out of the apartment and get my ass out of here in the blink of an eye, but then I'll be leaving with no answers. Or . . . I could reach down and take his phone and find the answers for myself.

Shit. What the hell is wrong with me? I swear, I'm really a smart girl. I make good choices, get good grades, and I don't sleep around. But since showing up here in Faders Bay, I've become a stranger to myself. I should run. I know that deep down, so why the hell am I lingering in the living room, holding my breath as I reach toward the phone?

Goddamn, I'm such a fucking idiot.

My fingers curl around the cool metal of Sawyer's phone, and I let out a shaky breath before quickly scurrying away, trying to keep quiet. I head into the kitchen before leaning up against the counter and glancing up at him across the apartment. He's still sound asleep, and a twisted grin stretches across my face, finally feeling as though I might just get somewhere.

Glancing down at the phone, I blow my cheeks out with a heavy breath. The likelihood that this thing doesn't require a passcode is not looking great, but I try my luck. Swiping my thumb across the screen, my jaw drops as the phone unlocks. I gape at it, unable to believe what I'm seeing.

Holy hell. Who doesn't have a passcode or even a pattern or thumbprint requirement for their phone these days? Having it freely available for snoopy little eyes is almost unheard of, but fuck, if he's going to practically offer it all up on a silver platter for me, who the hell am I to deny it?

Heading straight for the text messages, I start scrolling, opening the most recent and finding a text from some girl named Brandi that came through late last night, and within seconds I realize that Brandi is nothing but a thirsty hoe.

I hastily click out of it before going to the next. A text from Stacey, hitting up Sawyer only a few hours before Brandi.

It goes on and on, horny skank after horny skank, and by the time I'm reaching the tenth booty call in a roll, I start to wonder if I'm going to find anything at all.

"After you find what you're looking for," Sawyer says from the couch, his eyes still closed, "go cry to someone else."

My eyes bug out of my head, caught with my hand in the cookie jar. Hell, I can't even pretend I don't know what he's talking about. He's caught me right in the act, but he's got me wrong if he thinks I'm snooping through his phone to find out how many girls he's been screwing. I couldn't give a shit about that. The only thing I'm interested in is what the fuck this Empire thing is, and what I have to do with any of it.

Quickly realizing I'm not going to find anything substantial, I drop the phone to the counter with a heavy sigh before glancing toward the elevator door. I could probably still make it out of here.

I glance back toward Sawyer to find his sleepy, green gaze on me. "You won't even get to the lobby before we find you," he mutters. "And trust me, you won't like what happens if you try to escape us, so do us all a favor and just play along."

I narrow my gaze on him, frustration burning through my body. But I have to admit, at least he was nice enough to give me a warning. He could have just watched me try, only for me to end up in a situation that'll have me wanting to strangle them . . . you know, more than I already do. "Drop dead," I tell him.

He sits up on the couch, bracing his elbows against his knees. "Feisty this morning," he says. "What's up? Cross didn't fuck you hard enough?"

As if on cue, Cross comes sailing through the apartment, scoffing as he overhears Sawyer's comment. "You know damn well I fucked her just right," he says, striding past me to the fridge, not even sparing me a single glance. He grabs the bottle of orange juice and lifts it to his lips, taking a quick swig.

"Use a fucking glass," Zade spits from across the apartment, stepping out of a room I can only assume is his home office, though I have no idea what kind of business would be going on in there. Hell, up until this weekend, I assumed these guys were college students, though a niggling voice inside my head tells me I couldn't be further from the truth.

Zade's gaze falls to me before noticing the phone on the counter beside my hands. He's probably assuming I was up to something shady, which I definitely was, but he doesn't need to know that. "Well, if it isn't the big man in charge," I say, narrowing my gaze on him, not liking the disapproving stare in his eyes. "Kidnapped anyone this morning?"

"No one worth mentioning," he throws back at me, striding through the kitchen and heading for the espresso machine.

My jaw clenches, and I whip around, fixing him with a hard stare. "You're a real fucking asshole, you know that, right?"

Zade scoffs and steps into me, those psychotic eyes locked on mine. "Oh yeah? Considering this asshole is the only reason you're still fucking breathing, I'd suggest you shut your mouth and watch who you're talking to. Otherwise, you might just find yourself locked in a cement cell. I know how you like those."

A grin pulls at the corner of my lips. "Wow, you think so highly of yourself. *Watch who you're talking to*," I say with a scoff, mimicking his deep tone. "Here's how this is going to happen. You're going to stop with the tough guy act and be fucking real with me. Tell me who you are, what you want with me, why the fuck I was invited to that ball last night, and make it quick. I've had just about enough of you and your friends thinking you can come busting into my life, balls to the fucking wall, and start making demands. So please, hurry the fuck up and tell me what I want to know because I'd rather shoot myself through the eye than have to spend another minute here with you."

His eyes flash with something sinister, and I watch as he reaches behind himself. A gun appears in his hand and he presses it into my chest. "Go ahead then," he challenges. "Shoot yourself. Because the only way you'll be getting out of here before I'm through with you is in a body bag."

The room gets scarily quiet as I take the gun from him, our gazes locked with nothing but a fierce tension between us. The metal is both cold and heavy in my hand, and I realize this is a test.

He knows damn well I'm not about to put a bullet through my head, but what he doesn't know is just how far I'm willing to take this.

Positioning the gun in my hand, I let my finger slide through and rest on the trigger. My gaze lingers on the gun, taking it in before lifting my eyes back to Zade's. "You don't think I'll do it," I throw back at him, my tone matching the sinister gaze in his eye.

"I know you won't."

Lifting the gun, I raise it to the side of my head, letting him see the crazy in my eyes while noticing the way Cross and Sawyer become extremely still. "Are you willing to bet your life on it?"

Zade doesn't respond, and the longer I hold his stare, the quicker his face starts to fall. Unease flashes in his eyes, and I let a smirk twist across my lips. I watch as he starts to question himself, wondering if he's misjudged me, then just to prove my point, I put on the performance of a lifetime, jumping as a sharp gasp escapes through my lips.

His eyes widen, fear paralyzing him and he jolts toward me. "NO!" he roars, reaching for me just moments before realizing his mistake. That fear quickly morphs into rage and he snatches the gun out of my hand as my veins fill with power.

I smirk back at him, smugness consuming me. "Uh-oh. It looks like someone just showed his hand," I whisper, raising my chin as my chest presses up against his. "You may not give a shit about what happens to me, but after your little performance at the ball last night and your embarrassing act of desperation just now, it's clear that whatever you need me for, you need me alive."

Zade grips my chin, that stare of his sending chills down my spine. "I may need you alive," he admits, "but that doesn't mean I need you in one fucking piece. Fuck with me again, and I won't hesitate to make you wish you were dead."

With that, he releases me and walks away, shoving the gun into the waistband of his pants before balling his hands into fists at his side.

Unease consumes me, and I catch myself against the counter, trying to find a moment to breathe when a body moves in behind me. My back stiffens as Dalton's familiar scent wraps around me. "You're playing with fire," he warns me. "You need to back down before you find yourself in a shallow grave."

I whip around, not liking the tone in his voice, and come face to face with those blazing blue eyes. "Then tell me what the hell is going on," I demand, the desperation pulsing through my veins. "Because if you assholes expect me to fall in line and be the perfect little prisoner, then you're going to have to start offering some answers in return. If my life is at risk, then I need to know so I can better protect myself."

Dalton watches me a moment before glancing at Cross over my shoulder and then to Sawyer. The three of them seem to have some kind of silent conversation, and just as Dalton lets out a heavy sigh, seemingly ready to give me what I want, Zade comes striding back in.

"We can't give you the answers you're looking for, Oakley," he says, a hint of regret flashing in his eyes.

"Then what can you tell me?"

Zade presses his lips into a tight line before letting out a heavy breath. He steps back and pulls out a chair at his dining table, indicating for me to take a seat. I do just that, stepping out of Dalton's space and reluctantly moving past Zade.

I take a seat as Zade moves to the opposite end of the table, bracing his hands against the back of the chair while Dalton comes closer and leans against the edge of the counter. I can't help but feel as though I've been called to the principal's office, and when Sawyer and

Cross start to move in too, that feeling only gets stronger.

They glance between themselves before Zade finally gives it to me straight, a pain clear in his tone at having to tell me this, and I'm left wondering what the hell could be so bad. "My name is Zade DeVil," he starts. His surname makes me gasp, realizing he doesn't just own this penthouse, but the whole damn hotel. "And the four of us are part of an organization by the name of Empire. We're the largest and most powerful secret society in the country, built on blood, power, and sacrifice."

I arch a brow, not impressed in the slightest. "You mean a group of asshole college bros who couldn't get laid so they formed some exclusive club. Virgins united?"

Zade gives me a blank stare. "I don't care how you perceive our organization, but you know damn well that's not at all what we're about. You saw last night's event, and you saw the familiar faces in the crowd. You'd be a fool to belittle our reach."

I hate that he's right. I did see the faces in the crowd. Politicians, cops, judges. This organization is probably bigger than I could ever wrap my head around. "So, what?" I ask, playing ball. "You're a bunch of over-privileged rich pricks who have the ability to influence things within the community or politics."

Dalton nods from the edge of the counter. "That among other things."

"Okay. So when you say you have reach, just how far does that go?"

Zade shakes his head, not willing to discuss the type of strings

Empire can pull.

"Alright then, tell me this," I say, accepting there's a line drawn in the sand and that he won't tolerate me trying to cross it. I lift my gaze to his, my heart starting to race. "Have you killed people for this organization?"

He doesn't respond, but I see the answer clear in his eyes.

I nod, starting to grasp just how powerful this group really is while the knowledge of his callous nature really starts to sink in. He's killed before, maybe multiple times, and the fact that he's standing here before me means that he's gotten away with it every damn time. "And Empire allows for you to be able to do things like that without getting caught?"

He nods. "More or less."

Well, shit.

"Okay, so you're this big, powerful organization, but what the hell does it have to do with me?" I ask, glancing between them. "I've never even heard of Empire before, and I'm sure as hell not some undercover politician with a secret agenda to assassinate the competition. I'm just some normal girl, trying to pay her way through college without getting my ass grabbed at work."

Zade raises his chin, his gaze narrowing and becoming suspicious. "That's what we thought you could help us understand," he says. "Your name was given to me, as you saw from that photograph in my apartment. I've been tasked to protect you. Only, I can't figure out why."

I shake my head, my heart dropping right out of my ass. "What are you . . . are you saying someone wants me dead?"

"Seems that way, doesn't it?"

My chest heaves, and I feel a panic attack coming on. This is the type of shit you see in movies, not in real life. Besides, I'm a fucking treat, who would want me dead? I mean, I'm not great at paying my taxes, and I've been known to park in no-stopping zones, but surely that doesn't qualify for the death penalty.

"I . . . I swear, I—" I cut myself off, the fear making my eyes water. "What do I do?"

Cross scoffs. "You don't show up to balls you had no right being at for starters."

I stare at my hands on the table. "I thought you guys sent me that invitation. I found it at work when I was clocking in. It was like someone had been waiting for me to show up then stuck it there as though they knew I'd be the first to see it. You guys literally follow me there every shift, plus I found that calling card with that photo of me, so was it really such a stretch to assume it'd been from you?"

"If you thought it was from us," Sawyer says, narrowing his gaze on me. "Then why did you still show up without trying to let one of us know you'd accepted the invite?"

"Because I didn't want you to know I was going," I snap back at him. "It was my one shot to try and figure out who you were and what you were hiding from me. If I'd known it was sent from someone who wants to serve my head on a silver platter, then no, I probably wouldn't have shown up. And you know what? That's on you assholes too. You could have been open and honest with me from the start. Instead, you wanted to play your twisted little games."

"We did what we had to do," Dalton says, clenching his jaw. "That night we were locked up, these bastards were taking out the hitman who was sent to put a bullet between your eyes."

I gape at him. "What do you want from me? To drop to my knees and worship at your feet because you took out some asshole who's just as much the monster that you guys are? Perhaps you've forgotten that in the normal world, kidnapping someone and holding them hostage in a fucked-up little cell isn't normal. It's fucking terrifying. But what you did, Dalton, leading me into Zade's trap like that and pretending to have my back . . . that's just sick."

Guilt flashes in his eyes, and I stand from the table. "Is that everything I need to know, or are there more sordid details you're keeping from me?"

Zade shakes his head. "Unless you have any light to shed on the situation, then no. That's it."

I narrow my gaze on him, not believing him for a second, but for now, that's more than enough information. So much so that I feel as though I'm drowning in it. All that matters is that someone is out to get me. Someone in this fucked-up organization wants to take my life, and despite how much I despise them, these four assholes are my only chance at survival.

Letting out a sigh, I fix a sharp glare on Zade. "The guy who was working the door at the ball. When I gave him my name, his head snapped up as though he was surprised, and after checking the list and confirming my name wasn't on it, he still let me pass. Maybe he knows something," I suggest. "I doubt an organization as put together as yours would allow a random stray in off the street during such a big event. Plus, when I was walking around, a few people were giving me weird stares, like they recognized me but couldn't figure out why. But that's all I've got."

Zade clenches his jaw, his gaze shifting to Cross. Something passes between them that I can't even begin to understand. When they don't give me any sign of a response, I press my lips into a hard line. "I'm assuming you're not about to let me walk out the door?"

"No chance in hell," Zade tells me.

With that, I push out from the table and stride past them, my world burning to ashes around me.

CHAPTER 18

Sawyer

The basketball flies through the air, swiftly dropping into the basket. Dalton takes off after it, catching it on the rebound before heading back up the court. The fucker should have been in the NBA. He had the contract right there. All he had to do was sign, but apparently punishing himself is more important than securing his future.

I watch him move up and down the court, the rhythmic sound of the ball calming something inside me. After telling Oakley what she thinks she needs to know, she took off to Zade's spare room, needing some time to wrap her head around everything. Both Dalton and I have tried checking in on her, but it's something she's going to have to accept on her own.

I sit beside Cross on the rooftop court as Zade stands, arms crossed over his chest as he peers out at the city below, deep in thought. This past few weeks have been one big cluster fuck. We knew there was a possibility that Oakley's name would get out eventually and that someone would try to end her life before the night of the sixtieth moon, but there's no way we could have foreseen just how intense this was going to be.

Oakley fights us at every turn, though it's expected after the way things have been handled. She despises us, and I can't fucking blame her. People outside our world don't understand it. When they see a gun, they shit their pants. But for us, kidnapping, betrayal, and injustices are just a part of life.

Zade lets out a sigh as Dalton launches himself into the air, dunking the ball through the hoop. He swings off it before dropping back to the ground, letting the ball bounce away. "She's getting too close," Zade says, still staring out at the city. "This isn't how any of this was supposed to play out."

Don't I fucking know it.

"We couldn't anticipate how any of this has played out," Dalton says, striding back to us and grabbing his water bottle. "We're doing what we can, but—"

"No, you're doing what you can to get your dick wet," Zade snaps, turning back to us. "All three of you. This isn't a fucking whore house. There are plenty of bitches around here. You wanna fuck, find one of them. Getting involved with this girl . . . It's going to blow up in our faces. You're not thinking about the bigger picture."

Cross stands and narrows his gaze on Zade, not liking his decisions questioned. Cross doesn't do anything lightly, not even the girls he fucks. Every little thing he does is thoroughly planned and executed to perfection. "That's not what this is really about," Cross states, watching Zade with a thick curiosity. "You couldn't give a shit if we fucked her so hard she split in half. All that matters is that she's right there where you need her to be on the night of the sacrifice."

Zade clenches his jaw, and I see that Cross is right. Zade isn't always easy to read, but right now, it's as though he's written it across his face in permanent marker. "It's getting out of control," he admits. "I don't have a fucking handle on this. Every step we take feels like I'm scrambling just to keep everything together. The hitman at her apartment and then the ball. What next? We've got nothing but a fucking doorman."

I nod, agreeing with him. "Whoever is behind this knows what they're doing, but are we sure they're related?" I question. "The hit at her apartment was obvious. There was the warning card and a simple hitman through her window. The person behind that is small-minded, wanting a quick outcome. But inviting her to that ball where her murder would be witnessed by the whole organization? That's a calculated move with the purpose of making you appear weak."

Zade's brows pinch together, his hand dragging down his face. "You think these are two separate incidents? That we're looking for two people?"

I shrug my shoulders. "I'm saying it's a possibility we shouldn't write off. It's entirely possible that both hits were ordered by the same person. The first had the purpose of being quick and easy, it was done with respect to Empire in mind. They followed the traditions of giving a warning, but the ball? There were no traditions followed, no respect for who we are. They were willing to take a shot in the middle of an event, where members' families were in attendance, their lives put at risk. What if he'd taken the shot and missed? Or if he succeeded and put a bullet between her eyes in front of the eyes of our young? All hell would have broken loose."

Zade drops down on the bench, bracing his elbows against his knees, clearly frustrated. "We're going to lose her. She's slipping through our fingers and there's not a damn thing I can do about it."

Dalton shakes his head. "We're not losing her," he says. "We've told her what she needs to know, and that's enough for now. She's aware someone is trying to kill her, and unless she has a death wish, she'll stick to us like glue. We'll know when someone's coming."

Zade glances up at Dalton and scoffs. "Even if I kept her locked in the fucking cell for the next month, it still doesn't help me figure out who the fuck is behind this or which one of The Circle betrayed her name."

"We're not locking her in a fucking cell for a month," Cross mutters, almost seeming disinterested in the conversation. "But have you considered that perhaps we're looking at this all wrong?"

"What do you mean?" I question.

Cross lets out a heavy breath. "We've been taking the fight to Empire, questioning members and talking to The Circle, but it's getting us nowhere," he says. "They want Oakley dead, and something tells me her name wasn't randomly selected. We need to take this to her. Figure out why she was chosen as the sacrifice."

"We tried that," Dalton says. "She doesn't know anything."

"I know," Cross continues. "But if we dig into her background, we might just find the link, and who knows, that link might just offer us the answer we're looking for."

"It's worth a try," I say. "I'll get my guy on it."

"No," Zade says, holding his hand up. "We do it ourselves. If she's got the attention of The Circle, then whatever links her back to us is big. We can't risk it getting out."

"Can't risk what getting out?" Oakley's fiery tone rings out over the rooftop. We all glance back at her, our conversation dying quicker than it started. Oakley strides toward us and lets out a sigh. "Oh, I see. Discussing my imminent death I suppose."

Guilt tears at my chest. It's one thing to have to sacrifice her, but having to do it after getting the slightest window into who she is . . . man, it's going to suck.

Zade was right to warn us away from her. We can't afford to be making attachments. She's barely been here two weeks and already Dalton is in too deep. He won't physically admit it, but I see it in the way he looks at her. He's infatuated. He thinks he's just having fun with her, thinks he can handle it, but the day Zade carves her still-beating heart out of her chest will be the day something dies inside of him.

Despite how much it might suck for Dalton, having her hating on him right now might just be what's best for him. Oakley doesn't trust him, and nor should she. She shouldn't trust a damn one of us. If she knew why we were protecting her . . . damn, this whole thing would blow up in our faces. All that matters is while she's busy pushing him away, he's being saved from getting too attached.

Zade narrows his gaze at her, and it's clear just her presence is getting under his skin. "Is there something you need?"

She rolls her eyes as though just the tone of his voice offends her. "I've come to remind you that it's Monday. I have a lecture at two that I can't miss and work starting at five."

Zade shakes his head. "Absolutely not."

Oakley laughs, and the sound almost knocks me the fuck over, tightening something in my chest. "Oh, that's sweet you think I'm asking permission," she says while glaring at Zade, the two of them like fire and ice. "I'm telling you what my plans are as a courtesy. Believe it or not, I have a life outside of your twisted plans for me. I'm not your prisoner, and if I say I'd like to go to work to be able to pay my rent and keep my home, then that's exactly what I'm going to do. Not all of us have the luxury of being Daddy Warbucks with deep pockets."

Zade stands, and the rest of us watch on with bated breath, waiting for him to snap. She continues making her way toward us, and Zade intercepts her, stepping in front of her. "Maybe you've forgotten there's a target on your head," he says. "I'm not having my boys chase you around all fucking day."

She crosses her arms and stares up at him, not intimidated in the least. Not like she was at the start. "Then what do you suggest?"

Zade arches a brow before glancing back at us and letting out a heavy breath. "You'll stay here for the day and watch your lecture online, then we'll accompany you to work."

"You want me to just hang out in your apartment all day?"

"Did I stutter?"

Oakley groans and rolls her eyes. "Fine, but if I have to put up with your bullshit all day, I'm going to need charcoal. Both vine and compressed, and a large A3 sketch pad, too."

Zade scoffs. "The fuck do you think this is? You're here so you can avoid getting a bullet between your eyes. You're not on a fucking vacation, and I'm sure as hell not your little bellboy."

She grins up at him, her eyes sparkling, and just that look alone gets me hard. "Go fetch."

Ahh, fuck.

Zade clenches his hands into tight fists and Dalton flinches, ready to break it up when Zade ultimately decides to take her out ahead of schedule, only he somehow manages to calm himself. "Watch your fucking back, Quinn," he states, making her shrink away.

He doesn't say another word before stepping around her and stalking toward the edge of the rooftop, pulling out his phone to no doubt call the hotel concierge. We hear bits and pieces of his conversation, and he's just about to wrap it up when Oakley just has to go and stab a knife right through the fucker's back. "Could you get me a juicy burger too?" she calls out, making his back stiffen. "A nice big one with ketchup and fries. Maybe a Diet Coke too."

Ahhh, shit.

She just loves taking things from bad to worse.

Zade ends his call before whipping around and fixing Oakley with a death-defying glare. Fuck, it even sends a chill sailing down my spine, but not Oakley. She simply just turns to face us with a wide grin, so fucking proud of herself.

She strides toward us, collecting Dalton's basketball as she goes, and just the thought of her touching his balls has him discreetly moving back toward the court, already rocking a semi. "So," she says, bouncing the ball along the court. "Are you assholes going to put your bullshit aside so we can make today bearable, or are we gonna keep hating on each other?"

Dalton grins and holds his hand out for the ball, more than ready to force his way back into her good graces. She bounces it toward him and he catches it with ease, propping it against his hip. "Care to make it interesting?"

The mischievous grin that tears across her face is so fucking breathtaking, I have to look away. There's something about this girl that draws me in and makes me want to get to know her, and the more that happens, the harder this is going to be. I need to keep my distance. I can't afford to fall for a corpse.

"Alright," she says, stepping toward him. "I'm listening."

"You three," he says, nodding toward her then me and Cross. "Against me. I'll even sweeten the deal and only play with my left hand."

She narrows her gaze at him, knowing there must be a trap in here somewhere before glancing back at me and Cross, searching for some kind of acknowledgment. "What do you get if you win?"

"Payback," he murmurs, his gaze darkening. "Watching you fuck my friends was a nasty little game. If I win, I can take you any way I want."

She considers his proposal before pressing her lips into a hard line. "And if we win?"

He scoffs. "You won't."

"If we do?" she pushes.

He shrugs his shoulders. "What do you want?"

She thinks about it, taking a moment to really consider all her options. Something sparks in those soft blue eyes and she steps toward him, raising her chin. "I want you all in my debt," she says. "Each of you, including Zade, will owe me one favor in which I can collect at any damn time of my choosing."

My back stiffens, knowing just how dangerous this could be, and I snap my gaze toward Dalton. He knows better than to make this bet, and despite how desperately he wants to win, he wouldn't dare push this.

Zade has other plans though.

He steps up to the edge of the court, that same lethal challenge in his stare. "You got yourself a bet," he tells her, making my brow arch. "You win, and we'll be in your debt, but you lose, and you'll be in mine."

She shakes her head. "That wasn't the deal."

"It's my deal," he says. "You want to play with fire, then you better be prepared to get burned."

She swallows hard, and when she raises her chin, it's fucking on.

Cross and I stand, moving onto the court.

Then we play.

CHAPTER 19

Oakley

That was the longest basketball game I've ever witnessed, and I say witnessed because after the first eight minutes, I realized I hadn't touched the ball once and sat out instead. Hell, I don't even think they noticed. These assholes are competitive motherfuckers. At that point, I don't think they even cared about the deal. They just wanted to win.

There's no denying it though, Dalton Eros is a god on the court. He dominated, but when all rules were off the table and it was two against one, that cocky nature quickly faded. Now here I sit, happy as a fucking clam because as of ten minutes ago, these four assholes are now in my debt.

I sit across the court, leaning back on my hands with my ankles crossed out in front of me, the boys relaxing around me and soaking up the lunchtime sun. All except Zade, who's pacing by the edge of the roof and roaring demands through his phone. "Is he always like this?" I ask as Dalton notices my stare.

"Some days more than not," he admits. "He's got a lot on his plate. Couldn't be easy being in his position."

"And what position is that?"

Dalton spreads his arms out wide, indicating the very roof we're sitting on. "All of this. Rome wasn't built in a day, Firefly. This hotel is his pride and joy, and achieving this standard of luxury and maintaining a five-star rating isn't easy. He's worked his ass off for this."

God, I hate it when they say things that make me empathize with the devil.

I'm just about ready to admit that maybe Zade has at least one redeeming quality when a soft *ding* sounds across the rooftop. My gaze snaps back to the elevator, finding one of the many hotel employees striding toward us, a serving platter in his hands.

He glances at Zade, who points toward me, and his employee immediately adjusts his direction. Standing up, I meet the guy and he offers me the platter. "Miss," he says with a nod. "A house burger with fries, and a Diet Coke."

Taking it from him, I offer a polite smile. "Thank you," I say, astonished that Zade actually ordered it for me. But hey, what kind of asshole would he be if he didn't give his prisoner enough energy to try to escape him? After all, isn't that the fun of it?

I'm just about ready to set it down when the man fishes in his pocket and hands me two packets of charcoal sticks, exactly what I'd requested. I take them from him eagerly, recognizing the expensive brand across the packaging. A brand I've always had to skip out on. Motioning toward the platter, I give him a hopeful glance. "There doesn't happen to be a sketch pad hidden in here?"

"A sketch pad?" he questions, looking back at me in a panic. "My apologies, Miss. I was not informed that you required a sketch pad. I'll have someone go to pick one up. Is there any brand you prefer?"

"No, no," I say, glancing across at Zade, who watches me with a stupid smirk across his stupid face. He must have purposefully not mentioned the sketch pad when he put in the call. "I don't want you to go to any trouble. It's fine, I'll make do without it."

"As you wish," he says with a nod before Dalton whips out a fifty-dollar bill and hands it over. My eyes widen, watching the exchange, and a fierce longing rumbles through my chest. I'd kill to get tips like that on the regular. Perhaps I'm in the wrong field. I wonder if Zade would be so kind as to give me a job here. That way I could hit up all the rich pricks who come waltzing through the door. They couldn't be any worse than the assholes who frequent the bar. The only difference is the rich pricks have cash to blow.

The hotel employee scurries away to get back to work, and I drop back down to the court before diving into my burger. Those eight minutes of running up and down the court really killed me. Perhaps a little exercise is in my future.

The burger looks delicious, and I bite into it before noticing that Zade's stare is still firmly locked on me. "What's his probl—" I cut myself off as it hits me.

Chili. There's chili on this burger and a shit ton of it.

My mouth starts to burn and my eyes bug out of my head. "Holy fuck," I pant, scrambling for my Diet Coke and drinking half the glass through the skinny straw, feeling my eyeballs start to sweat. "Who the fuck puts that much chili on a burger?"

"Oh?" Zade questions, pure satisfaction in his dark eyes. "My mistake."

Rat bastard.

My mouth burns and I don't bother with a response, far too busy trying to scoop the ice cubes out of the glass and rapid-fire shoving them into my mouth, all while Dalton, Cross, and Sawyer just sit back and laugh.

Sawyer glances at the burger. "I take it you're not going to eat that?"

I shake my head, the burn slowly starting to ease. "Have it, but if you even look at my fries, you'll be on all fours with a collar and leash around your neck before you even know what's going on."

Sawyer just nods, already consuming the burger, not even appearing to notice how spicy it is. He annihilates it in seconds, and I pick at my fries as I grab the sticks of charcoal, trying to figure out exactly how this is going to work. I mean, there's a big court right in front of me. It's the biggest blank canvas I've ever seen.

"Don't even think about fucking with my court," Dalton mutters, watching me from across the massive green rectangle, reading me as effortlessly as though he'd been doing it for years.

Letting out a sigh, I glance up at him, needing to block the sun from my eyes. "Then where the hell am I going to draw? I don't have a canvas."

Cross glances at me with a strange curiosity in his eyes before pulling his shirt over his head. He turns his back and glances over his shoulder at me. "Will this do?"

"Your back?" I question, my greedy gaze shifting over the strong muscles beneath that beautiful, tanned skin, his back the perfect blank canvas. But I'd be lying if I said I didn't want to roam my hands all over it. "Are you sure? Charcoal isn't known for being tidy. It's messy as shit."

He gives me a blank stare. "Will it do or not?"

"I mean . . . yeah," I say, watching as he drops to the ground and sprawls across the court, offering his back for me to use as I please. Cross grabs his discarded shirt and shoves it under his head, getting comfortable for the long haul.

I don't hesitate, scooching toward him and laying the charcoal out beside him. I glance over his back, trying to figure out what to do with it, before leaning over his ass and starting my outline.

Over the next few minutes, a face starts to form, covering his whole back as we fall into a comfortable silence, but I find myself all too curious about this beautiful stranger. "Cross?" I question, almost certain he's going to fall asleep.

"Mmm?"

The charcoal sails over his strong back and I lean in a little closer, concentrating as I give definition to the girl's cheekbones, contouring the shit out of them. "What's your name?"

He glances back at me, barely lifting his head. "My name?" he questions, a strange hesitance in his tone. "It's Cross."

"No, I mean your real name," I say, not meeting his eyes. I don't want to seem like I'm prying for information, when I'm just wanting to have a casual conversation and know more about the man whose ass is fantastically close to my face. "I figured Cross was a nickname."

There's a strained silence before he gives a short nod. "It is," he murmurs. "My name is Easton. Easton Cross."

"Easton," I whisper, liking it so much more than I have the right to. It somehow feels so right on my lips. "Is it going to cause problems if I call you that, or do you prefer Cross?"

He waits a moment before letting that deep, raspy tone fly free. "You can call me Easton."

A strange flutter causes havoc deep in my stomach and I try to push it away, not wanting to make a big deal out of this. Yet, I can't help but feel as though we just made some kind of progress, and not just the *happy to smile at one another in passing* kind of progress, but the *I want to crush my lips to his and see if he can make me weak* kind of progress.

There's just something about this guy. He's so mysterious and quiet, yet broody and terrifying. But there's a softer side, something I don't think he often shows. Something I think he might be afraid of. It intrigues me, and I find myself drawn to him. It's almost as though I want to trust him. I want to believe that he'll always protect me.

"Can you tell me more about Empire?" I question, realizing this girl on his back is starting to resemble me.

"What do you want to know?"

I shrug my shoulders, having no idea where to start. "How does it work? Is there a boss or does it just run on a trust system?"

Sawyer scoffs, and I glance up at him, not realizing he was listening. "We might be a powerful organization, but there's no trust. Those motherfuckers will turn on you in a second if it means getting a step up in the world. If we didn't have such high standards when it comes to following traditions, we never would have made it this far."

"So how do you enforce it then?" I question, glazing over the woman's eyes on Easton's back and realizing it needs something more, something darker to match his vibe. "How do you make sure everyone stays in line?"

"It's similar to how a big company works," Dalton explains. "We have our board of directors who oversee all the day-to-day bullshit and enforce our rules and values. They're known as The Circle, twelve scary as fuck bastards. And then we have our leader who has the power to overrule, the one who The Circle goes to when they can't come to a decision. He's the big fucking boss."

"Well shit, how'd he get that gig?"

"Pretty simple, actually," Easton mutters, his gaze on Zade across the rooftop. "He was born with the right DNA."

"Oh, so it's an heir type of situation then, passed from father to son?"

"Exactly right," Easton says.

"No women?"

A grin pulls across Sawyer's lips, and his eyes sparkle with silent laughter. "Now what kind of misogynic organization would we be if we allowed women to enter our ranks? Haven't you heard? If your woman isn't in the kitchen or cleaning up after you, she should be in your bed with either her legs spread or her ass in the air."

My lips press into a tight line as disgust pulses heavily through my veins. "They don't really think that, do they?"

"A lot of them do, yeah," Sawyer says. "These are men in power we're talking about. They're all the fucking same. They want the world to kneel at their feet."

"Ugh, gross," I grumble. "So who's this big-time leader of yours?"

Something hardens in Easton's eyes as he continues watching Zade. "Up until three weeks ago," he mutters, "his father."

My eyes widen and my head whips back to glance at Zade, a strange type of understanding flourishing through me. That really explains a lot about why he is the way he is. It probably couldn't have been easy being raised by the type of man who would lead an organization like that. The pressure he must have felt growing up, the need to be the biggest, the best, the fastest. "What do you mean, 'up until three weeks ago'?" I ask, knowing damn well I'm toeing the line and at any moment they could pull the rug out from below me and clamp up like a steel trap. "What happened?"

A coldness sweeps over Easton and his stare almost becomes deadly. "Zade slit his throat."

The charcoal falls from my hands as a horrified gasp slips from between my lips, and I can't help but turn my gaze on Zade again. I knew he was vicious. I knew he had the ability to effortlessly take another man's life, but his father? His own flesh and blood? "Why would he do that?" I question in a low tone, my heart racing a million miles per hour.

"Why does anyone do anything?" Easton challenges. "For power."

Unease settles into my chest, and I pick up the charcoal, attempting to concentrate on what I'm doing, but the will just isn't there anymore. Sensing that this new information has rattled me, Dalton moves toward us and glances down at the portrait, his brows shooting up. "Holy shit," he says. "Are you some kind of artist? That's fucking amazing."

I glance over my drawing, taking in the subtle, feminine curve of my face, those haunted features perfectly depicting the fear I've felt over the past two weeks. My gaze travels up to the eyes and a proud smile settles over my lips as I realize just how perfectly I captured the similarities between Easton's snake and the one weaving in and out of the portrait's eye sockets.

It truly is a haunting image. Gothic and lonely, while also so poetic.

Hearing Dalton's remarks, Sawyer shuffles over to glance over it, and I watch as his brows shoot up too. He scoffs, the sound a strange mix of amused and impressed. "And you say we're fucked up," he comments before nodding to himself. "That looks just like Venom. It's uncanny."

"Venom?" I question.

"My snake," Easton says before passing his phone back to me. "Show me."

I take a quick picture and hand his phone back almost faster than he gave it to me, not wanting him to think I'm holding onto it any longer than necessary. "Not bad," he says. "You finished?"

I shrug my shoulders. "I mean, there's always more details I could add, but yeah. I think I'm done."

Easton nods and pushes to his feet. "I gotta get out of here," he says, reaching down for his shirt, but thankfully not pulling it on. After all, to see him put his shirt on and ruin the drawing so soon after finishing it would break my heart. I don't know what I was hoping for though. It's not like he's going to be able to do much with all that charcoal on his back.

Easton doesn't bother with a goodbye and just takes off, leaving me alone with Dalton and Sawyer while Zade continues to make demands on his phone. I stretch up, my body cramping from leaning over Easton for the past hour, and as soon as I feel the blood starting to pump again, I reach for the napkin that lays discarded from my lunch.

Getting to my feet, I try to wipe all the charcoal off my fingers, but it's no use. I'm going to need a good shower and a scrubbing brush if I want to feel clean again. "I'm umm . . . I'm gonna go back down to Zade's apartment and try to get this shit off," I say, my mind focused on my fingers.

Dalton nods. "I'll come down with you."

I give him a smile that doesn't reach my eyes as I grab what's left of the charcoal sticks and dump them on my lunch tray. I hoist it all into my arms and make my way back to the elevator when Sawyer falls into my other side. I glance up at him with a questioning stare, and he looks back at me as though I'm a fool to be questioning him. "What?"

he mutters. "You think I'm staying up here so I can listen to Zade talkin' shit on that phone all day? Fuck that."

"Good point," I laugh.

We step into the elevator and the second the door closes, the tension in the small metal box skyrockets. I suck in a breath, watching Dalton from the corner of my eye as he discreetly moves in behind me.

I close my eyes, feeling his closeness despite not laying a single finger on me. "Is there something you need?" I question, already panting. I know exactly what he wants, and damn it, I'm going to give it to him.

He groans low and I feel him move into me, his sweet breath brushing across my neck. My knees shake, and I feel his rock-hard cock grind against me. "You know damn well what I need."

My head tilts, inviting him in when the elevator jolts, coming to a violent stop. My eyes spring open as a soft gasp escapes my lips. I glance over to find Sawyer's finger on the emergency stop button and his hungry stare locked on me.

Oh my.

Dalton's hand falls to my waist as Sawyer saunters toward me like some kind of predator, an electrifying thrill shooting through me. He steps into me and takes the tray out of my hands as my tongue rolls over my bottom lip. He puts it down and kicks it aside, giving us the space we need, and as he moves back into me, I can't help but slip my hand up the front of Sawyer's shirt, feeling the tight ridges of his abs.

I don't say a word, my heart racing as the anticipation builds between us, and every moment of silence makes it harder to breathe.

Dalton's hand slips down the back of my hip and pushes inside my sweatpants as he kicks my legs apart. I feel his warm fingers against my ass before he takes them lower, slipping between my legs and cupping my pussy. He gives it a firm squeeze and damn it, I know he feels just how wet I am. He doesn't hesitate, pushing two thick fingers deep inside me, and I gasp as I watch Sawyer slowly pull his shirt over his head, his stare becoming hooded as he watches his friend pleasure me.

I grind down against Dalton's hand, needing so much more as Sawyer motions to my shirt. "Take it off," he says in that chilling, demanding tone that has me ready to drop to my knees. "Let me see you."

Gripping the fabric at each hip, I draw it up my body, feeling Sawyer's razor-sharp stare as he takes in every inch of exposed skin. I toss it aside, unable to look away from those haunting green eyes before hooking my thumbs into the waistband of my sweatpants. I take my time pushing them down, each movement allowing Dalton's fingers to dive deeper.

Dalton pulls his fingers back and trails them to my ass, slowly spreading my arousal, and I push back against him as I watch Sawyer reach into his pants and free that deliciously thick cock. He slowly strokes it, watching me as though he knows exactly how this is going to go.

The hunger in his eyes is addictive, and the very thought of being the one who gets to satiate that need is like the best kind of high.

Dalton's other hand weaves into the back of my hair, gripping it firmly and tipping my head back as his lips brush across my neck. His fingers push into my ass and I groan, my pussy clenching with need. "This is gonna be fast, Firefly," he warns. "Have you ever had someone fuck this tight ass?"

I nod, my whole body jolting as Sawyer reaches between my legs, his fingers brushing across my sensitive clit. "I have," I say with a breathy gasp, Sawyer's fingers like magic against my body as they push into my cunt, his thumb pressing against my clit. "But no one as big as you."

A low growl of approval sounds through the elevator, and I reach for Sawyer, curling my hand around his cock as they both fuck me with their fingers, preparing me to take them both.

Nervousness flutters through my chest as Sawyer steps closer into me. "Are you fucking ready for this?" he questions.

My eyes roll as his thumb continues to circle my clit and I tighten my grip on his cock, the tension like nothing I've ever felt. "The question is," I pant, wishing he'd hurry up and rail me, "are you?"

A wicked grin kicks up the corner of Sawyer's lips, and without hesitation, he reaches down to grab my ass before hauling me up against his body. I hook my arms around his neck, holding myself up as he quickly adjusts me, slipping his strong arms beneath my knees and giving him all the control to bounce me on his cock.

I'm completely spread apart, at both of their mercy, and I can practically feel myself dripping as my desperation reaches new levels. Sawyer lines himself up with my entrance and brings me down, his tip pushing into me and slowly stretching me wider the deeper he goes.

A satisfied moan pulls from my chest as he raises me back up. "Oh God," I mutter, this position making me see stars.

Dalton moves in closer, his chest right up against my back as he reaches down, making sure I'm ready for him. He takes my waist as I release one of my arms from Sawyer's neck and twist to hook it around Dalton's, holding myself up on them both.

Sawyer holds me still, locking me against his strong body as I feel Dalton at my ass, the cold piercing like a promise of just how good this is going to be. He pushes inside of me and the pressure intensifies, but he takes it slow, knowing damn well a guy like him needs to be careful.

I suck in a breath and relax around him. "Holy fuck."

As Dalton pulls back, I dig my nails into Sawyer's shoulder, unsure if I'm about to come or be torn apart, but Sawyer starts to move again, slowly thrusting in and out of my cunt and making my eyes roll. I quickly get used to his size and the pressure morphs into undeniable pleasure.

I hold on for dear life as they fuck me together, matching each other's pace, both my ass and pussy so damn full. It takes only a minute to feel that familiar tightening deep in my core, and without a doubt, this is going to end with a bang.

It builds and builds as I grip their shoulders, unable to catch my breath. My head tips back and I groan loudly, the overwhelming pleasure like nothing I've ever felt. I've been with guys and done all sorts of things, but this . . . fuck, I've never done this.

"Uh, fuck," Sawyer grunts, just as close as I am.

He thrusts into me again and I see stars. "Shit, I'm gonna come."

"Give it to me," Sawyer demands. "Let me feel that sweet cunt squeeze me."

His words are my fucking kryptonite, and as they both slam back inside of me, I come hard. My orgasm rocks through my body, my pussy convulsing around Sawyer's thick cock, and as if on cue, he comes with me, shooting hot spurts of cum deep inside my pussy.

My high pulses through my body like electric currents, and as they continue to fuck me, it only becomes more intense.

Dalton's hands dig into my hips, and I recognize the tone in his grunts—he's about to come. And not a second later, he finishes with a raw groan, spilling his seed into me. They slow their movements as I come down from my high, the three of us gasping for air.

They hold on to me a moment longer, each of us just needing a minute to collect ourselves. Well before I'm ready for him to, Dalton pulls out of me, allowing space for Sawyer to lower me back to the ground. I keep my hand on his shoulder, finding my footing, and before I can even look for my clothes, Sawyer releases the emergency stop of the elevator.

We sail back down to Zade's penthouse apartment, the doors opening barely a second later while I stand naked as the day I was born, my clothes clenched between my fingers as hot cum slowly drips down my leg.

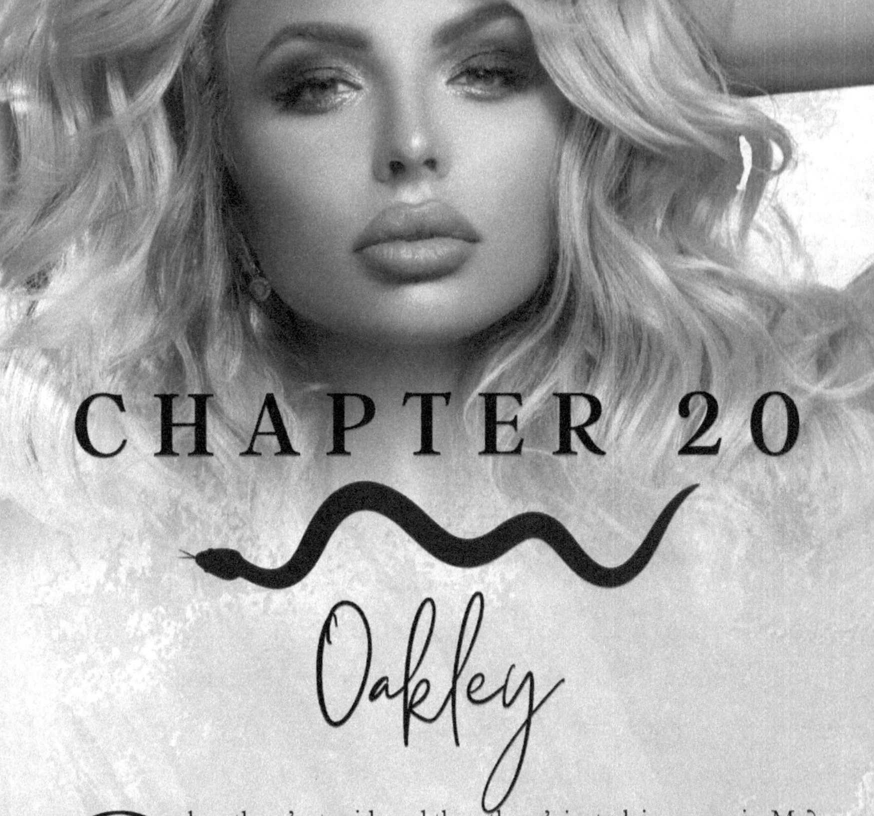

CHAPTER 20

Oakley

Okay, there's stupid, and then there's just plain moronic. Me? I'm both.

I knew this was a bad idea the second it entered my brain, yet the more I thought about it, the more it became my only option. There I was standing behind the bar, serving up beers on Monday night to a crowd full of people who had no idea what kind of bullshit I've been dealing with, and then BAM, the idea formed, and suddenly getting an impromptu double dicking was the furthest thing from my mind.

I should bail. Hell, I should bail and then run for the fucking hills. If Zade finds out about this, a hitman will be the least of my concerns.

This is going to end badly for me. Fuck, everything seems to be ending badly for me . . . Well, except for becoming a human cum bank in an elevator and then again during my online psychology lecture. Though that shit was long and boring, and these days I prefer long and hard.

As promised, the boys sat at Danny's Bar throughout my shift and the minute it was over, they surprised the hell out of me and took me back to my own apartment. I could have sworn they'd pack me up, shove me in the car, and take me back to Zade's penthouse prison, but apparently I've started to earn their trust.

Don't get me wrong, the lecture I received from Zade in my living room, warning me not to put a foot out of line was one for the ages. I was given all their cell numbers and ordered to call for help if I heard even the slightest twig break outside, and I wouldn't be surprised if I found one of them sleeping on my couch, just to keep an eye on me. To be honest, I think Zade just couldn't be fucked driving back into the city . . . or this is some kind of test. One I'm sure to fail. Either way, if this means I can start getting some semblance of a normal life back, then I'll seize it with both hands and never let go.

Except for right now.

Staring up at the ceiling of Zade's Escalade, I wonder about all the different ways this could get me killed. Or worse, have to face Zade's bullshit ranting. He's not going to like this. None of them are, but I have to give it a try.

The minute I mentioned the doorman at the ball, I knew they would chase down that lead the first opportunity they got. So here I am, hidden in the back of Zade's car, waiting for them to take the bait.

They're going to lead me right where I want to go. Right into the heart of Empire.

I've been laying here for forty-five minutes after somehow convincing them that I'm at home, tucked into bed and as safe as can be. I've been going back and forth a million times, trying to convince myself just how bad of an idea this is. But I need to know. I need to see it with my own two eyes. If somebody within that organization is planning on having me slaughtered like cattle, then I have the right to know why. And hell, perhaps even learn his name so I know who to haunt from the grave.

A loud yawn comes tearing out of me just as all four doors open, and I cut that shit off faster than I binged *Wednesday*. The guys get in, and I listen to the four heavy thuds as they pull their doors closed behind them. The engine roars to life before settling into a subtle purr, and before I know it, bailing is no longer an option.

My heart races like never before as Zade backs out of his parking space and I do what I can to keep hidden in the back. It's nearing midnight and they don't say a word, making the silence seem so damn loud. I mean, shit. I've never noticed how loud I breathe before, but it feels like every soft exhale sounds like a random neighbor's two-stroke lawn mower screeching to life first thing on a Sunday morning.

We drive for no more than fifteen minutes before coming to a stop in the middle of nowhere. Zade cuts the engine and my brows furrow as the guys silently get out of the car. I wait a few moments before peeking up over the window and realizing we're in an abandoned parking lot, and I watch as they walk away, into the darkness.

I've got to be out of my fucking mind for even considering this.

I should stay here. I'll be safer here. But it's also really fucking dark, and considering someone wants to play target practice with my head, perhaps I should stick with the guys. Besides, who doesn't love a surprise every now and then?

Slipping out of the Escalade, I stick to the shadows and hurry after them, my brows furrowing as I notice them creeping closer toward an old train tunnel. Without any warning, they disappear inside.

What the hell is this?

Not wanting to lose sight of them out here in the darkness, I quickly hurry to the opening of the tunnel and peer in, seeing absolutely nothing. The only sign they're in there is the sound of their echoing footsteps.

My hands shake, nervousness sweeping through me. If I don't do this now, if I don't take this risk, I'll never get the chance again. I have to know who these people are. I have to know why they have such an interest in me. If I don't, it's my life on the line. I can't trust Zade. I can't trust that he's always going to be there, and I sure as hell can't trust that one day he isn't going to grow tired of me and throw me to the wolves.

Sooner or later, Zade is going to replace his father as the leader of Empire. I can only hope when that time comes, he'll be able to put a stop to all this bullshit. But in reality, I don't know him. I don't know what makes him tick, what calms him, or what makes him feel at peace. So who the hell am I to make assumptions about how he'll lead his Empire? I could be walking right into a trap. It wouldn't be the first time where Zade DeVil is concerned.

Sometimes all a girl has is herself. Best case scenario, the guys figure out who's behind this and put an end to it. Worst case scenario, I'm out on my own, running for my life, hoping to God they don't find me.

Knowing this is a bad idea, I slip inside the tunnel anyway, and a feeling of dread washes over me. Not wanting the boys to hear my footsteps on the concrete, I tiptoe after them, the tunnel getting colder the further we walk.

Goosebumps sail over my skin as the cold seeps into my bones. We walk for a few minutes before the boys stop up ahead and I pause, my heart racing erratically. It's impossible to see what they're doing from back here, and as the boys look around, I press myself up against the wall of the tunnel, willing myself to disappear.

There's a heavy metal clang followed by a strange scraping, and right before my eyes the boys step into the wall, leaving me gaping after them. "What the fuck?" I mouth to myself, the darkness playing tricks on my eyes. I know those assholes didn't just step through some type of magical portal.

Not wanting to lose track of them and end up alone in this creep-tastic tunnel, I quickly scurry along, my heart thumping in my ears. My breath comes in sharp, heavy pants as paranoia slinks up on me, certain that someone is about to jump out and drag me even further into the darkness.

I stop at the place where the boys disappeared and glance over the tunnel wall. My eyes finally begin to adjust to the dark, and I find an old door that looks as though it must be centuries old. There's a keyhole to the side and a flare of frustration fires through me. Trying my luck, I shove my hands up against the old door and give it a hard shove, my eyes widening as it starts to move.

"Oh shit," I breathe. The door is heavy as hell, but when I lean right up against it with all my weight, it opens just enough for me to slip through the gap.

Inside is dimly lit, and I quickly notice a narrow set of stairs carved from old stone blocks. Instinctively I walk toward it, bypassing some expensive-looking tech. Assuming it's some kind of security system, I don't touch a thing. I might be a whiz when it comes to stealing people's phones and magically unlocking them, but when it comes to shit like this, I'd probably send the whole system into a meltdown.

Taking myself down the stairs, I come to an old iron gate that looks to be gold-plated. Heavy chains hang around it, but they've been left unlocked as though the boys are anticipating a hasty getaway. My fingers curl around the cold iron and I give it a small push, fear pounding through my body.

The gate isn't anywhere near as heavy as the first door, and as I pass through it, I can't help but notice the similarities between the intricate design in the gate and the tattoos across Easton's chest. I study it closer but don't linger, not wanting the boys to get too far ahead.

There's no telling what I could find down here. It could be a maze of tunnels, or I could be walking right toward a trap. So as long as I try to keep the boys in sight, I might just have a chance of seeing daylight again.

More stairs lead me further underground, and at the last step, I can see a faint glow of light ahead. A booming laugh interrupts the soft conversation, followed by a stern voice echoing through the long corridor.

I follow the sounds and the closer I get, the clearer it becomes that this is the home of Empire. Or, at least somewhere safe for the members to come and openly converse. Turning the corner at the end, the corridor opens up into a wide space filled with dark colors and dim lighting.

Men in suits fill the room, lounging back in armchairs with cigars between their fingers while girls dance for them, making them feel like kings. I swallow hard, disgust brimming in my chest. These men are not kings. They're frauds who get ahead in life because of the connections they make in underground organizations like this. They don't deserve anything they've got. Especially when there are honest, hard-working people out there who are putting in the effort.

Obnoxious laughter draws my attention, and I glance across the room to find the chief of police lounged back on a leather-studded couch, one hand holding his drink, the other gripping a young waitress's ass. Unease flashes in her eyes, and the need to save her slams through me, but I watch as she discreetly slips out of his reach as though she's been doing it all night. She barely looks eighteen, and I find myself wondering how the hell she ended up here.

Not wanting to linger on anything, I move into the room, keeping to the edges and trying to blend in. There are plenty of people in this fucked-up little gentleman's club, so sliding in unnoticed isn't a problem.

I get halfway across the room when something catches my eye. I glance up just in time to see Dalton step out of the shadows, a chilling look in his eyes. He moves in front of a door, discreetly checking that no one is watching him before disappearing through it.

Gotcha, motherfucker.

Cutting through the room, I hurry past arrogant men and narrowly avoid getting my ass grabbed by someone's grandfather before reaching the door. It's been left cracked, and I peer through it to find a dark corridor. It's somehow even creepier than the old train tunnel, but I've come this far. I'm not about to give up now.

Letting out a shaky breath, I slip through the door and into the corridor, gently closing it behind me. I follow it along, walking around a bend and down a small flight of steps. The corridor is lit with old oil lanterns, and the further down I get, the more it feels like some kind of dungeon.

My stomach twists and clenches, and the further down I go, the harder it gets to continue. Chills sweep over my skin and my breath catches in my throat. The odd mix of fear and anticipation makes me want to throw up.

As I reach the bottom of the old stone stairs, I turn the corner into a darkened room and come to a screeching halt. Dalton, Sawyer, and Zade all stand around a man who's been bound to a chair.

My eyes widen, and I hastily back up before they see me. "I want a fucking name," Zade roars, the terrifying rumble of his tone making my knees shake—and not in a good way. Zade adjusts himself, taking a step toward the man, and at this new angle, I get a clear view of his face. Horror blasts through me as I recognize the doorman from the ball.

This is on me.

I knew they'd question him, but I never expected it would go this far. I've all but signed his death certificate, and if they don't kill him, he's gonna wish they had.

He doesn't deserve this. He didn't do anything wrong. He showed me kindness at the door of the ballroom, allowing me to walk through despite my name not showing up on his list. He didn't have to do that, and hell, a part of me kind of wished he hadn't. But should he be held and interrogated by the likes of Zade DeVil? Absolutely not.

The guy shakes his head, terror in his eyes. "I don't know what you're talking about. The bitch showed me her invitation. I figured her name was accidentally left off the list. I swear. That's it. That's all that happened."

Zade scoffs and leans into him, bracing both hands on the armrests of the chair. His voice drops scarily low, and I swallow hard, only now just realizing what it means to be targeted by this man. Up until now, Zade has only been playing with me. "Someone approved you to let her in," he says, his words like ice sliding down my spine. "Give me a name, and I might allow you to walk away from this."

The doorman shakes as his gaze flicks between the boys, silently begging for some kind of relief. Realizing it isn't coming, he starts to hyperventilate, panic gripping him. "I . . . I . . . I told you what I know."

Zade tsks, pulling out a silver dagger. The designs on the hilt are so elegant, and yet so utterly terrifying. He presses the tip of his finger to the top of the blade and spins the dagger between his hands. The doorman's gaze locks on the sleek blade as it catches in the haunting glow of the lanterns.

"Last chance," Zade croons.

The doorman sobs and Zade shakes his head, almost looking disappointed. He lets out a heavy sigh and rears back with the blade. My eyes bug out of my head, fear paralyzing me. Zade's hostage blanches before wetting his pants, and my heart breaks seeing what Zade has reduced this man to. "Okay," he cries. "Just please . . . I'll tell you what you want to know."

"See? That wasn't so hard now, was it?" Zade taunts. "Give me a name."

The doorman swallows hard, nervousness flashing in his eyes. It's almost as though he's more terrified of this other person than he is of Zade, but that couldn't be right. Zade is the most callous and cruel monster this planet has to offer. The future leader of Empire.

The doorman lets out a sigh, his gaze dropping away from Zade's in defeat. "Percival Winchester," he finally says, his voice breaking as he chokes out the words. "He approached me before the ball and gave me a hundred bucks to let her through the door. I didn't think it was a big deal."

Zade sighs, looking at the man in pity, and then in one lightning-fast swipe, the blade slashes across his throat. Blood spurts like a waterfall, and as I try to scream, a strong hand clamps down over my mouth. My hands fly up, my nails digging deep into his skin as I desperately try to get away, but he pulls me in harder, my back slamming up against his wide chest. "Hush now, Pretty," I hear Easton in my ear, slowly pulling me back into the darkness. "You don't want anyone finding out you're here."

I can't take my eyes off the blood, watching as it pours out over the doorman's clothes, soaking them as he chokes and drowns in his own blood. My eyes are wide, terror gripping me like never before.

He killed him. He took his blade and slaughtered him like cattle. And what's more, Zade doesn't even seem fazed about it.

Turning around, Zade locks his cold stare directly on mine and strides toward me, Sawyer and Dalton right on his heels. He stops before me and I gape up at him, my knees failing me as I fall back against Easton. Something sparkles in his eyes, and in an instant he moves past me, starting his trek back up the old stone steps. "Come on," he throws over his shoulder. "We're leaving."

With that, Easton gives me a nudge in the back of my ribs, propelling me forward. I quickly follow, knowing damn well I have no other choice. As we leave the gruesome sight behind, I realize without a doubt that Zade knew I was there the whole damn time. He knew I was watching and still killed that man right in front of my eyes.

Zade DeVil truly is a monster. A cold, callous murderer. And yet despite all of that, I can't help but want to know him.

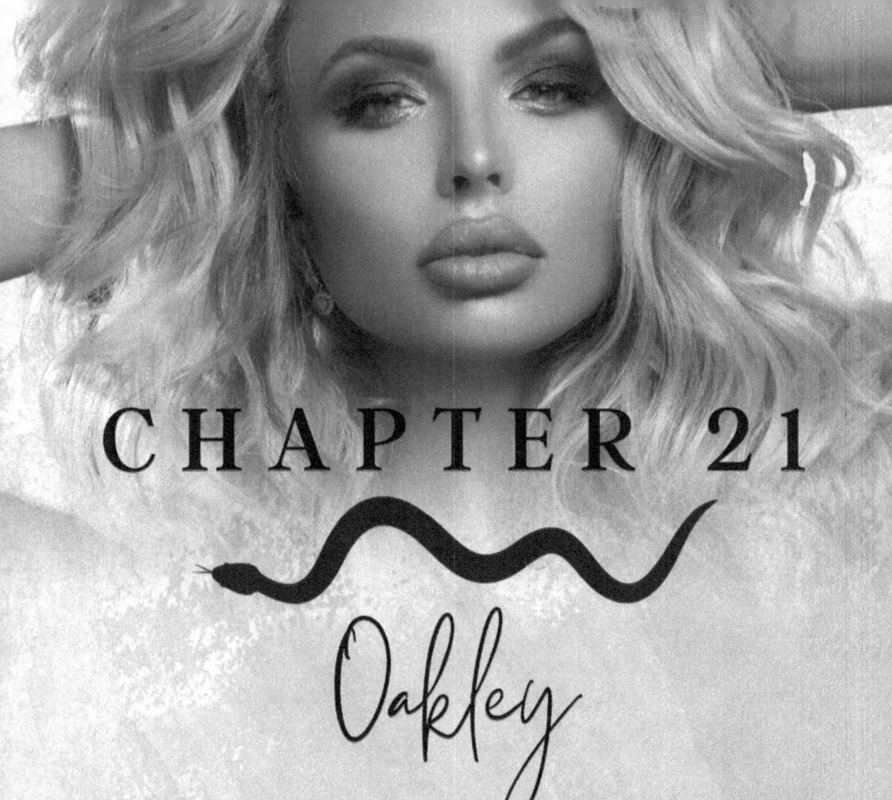

CHAPTER 21

Oakley

My hands shake as I sit between Easton and Sawyer in the back of Zade's Escalade, Easton's knee pressed up against mine. Zade watches me through the rearview mirror, and despite not once looking up to meet his rattling stare, I can feel it like lasers on my skin.

What the hell have I allowed myself to be involved in? These people, this organization, it's too much.

The Escalade pulls to a stop, and for the first time since getting in the car, my gaze lifts to the window, and I'm surprised to find us back at the college apartment complex. I could have sworn after catching me at the Empire compound, I'd be back in that cement prison. My brows furrow, but I don't dare question him on it. If I get to be at home in my own bed, with privacy, then I'll take it. It beats being Zade's prisoner.

I'll never be able to understand Zade or the decisions he makes. There's no rhyme or reason to this—at least not one I can see. Though something tells me he has a reason for every last thing he does.

We get out of the Escalade and hover, unsure if Zade would actually allow me to go if I started walking. Easton stands beside me and Zade nods to him. "Go with her. Sweep her apartment and then meet me back in mine. We've got some shit to deal with."

Easton nods and I don't hesitate, taking off at a brisk pace to get back to my apartment. Dalton watches the way his friend falls in beside me as his arm brushes against mine.

My gaze falls to the ground, so confused by all of this. Dalton is giving me mixed signals. He's so hard, so demanding and forceful, but at other times, I'll catch him watching me, teasing me, wanting to be near me. I don't get it, but it doesn't matter. He betrayed my trust. He destroyed any chance of something growing between us, whether it was friendship or something else.

They've all been dishonest. Dalton set me up to be kidnapped and Sawyer stood before me, insinuating that he'd take me by force. Now that I know him a little better, I realize that's not who he is. Sawyer is sweet and kind-hearted, and while he's just as cruel and callous on the outside as the rest of them, there's something softer hidden beneath. But there's no denying that back in the concrete prison, his words were terrifying.

Easton Cross is the only one who seems to have been honest with me. He was real from the start, and while something warns me to run from him, I'm drawn to him as well. Down in that dungeon with the blood spurting from the doorman, Easton's arms around me somehow made everything alright. I know he'd never hurt me, and something has me wanting to cling to him. But that doesn't mean I should trust him.

Zade, on the other hand, has done just about everything humanly possible to ensure I despise him. Kidnapping, holding me hostage, and my all-time favorite, his hand locking around my throat and squeezing the life out of me. I could see it in his eyes. If I had pushed him just a little more, he would have not thought twice about killing me.

All I know is Zade DeVil is a different breed. He's unpredictable and wild, and that scares the shit out of me.

Easton and I walk side by side and he holds the door open for me as we make our way into the hallway of our apartment complex. My arms are crossed over my chest, concealing the fact that my hands haven't stopped shaking since watching Zade slaughter that man.

Easton clears his throat and pulls his hand up in front of him, and it's only then do I realize that Venom is wrapped around his wrist. Has she been there this whole time? Down in the dungeons, the tunnels? I hadn't even noticed, but why would I notice a snake when there was someone being brutally murdered in front of my eyes?

We move in front of my apartment, and I fish my key out of the back pocket of my jeans. Lifting my hand to the door, I try to slide it into the lock, but my hands are shaking more violently now, every passing second only getting worse. "Here," he says, laying his hand over mine and steading it before guiding the key into the lock. He gives it a twist and the door unlocks, slowly swinging open before me.

We stand out in the hallway, a heavy tension growing between us. "You know," he starts, those dark eyes looking down at mine. "We may be monsters trained to kill and do the things others don't have the stomach for, but we're your best shot at survival."

I swallow hard and drop my gaze to the snake in his hand, watching as she slowly weaves through his fingers, unable to bear the look in his eyes. He was so earnest, so honest and real, and yet I can't help the feeling that he doesn't believe a damn word he's saying. "I, umm . . . I just want to get to bed and try to forget any of this ever happened."

Easton scoffs as he pushes the door further open and waves me in before him. "Easier said than done," he tells me. "That image is going to be ingrained in your mind for the rest of your life. Witnessing something like that for the first time isn't easy. But for the record, you're doing better than I did."

"Yeah?" I question, watching as he starts his sweep of my apartment.

I find myself following close by, not trusting the rest of the apartment until Easton's checked it out. "I was twelve when my old man thought it'd be a great bonding experience to take me on a hit. He had me hold down some guy and watch as he gutted him right there on his kitchen floor, his organs slipping out as though they had a mind of their own," he says, moving down to Cara's room and quickly checking over it, somehow not making a sound as she sleeps inside. He gently closes her door before turning back to me as though he hadn't just told me the most gruesome thing. "I threw up all over the poor bastard. It wasn't a pretty sight."

My lips scrunch in distaste. "That's . . . wrong in so many ways.

Why'd you have to tell me that?"

He shrugs his shoulders, finishing his sweep and hovering in my living room. "I thought we were sharing stories," he admits before giving me a tight smile. "Your place is clear, so you're good to do whatever you gotta do. But don't be surprised if you find one of us sleeping on your couch."

He goes to leave when I find myself calling after him, and he turns back, waiting patiently for me to figure out what I need to say. "I . . . I don't understand why Zade killed the doorman," I question, my voice breaking. "He gave him what he wanted. He got the name. He didn't need to do that."

Easton presses his lips into a hard line before shaking his head. "Zade was never going to get what he needed," he admits. "The name he gave . . . the motherfucker was lying in a desperate bid to save himself."

"How do you know that?"

"Because giving us Percy's name is about as useless as if he'd given us one of ours." My brows furrow as Easton takes a second to consider what details he's comfortable sharing. "Percival Winchester is Zade's mentor. He's . . . Well, he was more a father to Zade than his old man ever was."

My brows shoot up, my mind whirring with the possibilities. "And there's no chance he could be behind any of this?"

Easton shakes his head. "None," he states. "Percy is in palliative care, dying of late-stage lung cancer, and can barely walk, talk, or feed himself. There's just no way. He'd rather put a bullet through his own skull than betray Zade. Besides, in his current state, he couldn't physically or mentally pull off something like this. Giving us his name was a slap in the face."

"So why the hell would he do it then?"

"Who fucking knows," he mutters, shrugging his shoulders. "Not many are privy to the state of Percy's deteriorating health. Most people think he's been having some time off at his beach house up north. Perhaps he thought he could use Percy's absence as an excuse to pin it on him. All I know is every fucking step forward we take, is another five back."

I swallow hard and raise my gaze to his, letting him see the raw honesty in my eyes. "I'm going to die, aren't I?"

His face drops and he doesn't respond, but I appreciate that he's not trying to sugarcoat some bullshit answer. Even with their protection, the reality of the situation is they don't know who's behind this, and without that, there's no way to predict these attacks. Yet, I still find myself wondering why they want to protect me at all. I mean nothing to them.

A heavy moment passes between us and the tension dissipates, leaving nothing but hollowness. Seeing the defeat in my eyes, Easton gives me a tight smile. "You're stronger than you know," he tells me. "You've made it this far, haven't you? We might not be able to protect you at all times, but you can protect yourself. You just need to believe you can."

With that, he turns and strides back through my apartment toward the door. I don't hesitate in heading to my room, hating how fucked up this man has got me. One minute I want to tear his balls out through his throat, and the next I want them in my mouth.

Letting out a heavy sigh, I shove through my bedroom door, flipping the light switch as I go and come to a startling stop, finding a man standing in the corner. He moves like lightning, a gun whipping toward me as I let out an ear-shattering scream and run for my fucking life.

My feet don't move fast enough and this strange man is on me in seconds, gripping my hair and yanking me back. I ram my elbow into his stomach and he grunts, but his grip on me is too strong. "Fuck, you little bitch," he spits.

He starts dragging me back, his hand clamped over my mouth like a goddamn vice. I try to scream around it as he reaches my bedroom window and quickly breaks the glass with his gun, realizing this is going to be his only way out of here.

He starts pulling me through it as I try to fight him off. I grip the side of the window frame, broken glass slicing through my palm like soft butter. I cry out and just as quickly as this motherfucker got me, Easton comes barging through my bedroom door, his eyes wild and sharp.

My captor lashes out in a fit of panic, his gun blasting by my ear. I watch in horror as Easton roars, the bullet shooting directly into his shoulder, the force of the blast knocking him back against my wall. He grips his shoulder, blood seeping through his fingers, but it doesn't seem to faze him. It only serves to piss him off more.

I grip the window frame tighter, the jagged glass shredding my palm as I try to fight my attacker off. Easton raises his arm, his jaw clenched with fury in his eyes. The bullet flies from its chamber and I feel it whooshing past my face before hitting my attacker right between his eyes.

His hold immediately goes slack as a blood-curdling scream tears from the back of my throat. The fucker's lifeless body falls back onto the grass outside my window and I quickly scurry back inside, blood pouring down my arm.

"EASTON," I cry, trying to wipe the tears off my face as I barrel toward him, watching in horror as he slowly falls down my bedroom wall, the pain too great to bear.

He grunts as I fall to my knees beside him, my eyes going wide as I take in the gaping hole in his shoulder. "Fuck," I panic, desperately searching for something to stop the bleeding. Finding a discarded tee, I grab it and shove it against his shoulder, pressing hard in an attempt to stem the blood flow. I try to calm myself, knowing I'm not helping anybody by being scared, but I struggle to keep my hands steady on Easton's shoulder. "What . . . what do I do? Are you dying?"

"No," he grunts, clenching his jaw, "but I'll fucking pass out if we don't do something soon."

"FUCK."

"Zade," he says, the pain tearing at him. "Get me to Zade."

I nod, my gaze snapping to my bedroom door. How the fuck am I supposed to get him to Zade? He's twice my size, maybe six-foot-four, and packed with muscle. "You're gonna have to help me," I tell him, hurrying to my feet and gripping his other arm. "I can't drag you."

Easton grips his shoulder and I pull hard, trying to get him to his feet while blood soaks into the carpet. He gets himself up and heavily leans against me, each movement causing him to grunt and groan. "Come on," I say, his large frame weighing me down.

I kick the door open again and start dragging him out, each step feeling as though I'm getting smaller. Tears linger on my face, and the harder it is to hold him up, the more pain that tears through my shredded palms.

I get him through the living room and as we try to get to the door, I can't help but glance toward Cara's door. How the hell is she sleeping through all of this? Surely she must have heard the gunshots.

We reach the door, and as I struggle to open it while trying to keep Easton up, thoughts of Cara fade to the back of my mind. It feels as though it takes a lifetime before we're breaking out into the hall and I scream out, finding Zade, Dalton, and Sawyer coming through the main door at the other end of the corridor. "HELP," I cry, my knees buckling under Easton's weight, falling to the ground. "He's been shot."

They're running before the words are even out of my mouth.

Zade reaches us first, his eyes scanning over Easton in horror. "What the fuck happened?" he demands as Sawyer barges through to my apartment, going to see for himself.

I shake my head as Zade and Dalton dive in, relieving me of Easton's weight and hauling him back to his feet. "I don't know," I tell them as Zade kicks in his apartment door, not wasting time searching for his key. "Easton did the sweep, he checked my room and made sure it was clear, then when I was going to bed, there was someone in there waiting for me."

"How the fuck did he get shot?" Zade spits, clearly not interested in the smaller details.

"How do you think he got shot?" I throw back at him, quickly following the guys into Zade's apartment and pulling out a chair before they dump Easton on it. "The asshole was trying to drag me out the window and when he saw Easton, he took his shot."

"Fuck," Dalton mutters, his head whipping back toward the door, ready to race in after Sawyer.

"The fucker's dead," Easton grunts, his skin clammy and pale.

Dalton crosses to the kitchen and searches through the cabinets before pulling out a first aid kit and bringing it back to the table. He tears it open, pulling out all sorts of medical equipment, and my eyes widen, realizing these idiots fully plan on handling this themselves. "What are you doing?" I question. "We need to call an ambulance. He's going to need surgery."

Zade grabs Easton's shirt and tears it off him, and it doesn't go unnoticed that the charcoal drawing I did this morning is still faintly there. Drawing that feels like a lifetime ago. My gaze lingers on the portrait, and I quickly realize there's something different about this. It's not charcoal at all. It's ink.

My gaze widens, realizing that after taking off on the rooftop today, he went to have my drawing tattooed on his back. Before I can mention it aloud, Zade curses. "Fuck, no exit wound."

"Shit," Easton says with a heavy sigh as Dalton takes off to the kitchen again.

"What?" I rush out as Sawyer comes hurrying back through the door, his eyes wide as he glances over Easton, taking in the bullet hole and the blood seeping from it. "What does that mean?"

"It means," Zade says, clenching his jaw as he searches through the first aid supplies and picks out a pair of tweezers that look scary as fuck, "that the bullet is still in there and we've gotta go in to get it out."

My face falls, realizing how painful that's going to be. I gape at Easton just as Dalton returns with a bottle of whiskey and hands it to him. Easton eagerly lifts it to his lips, not waiting a damn second.

I shake my head in shock. Surely they're not actually considering doing this themselves. "This is insane," I tell them as Sawyer joins us, standing at my side. "He needs a doctor."

"Zade knows what he's doing," Sawyer says, before getting a full view of Easton's back and scoffing. "Man, you're fucking addicted to ink."

Easton shakes his head, his eyes getting heavy. "It's not an addiction unless you've sucked dick for it," he says, just as Zade steps into him, holding the tweezers. My eyes go wide as horror grips my chest. This is really happening.

"Where's Cara?" Zade asks. "Why wasn't she helping you?"

Sawyer lets out a frustrated sigh, answering before I get the chance. "The fucker slipped her something. She's out cold, but all her vitals are fine. She just needs to sleep it off."

Understanding dawns on me, answering the question I'd wondered about earlier as Easton glances up at me, looking like death warmed over. "Show me your hand."

I gape at him and reluctantly lift my hand, showing him the deep cuts across my palm from the glass, knowing he needs this distraction. He presses his lips into a hard line before muttering something under his breath. He shakes his head, and before I know it, Dalton scoops up my hand. "Why the fuck didn't you say anything?" he demands, grabbing another chair and forcing me into it. "You're going to need stitches."

"Then drop me off at the hospital," I say. "And while you're at it, you can drop Easton off too."

Zade lets out a huff, not bothering to look my way. "Shut up and let him fix you," he says. "You're bleeding all over my apartment."

I scoff. "Right, because you really give a shit what happens to this apart—AH FUCK," I cry out as Dalton pours something over my cut, cleaning it out. I try to tear my hand back but he has a death grip on it. "Was that necessary?"

Dalton doesn't respond as he focuses on what he's doing, and I watch in horror as he fishes out a needle and thread from the first aid kit. "Tell me you're gonna do something to numb the pain first?"

Easton scoffs beside me and hands me the bottle of whiskey. "Drink up, Pretty."

Fuck.

I take the whiskey and bring it to my lips, taking a deep swig as Zade gets to work searching for the bullet lost in Easton's shoulder. My stomach clenches as the tweezers disappear inside his shoulder, but I keep my stare on it, distracting me from the needle clutched between Dalton's fingers.

Easton clenches his jaw, sucking in a sharp breath through his teeth, reaching for the whiskey and tearing it out of my grasp. He takes a long, drawn-out swig before cutting himself off, his eyes wide as he looks at Sawyer. "Venom," he says. "She's not here."

"Fuck," Sawyer says, turning on his heel. "I'll find her."

I barely get a chance to think about the fact there's a snake loose in my apartment with my knocked-out roomie when Dalton digs down with the needle, and I realize just how low my pain threshold really is. I cry out and Easton hands me the whiskey once again. I drink up, the liquor burning my throat on its way down. "Fuck me, this hurts so bad."

Easton scoffs, glancing at me with his brow arched. "You think that hurts?" he questions. "You should try being shot."

Okay, he has a point. He's definitely in more pain than I am.

I try to keep my mouth shut when Dalton subtly shakes his head, keeping his attention on my hand. "We can't keep her safe here."

"My thoughts exactly," Zade mutters, digging a little deeper into Easton's shoulder. "We're out of options. We need to move her into the penthouse."

"What?" I demand, my head snapping up, the very thought of living in that big penthouse sending chills sailing down my spine. Even more so now that I've seen exactly how cruel Zade really is. "Over my dead fucking body."

Zade scoffs, irritated by my refusal. "If that's what it takes."

I clench my jaw, glaring at the asshole. "I'm not living with you," I say, putting my foot down despite knowing that this place really isn't safe for me anymore. "I have a job and college to think about."

Zade grunts, tugging on the tweezers until the bullet emerges from Easton's shoulder, blood pouring out after it. Putting it down on the table, I hear the heavy metal of the bullet rolling around before Zade's callous stare locks onto mine. "What good will your precious job and college degree be if you're dead?"

Holding his stare, I clench my jaw, fury rippling through me as I realize my own needs and wants don't even begin to register on his radar. He arches a brow, silently daring me to fight him on it, but he's right. Fighting and refusing only puts me in a worse situation.

I let out a sigh and glance down at my hand, cutting the conversation short. Just when I think he's about to gloat for yet another win, Sawyer comes busting through the door, Venom wrapped around his hand and her fangs lodged deep into his wrist. "The little fucker bit me."

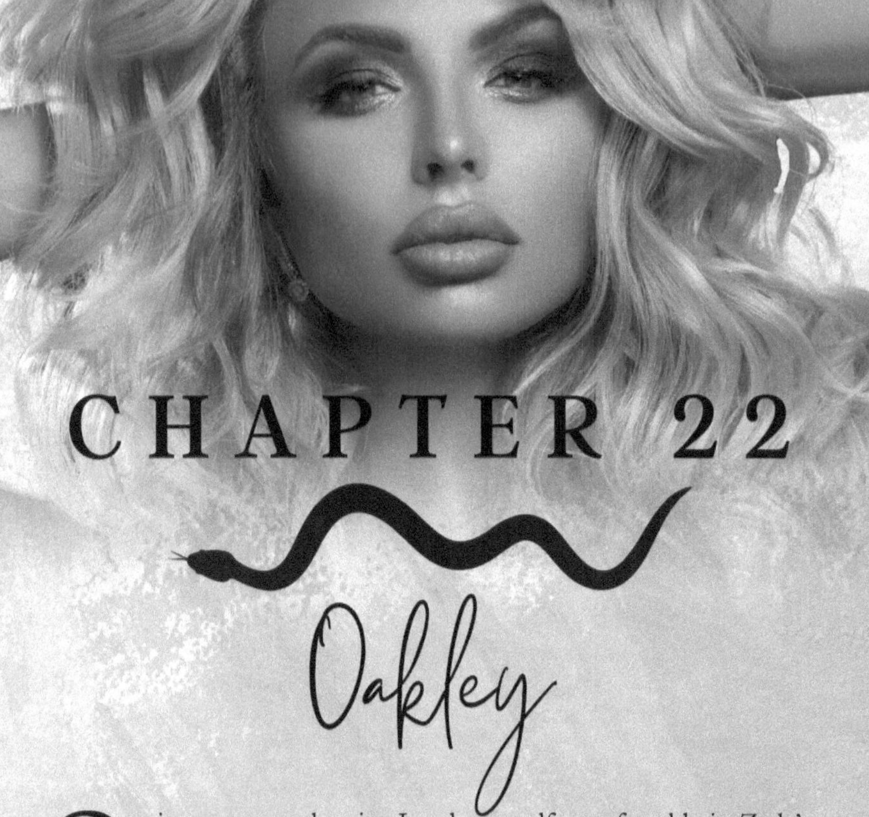

CHAPTER 22

Oakley

Staring out over the city, I make myself comfortable in Zade's den, pulling my feet up onto the couch. I clutch a glass in my hand, mindlessly swirling the frosty liquid around and listening to the ice cubes as they clatter against the edge of the glass.

The lights are dimmed and the city below is just starting to come alive for the night. I've been here less than a day, and I'm already desperate to get out, even though that's not possible. I suppose it could be worse—Zade could have me chained and locked up. This view beats his fucked-up cement prison any day.

Bringing my glass to my lips, I take a quick sip just as Dalton appears in the entryway, leaning against the frame and gently knocking against the wall. "Want some company?" he questions, a subtle hint of guilt hidden within his bright blue eyes.

I shrug my shoulders and glance back at the view, the city lights sparkling. "I suppose."

He strides through the den and drops onto the couch next to me, leaving space between us. I watch him out the corner of my eye, not wanting to let on that he has my full attention. "I, uhh . . . I came to check on you," he says while getting comfortable, putting his feet up on the small coffee table and stretching his arms out along the back of the couch. "How are you doing?"

"How do you think I'm doing?" I question, sparing him a quick glance and seeing something real in his eyes. He still seems like that cocky, too-sure-of-himself asshole I first met outside the apartment complex, but here and now, there's something raw and honest.

"Stupid question, huh?"

"The worst," I agree.

His gaze lingers on me before letting out a heavy breath. "You really hate me, don't you?"

I consider his question before finally shaking my head. "How can I hate someone I don't know?" I murmur, my voice like a whisper floating through the room. "Was that cocky-as-fuck guy who took me riding on his bike and told me that sad chicks give the best head the real you? Or were you doing your part in this sick little game, trying to draw me in? See that guy, the one up on the roof that night? I liked that guy. He was carefree and fun. But something tells me that's not who you really are."

He nods as if really hearing me. "Let me make it up to you," he offers. "That guy on the roof, that was the real me, and I know I haven't given you a reason to believe that, but give me a chance to show you."

I adjust myself on the couch, turning to face him more directly before placing my glass down on the coffee table. "You set me up to be kidnapped by men who scared the shit out of me, and then sat in that cell with me and lied about who you are. You saw how fucked up that was and you let them do that to me. You did that to me."

His gaze drops, and I see self-loathing in his eyes, the guilt that's been building and eating at him. "I know," he tells me. "The truth is, I was more than happy to play along. I'm not a good guy, Firefly. The way I was raised, shit like that comes naturally to me. It wasn't until I received that text from Zade, telling me it was time, that I realized how badly I didn't want to hurt you."

"But you still did it anyway."

He nods. "I did."

"Fool me once and that's on you," I tell him. "Fool me twice and . . . well, that just wouldn't happen."

He watches me, the silence growing heavy until a curious suspicion flashes in his eyes. His head tilts just a little, the curiosity getting stronger. "You want Cross."

My brows furrow as I consider what he's asking, and I shake my head. "No, I don't think I do," I tell him. "I mean, don't get me wrong, he's hot as fuck. You all are, and goddamn, the way he fucked me during the ball was insane. My knees shake every time I think about it. But I don't want to be with him. I don't want to be with anyone. I'm just trying to not get killed."

"But there's something about him that's drawing you in," he states. "It's the snake, isn't it? That fucked-up little bond he has with Venom. Chicks dig that kind of shit. I can get a kitten if it'll help."

I laugh and roll my eyes. "For the love of all things holy, please don't get a kitten. You'll end up turning it into an attack demon, and there's nothing cute about that. Besides, Venom will probably think it's lunch." Dalton laughs and I let out a sigh, knowing he's still waiting for an answer. "For what it's worth, the only reason I'm so drawn to Easton is because he's the only one who hasn't messed with me yet."

His brows furrow as I go on. "Sawyer had me believing he was going to rape me in that cell and Zade . . . well, what hasn't he done?"

"Sawyer never would have touched you. You know that, right? He was just trying to fuck with your head."

"It worked," I mutter darkly. "But yes, I know that now. Doesn't mean I have to forgive him."

"Sure as hell seemed like you did when you sucked his cock like that."

A grin pulls up the corner of my lips. "What's the matter, Dalton? You sound jealous."

He shrugs his shoulders. "So what if I am?" he questions, reaching for me and brushing the back of his finger over the curve of my face. His gaze drops to my lips before coming back to my eyes. "Don't lie to me, Firefly. Up on that roof, you felt the connection between us."

My heart starts to race, and for the first time, it's not because I'm terrified of imminent death. Not knowing how to respond, I move across the couch and straddle his lap. Dalton's hands fall to my waist as he watches me, those blazing blue eyes so intense and warm. "I specifically recall you telling me you weren't interested in anything more than the occasional screw."

"I'm gonna be real with you, Firefly. I don't know what the fuck I want, but what I do know is that every time you're around me, I want to be close to you. I want to hear your thoughts, and when you get all fired up the way you do . . . fuck, babe, it gets me hard."

"Is that right?" I ask, reaching down between us and slipping my hand into the front of his pants.

A sly grin cuts across his face and he bounces his knee, making me fall into him. He catches me before I break his face, his hand gripping the back of my neck. My face hovers just in front of his as I curl my fingers around his hardening cock, his piercing sending a thrill shooting through my body.

There's a pause between us as his eyes lock on mine, and as the moment becomes too intense, he crushes his lips to mine, kissing me deeply.

My eyes roll to the back of my head as I sink into him, his kiss as magical as the first snowfall of winter. He's dominant and forceful, just as he was up on the roof and in the elevator, but there's something different here. Something real.

My hand moves up and down his thick cock, my fingers unable to wrap the whole way around, and as he groans with approval, he grips my ass and pulls me in, locking our bodies together.

As I continue working him, my movements rub against my pussy and I suck in a breath, already so hot for this.

Needing to see and feel that perfect body against mine, I break our kiss, panting with desperation as I pointedly drop my gaze. "Lose the clothes, hot shot."

A wicked grin stretches across his face and he reaches over his head, gripping the material at the back of his neck and shrugging out of his shirt. I let out a soft exhale. Looking like this should be a crime.

Not wanting to miss out on the fun, Dalton gets busy stripping me bare before making things easier and losing his pants. I don't dare stop working him, only now without his clothes, getting off on him is a shitload easier.

Watching me closely, he rolls his tongue over his bottom lip. "I'm not fooled, Firefly. I know you're running the show, so I'm not going to try making demands. But the very next time I get you alone, you'll be spread out with that cunt on display, and you're going to show me exactly how you fuck yourself."

A blast of arousal sails through my body like an electric shot straight to my core, and I grind my pussy against him, both of us groaning with desperation. "I'll show you mine if you show me yours."

Starvation flashes in those blazing eyes, and in a flash of need, his arm tightens around me and he lifts me before bringing me down directly on his monster cock.

He fills me to the brim, stretching me so damn wide, that delicious piercing doing wicked things to me. I throw my head back while sucking in a deep breath, the unadulterated pleasure making me come alive.

And then I start to move.

Easton was right. It's not an addiction until you've sucked dick for it, and good lord, you can guarantee I've sucked this man's dick until he came down my throat. It's official; I am undeniably addicted to Dalton Eros.

My arms lock around his neck, and as I come up on my knees, Dalton sucks my nipple into his mouth, flicking it with his tongue. I groan low, bouncing on his cock and rolling my hips.

His hands roam over my body. My tits. My waist. My neck. My ass. It's everything and more, yet somehow not nearly enough.

I ride him up and down, bouncing, grinding, rolling, putting my body on show and letting him know just how I like it. My pussy clenches around him, squeezing tight, and he groans low, his fingers biting into my hips. "Fuck, Firefly. If you keep grinding your fucking hips like that, I'm gonna come, and I'm not nearly finished with you yet."

I grin wide and grind my hips a little more. "You'll fucking come when I say you can come and not a second before, hot shot. Is that clear?"

His hand drops to my ass, gripping it tight before pulling back and spanking it hard, making me yelp with pleasure. "Watch yourself, Oakley. Just because I'm giving you control now, doesn't mean I won't take it back and fuck you into submission."

Well damn. Maybe that's exactly what I need.

"You talk a big game, hot shot," I murmur, letting him hear the overwhelming desire in my throat as my pussy tightens around him. "But we both know that by the end of this, you'll be the one fucked into submission."

Before Dalton can get another word in, I give him exactly what he needs.

I fuck him so hard and fast my thighs burn, but I don't dare stop, his fingers on my hips only spurring me on. "Oh fuck," he grunts, raising his hips to take me deeper, but it's not enough. I grab his shoulder and shove him down on the couch.

He adjusts us to lay flat, and we both groan as I lean forward, bracing my hands against his wide chest and sinking into this new position. He reaches up and presses his thumb to my clit, rubbing tight, fast circles that make my eyes roll.

It's too much. I can't take it anymore. "Oh God," I pant, my nails digging into his pec. "I'm gonna come."

The words barely get through my lips when he applies more pressure to my clit and my world detonates, my orgasm exploding through me. "Fuck," I cry, throwing my head back, the elation too much to take.

My pussy convulses around him and as I squeeze hard, he comes right along with me, shooting hot spurts of cum deep inside of me while groaning my name.

"Holy fuck," I breathe, slowing my movements and riding it out.

Dalton takes a breath, his eyes briefly closing. "You can say that again."

I keep my hips moving slowly, rocking back and forth as we both try to catch our breath, and as I sit up a little straighter, something draws my attention to the door. My gaze shifts across the room and my back stiffens, finding Zade DeVil leaning against the doorframe, those strong arms crossed over his chest and his sharp stare locked on me.

A flash of shock and embarrassment surges through me, but I shake it off. I don't have anything to be embarrassed about, and hell, from the hunger in his eyes, I'd dare say he enjoyed the show. I don't say a word, don't let on that he's here, enjoying how that lethal stare takes me in. In return, he remains silent, more than content on watching the show.

Wanting to give him one, I glance down at Dalton, rolling my tongue over my bottom lip. "So?" I question. "What were you saying about fucking me into submission? Wanna show me what you mean?"

Dalton eagerly grabs me and lays me out over the coffee table, my legs pushed up to my chest, allowing the perfect view for my captivated audience.

CHAPTER 23

Zade

Oakley Quinn is a fucking nightmare. Keeping her in check shouldn't be this complicated, and yet she's defiant and strong-willed. It won't be long until I break her down. She'll become submissive, weak, wounded, and scared. Breaking her is going to be the most enjoyable thing I've ever experienced, but keeping her alive might just be the hardest.

Standing outside the Thorne estate, I stare up at the home where the boys and I practically grew up. This was a safe space. A place where we could escape the harsh realities of our own homes, but things are different now. We're not kids fucking around, trying to win our fathers' approval. We're grown and able to see through their manipulation and lies, and they learned pretty damn fast that we're not the type of people they want to fuck with.

A quick check of my phone shows it's creeping closer to 3 a.m. I let out a sigh, slipping around the side access and into the backyard. After Cross was shot in Oakley's apartment, I called a meeting with The Circle.

I've had enough. This shit ends now.

The calling card and break-in at Oakley's apartment were cute, and the blatant attempt at humiliation during the ball was creative, but now it's fucking business. Now one of my closest friends has become collateral damage in this war, and I won't stand by and allow this shit to slide. Don't get me wrong, it's not the first time Cross has been shot. But he got shot trying to protect my interests, and that can't happen again.

Not wanting these assholes to see me coming, I make my way to the back door, keying in the familiar password, and slipping inside the mansion. I've been standing out front for the past hour, watching and waiting for everyone to arrive. Now that I know they're all here, it's time to get this shit started.

Moving through the mansion like a ghost, I slip through back passageways and secret rooms, weaving through the hallways where the boys and I once ran like a herd of elephants. I'm closing in on Nikolai's home office when my phone buzzes in my pocket, and I pull it out to see a fresh text.

Pausing in the hallway, I unlock my phone and find a text from Cara. I consider swiping the notification away and ignoring it before letting out a sigh and opening it.

Cara - What the fuck is going on? I haven't seen Oakley in days. What have you done to her?

Zade - She's fine. Mind your fucking business.

Cara - I swear, if you hurt her…

Zade - You'll what?

There's no response and I scoff, shoving the phone back into my pocket. Cara knows we have an interest in Oakley. Hell, it's the reason why she's been living in that shitty apartment for the past few weeks, posing as her roommate. She just doesn't know why, and she never will. But that doesn't mean she's not curious and will do whatever she can to try and figure it out, and in doing so, she's allowed herself to form an attachment. Exactly what I asked her not to do.

Hell, it's exactly what I asked them all not to do. First it was Dalton, and now the dickhead is practically drooling over her. Next, Sawyer, but he won't admit it. He's too scared of his own fucking emotions to understand how he feels, but nonetheless, it's there. But then Cross. Fuck, that one stung. Cross was the one guarantee I had, and he went and fucking blew it. Just like Sawyer, he doesn't realize he's getting attached, but he'll figure it out soon enough.

Slipping through the back entrance of Nikolai's impressive home office, I hide in the shadows, and not a damn one of them notices I'm here. I listen to their conversation, hearing the tone in their voices as my name is mentioned. "What is all this about?" Ira Abrahms demands. "It's three in the morning. This is absurd."

Hartley Scott lets out a frustrated grunt as he helps himself to Nikolai's liquor cabinet. "Too right," he spits. "He's a hot-headed kid, not ready to take on such a profound role. The power he's going to wield . . . He's going to burn this organization to the ground. Lawson would never have played these ridiculous games."

The mention of my father's name grinds on my nerves, and as I go to step out of the shadows, Nikolai holds his hands out in peace. "Come now, this is our future leader you're talking about. Show some respect. You may not like him, but you will show loyalty to the blood of Empire under my roof."

The corner of my lip twitches with a small smile. I've always been able to rely on Nikolai to have my back, even during the worst of times. I've always seen him as a father figure to me. At least, he's who I always wished my father could have been. Maybe things would have been different. Perhaps I would have had a healthy respect for the dead bastard and the overwhelming need to slice my blade across his throat would have never existed.

Stepping out of the shadows, I let myself be known, keeping my gaze locked on Hartley Scott. I take in his tired business suit and his disheveled, messy appearance. He's in politics and is a master manipulator of the public, but in this room with these people, he's nothing. "Is there something you would like to say about the way I conduct business?"

Hartley's gaze drops, and I don't miss the way the remaining eleven members discreetly form a circle around the room. "No, Zade. Of course not. I appreciate your promptness in calling this meeting. It shows an eagerness and drive for the position you will be moving into. As part of The Circle, this is very pleasing to see. You have a strong loyalty to our traditions, and I look forward to seeing how you take on this role. However, I must admit, I am at a loss for why we are here."

I hold his stare for a moment longer. Fucking ass kisser.

He's a snake in sheep's clothing. That's all he'll ever be.

Taking a step into the circle, I begin to pace, slowly making my way around the twelve men before meeting each of their stares.

Aleksander Torrini. Chin raised in defiance, eyes narrowed and suspicious.

Clifford Langdon. Timid and nervous, clearly has no clue what this is about.

Gideon Harvey. Tired and bored.

I keep going around the circle, taking them all in one by one. I have grown up with these men. They would frequent my home for meetings with my father. They watched me grow and mature and then watched me become cold and relentless. They know who I am, know what I'm capable of, and my bad side is not where they want to be.

"As you are all aware," I start, my tone letting on just how serious I am. "There are exactly thirty more days until we reach the end of our mourning period, and in that time I will stand before you as the only heir of Empire and carve the still-beating heart out of the chest of an innocent to complete the leadership ritual. The woman who has been so carefully selected is Oakley Quinn. Twenty-year-old college student, recently returned to Faders Bay. However, I do not need to share this information with you as tradition dictates that all of you have personally signed off on this young woman becoming my sacrifice."

Nervous glances are shared between one another, and a thrill shoots through me. They don't know where I'm going with this, nor how it will end for them. "What tradition does not dictate is that the name of my sacrifice become common knowledge among our members," I state. "Over the past two weeks, there have been multiple attempts on her life in a bid to ensure I do not complete my sacrifice, therefore making me unable to take my rightful position at the head of this organization."

I step directly into the center of the circle, shifting around and letting my hard stare lock onto each man, letting them feel my wrath. "Let me be very clear," I state, each word loud and authoritative, reverberating through the office. "One of the twelve men standing before me tonight has betrayed me by sharing Oakley's name with those who mean us harm. In doing so, that person has betrayed Empire, our blood, and our way of life. A betrayal against me is a betrayal against your brothers, and you will be punished." I pause, shifting around the room to see the true fear in their eyes. "Do not be fooled, brothers. I will find who is responsible. And when I do, I will enjoy holding this person to the full extent of our laws. There will be no trial, no vote . . . no hope. Just my dagger across his throat."

With that, I turn and walk out of the room, each step echoing through the silence.

Making my way out the front door of the mansion, I hit the grand entry stairs and sail down them before leaning up against a post at the bottom. One by one, The Circle members exit the Thorne estate and quickly hurry to their cars. Those who are usually quite vocal are now quiet and timid.

A moment passes before the last Circle member is gone and a shadow steps in beside me. "Starting strong," Nikolai says. "Some aren't going to take well to that."

"I don't give a shit what they take well to," I tell him. "If I don't set the tone now, they're going to walk all over me, and I don't take kindly to that. Within a week, they'll be dead and buried. I won't hesitate to make an example of anyone who refuses to fall in line."

Nikolai watches me for a moment, both concern and curiosity deep in his stare. "Come and join me for a drink," he says. "It's about time you learned some things."

Nikolai doesn't wait for a response, simply turns on his heel and climbs back up the grand entryway. I trail back into his estate behind him and to his home office. He offers me the leather-studded armchair across from his desk and I take a seat, watching as he crosses to his liquor cabinet and pours two drinks.

"What's this about?" I question as he hands me a glass.

Nikolai takes the armchair beside mine, taking a slow, heavy breath and reaching for the pack of cigars on the small table between us. He cuts the end before resting it between his lips and lighting it. Impatience gnaws at me, and as a cloud of smoke puffs out in front of him, I have to ball my hands into fists to keep from ripping the fucking thing right out of his mouth. "Nikolai," I warn.

He glances my way, and after getting his fix, he lowers his hand, the edge of his cigar dangling over the ashtray. "You mustn't tell Myra

I was smoking in the house. She'd have my balls for it."

"To be quite honest, I don't give a shit what your wife does with your balls. I am, however, interested in what things you feel I need to know."

"Patience is a virtue, Zade, and unfortunately, it's not a lesson you were ever fond of learning," he states before his face becomes shrouded in seriousness, finally getting down to business. "What do you know of Oakley Quinn? Have you looked into her background?"

My brows furrow. What kind of stupid question is that? Of course I've looked into her background. I nod. "There's absolutely nothing interesting about her. She lived here as a kid. Her father died and she went to live with an aunt in Missouri. She had issues with a troubling ex-boyfriend, then decided to move back here."

"What do you know of her father?"

I try to rack my brain for what I found on the man. "Not a lot. Matthias Quinn seemed to be some kind of hero within the community of Faders Bay. He was dumped with Oakley as a newborn after a one-night stand and worked as a local firefighter. Wasn't winning awards for his lifesaving work, but he wasn't exactly the runt of the station either."

"And if I told you the background check you did on him was all fabricated?"

I watch him cautiously. "What aren't you telling me?"

Nikolai lets out a heavy breath before taking his glass and lifting it to his lips. He tips all its contents down his throat before settling his stony gaze back on me. "Matthias Quinn is the illegitimate, only-born son of your grandfather, Julius DeVil."

I stare at him, not following along. "The fuck did you just say?" I question the words only-born son on repeat in my head. "Because it sounds a lot like you're trying to tell me that I am not the legitimate heir of Empire."

"That's exactly what I am trying to tell you, Zade. You are not the rightful heir of Empire. The blood does not run through your veins. It runs through Oakley's."

I fly up from my armchair and slam Nikolai up against the wall, my dagger at his throat. A drop of blood slips from beneath his delicate skin and stains my blade. Fury consumes me, and as I press my blade into him, I feel everything I worked for slipping through my fingers. "How dare you spread such vile lies."

"They are not lies, Zade," he says in a comforting tone, not fazed by my outburst in the slightest. It's almost as though he had expected this of me, this childish outburst over power. "Release me, and I will share what I know."

Letting out a breath, I reluctantly step back, needing to hear exactly what the old bastard has to say. He pulls a handkerchief from his pocket and gently dabs at the base of his throat as he strides across his office.

I follow, watching as he reaches into the neckline of his shirt and pulls a small brass key from a low-hanging chain. Nikolai glances at me, making sure he has my full attention before pushing open his desk drawer and using the key to release a false bottom.

Nikolai reaches in and produces a manilla folder full of papers before handing them to me. "What's this?" I question, snatching it from his hand with no intention of giving it up.

"In that folder, you will find evidence of your grandfather's affair. I am sure you have heard the stories and are aware that your grandparents had an arranged marriage, and in those early years, they were not fond of one another. Your grandfather had an affair with a younger woman, a Miss Marietta Quinn. She was barely eighteen and he was forty-three, and upon discovering her pregnancy, he hid her away and paid her to keep quiet. She died soon after the birth of her son, Matthias. Cause of death not provided."

Every word out of his mouth is like a shot straight to the chest, but it's like watching a train wreck; impossible to look away. "My father is Julius' son, Lawson DeVil. The blood of Empire lived in his veins," I state, knowing that as fact. "I am his son, the heir of Empire."

"I'm sorry, Zade," he says, shaking his head. "You are indeed your father's son. However, your father is not biologically Julius' son."

"And what proof do you have of that?"

"It's all in the folder," he tells me, waving toward the papers in my hand. "Your grandparents tried for a child for a very long time, and upon realizing his wife could not conceive an heir, he turned to other avenues. Your father is the result of a junkie living on the street who'd been abused by her stepfather. He was abandoned as a newborn at the door of a fire station, and within three hours, he was the new heir of Empire."

My world starts to implode, everything I knew to be true suddenly burning to ash at my feet. My heart races and I shake my head. "That can't be right."

"I am sorry, son. I know this isn't the news you were hoping to hear, but every word I speak is true. You'll find an autopsy report for your grandmother, Iris, stating no evidence of ever birthing a child. Your father is Julius' adoptive son, and he does not share the same blood that runs through his veins. Your father never belonged to Empire, and when this was brought to his attention all those years ago, he took Matthias' life and buried the evidence."

My face falls. "He murdered the rightful heir."

"Indeed," he says, giving me a pointed stare. "And in thirty suns and thirty moons, you will do the very same thing."

Oakley.

Fuck.

Falling back a step, I drop into the leather-studded armchair. "What do I do?" I question. "If Empire finds out about this, I'll be put to death. Right along with anyone who helps me."

Nikolai's head snaps up, his eyes coming to rest on mine He knows damn well that despite Sawyer not knowing any of this, it will be assumed that he does. All my friends will be hunted right along with me, whether they're involved or not. "Do not mishear me, Zade. I am loyal to the blood of Empire," he states, specifically telling me he will not be loyal to me. "However, I will do everything in my power to keep my son from suffering this fate. I do not believe you should be punished for a position you were put in by those before you."

"Thank you," I tell him, sitting back in the chair, trying to figure out where the hell to go from here. I will my brain not to think about the fact that the only true living heir of Empire is currently being held prisoner in my penthouse, busily fucking my friends. "Oakley will never belong in this world."

"No," he agrees. "She will not."

"What do I do?"

"Exactly what we intended for you to do," he tells me. "In thirty days and thirty moons, you will take her life and put an end to this. There will be no living heir and you will rise as the new blood of Empire."

The ashes at my feet begin to shift together and I rise like a fucking phoenix. The power of what's to come blasts through my veins. I will become the new blood of Empire, and I will do whatever the fuck it takes.

Nikolai meets my eyes. "You must know, there are a few outside of The Circle who believe they know the truth. They're only guessing, but nonetheless, I have tried to keep them quiet. But they are getting restless," he admits. "This news getting out will not fare well for Empire. There are ones who believe you do not belong in power, who do not wish to follow someone so . . . young. Those are the ones who will come for your back. Your father was a callous ruler, one who never should have worn the crown of our people. But you, Zade, you will lead this organization the way it was intended to be led."

My gaze lingers on his, and the longer I watch him, the clearer it becomes. "You know who this is," I state. "You know who's been making these attacks on Oakley."

He shakes his head. "I do not."

"But you know something." He watches me, not responding,

seemingly mulling over how he's going to play this. "You know which of The Circle betrayed her name."

Something flashes in his eyes, and I see a slight tightening in his jaw.

"Give me a name, Nikolai," I prompt, not playing games.

He lets out a sigh. "Can I trust that my admission in this matter will remain confidential?"

"Of course," I say, giving him my word. My word is my bond.

Nikolai's lips press into a hard line, his heart on his sleeve. He takes a breath, knowing the next words out of his mouth will be nothing short of a death sentence for a brother who has stood by his side as a member of The Circle for twenty-odd years. But what choice does he have? Either let this fight continue and allow Oakley Quinn to rise as our leader and burn everything we've built over the centuries to the ground, or save us all? "The name you're looking for is Aleksander Torrini."

And with that, I rise, clutching the manilla folder in my hand. Without another glance toward Nikolai, I stride out of the office and back through the front door. My phone is already in my hand and my thumb madly roaming over the screen, a new text sent off to Dalton and Sawyer before my feet leave the final step of the property.

Zade - Meet me outside the Torrini estate in 30. Leave Oakley with Cross.

The moon still shimmers high in the sky when a black SUV comes flying over the hill, hurtling toward me. It pulls to a stop beside my Escalade, and as Dalton and Sawyer step out of the car, we each look up at the Torrini mansion.

It's not as grand as the Thorne estate, but it's also nothing to sneeze at either. "You ready?" I ask the boys, glancing back as they stride toward me.

Dalton grins, a gun already in his hand, though we both know he won't be needing it. This one is all mine. "Fucking born ready."

Sawyer nods, and without hesitation, we take off toward the house. "Who squealed?" he questions, glancing my way.

My jaw clenches, holding up my word of keeping this confidential, and Sawyer just grins some more. "Ahhh, my old man, huh? I knew he'd crumble."

Getting closer to the house, I go to the front while Dalton takes the left and Sawyer heads to the right, covering all bases. Although, it's barely 4:30 in the morning. I doubt anyone will be awake inside, but either way, we need to make this quick.

Aleksander lives by the bay, the shore practically on his front doorstep, and soon enough, the street will fill with early morning joggers and surfers trying to start their day off right. Despite how I had wanted to take my time with this, we need to play this smart. In and out. Get the job done and make sure no one sees us.

Making my way up the steps, I move toward the front door and hover in front of it. Aleksander has one hell of a security system set up here, just as all The Circle members do. I won't risk touching that door until I know we can get in undetected.

I wait barely thirty seconds, watching the red light on the front of the automatic locking system on the door. There's a soft whirring sound before the light turns green.

My phone buzzes in my pocket, and I take it out, my lips pulling into a sly grin.

Sawyer - All clear.

Fuck yeah.

My hand closes over the handle, and I'm in.

Striding through the house, I notice a soft strip of light shining from beneath a closed door just as Sawyer comes in from the back. I nod toward the door, and his brow arches just seconds before a grin pulls at his lips. As he glances back at me, I have to resist laughing.

This fucker is always on the same wavelength. Besides, there's nothing like a good trap.

We wait barely twenty seconds before Dalton shows his face in the hallway, each of us blocking every direction. I don't even get a chance to tell him what's going on before he notices the light under the door and rolls his eyes. "Fuck, man," he whispers. "I'm still paying for the last trap I set."

"Stop being such a fucking pussy," I tell him.

Dalton has the audacity to look offended as I search the room for something to use to our advantage. Something that will make just enough noise to alarm whoever's in that room, but not enough to wake their sleeping family upstairs.

I find nothing but a glass vase and cringe, knowing it'll have to do before Sawyer shuffles further down the hall and crouches down to a mini robot vacuum. He glances back at me, his eyes dark, sick, and twisted. Perfect.

Giving the nod of approval, Sawyer scoops up the robot vacuum and brings it out into the foyer. He positions it directly between the three of us so that whoever's in there doesn't come running out and head in the wrong direction. What fun would that be?

He hits the big red button in the center, and like a good little robot, it beeps three times before getting to work. The soft whir of the machine is like music to my ears.

Sawyer quickly shuffles back into position, and just as he gets there, the door whips open, sending the light spilling out into the foyer. Aleksander comes barging out, his eyes wide and in a panic. As he sees me and notices his escape routes are gone, his stare only becoming more frantic.

Without saying a word, he knows what this is about. He knows his time is up.

"Let's make this fast, Alek," I say. "I don't want to be here longer than necessary."

His gaze shoots around the hall, searching for some way to try and help himself, and when he glances toward the stairs, I let out a heavy sigh. "Don't be foolish. I don't want to include them in this, but if you push me, you know damn well I'll line them up across the wall and have them watch."

Regaining a little composure, Aleksander strides closer, putting himself directly between the boys and me. "Assuming this is about your little performance at Nikolai's estate, then you have your wires crossed somewhere," he states, not bothering to tell me to leave his family out of this, simply jumping to the defense. "Who gave you my name? Was it Abrahms? Harvey? Those bastards are just out to save themselves. It's their home you should be breaking into, not mine."

"Wow, you made vows to protect the brotherhood of The Circle, and yet you're so easily throwing them under the bus," I say, taking a single step toward him and watching as his eyes shift around the room. He knows damn well just how much trouble he's in. "You know what that tells me, Aleksander?" I question, drawing my dagger. "That your word is not something I can rely on."

I take another step, and Dalton and Sawyer do the same, closing in on him. "You betrayed me, Alek, and in doing so, you betrayed the blood. Betrayed your brothers."

My words send a sharp pain through my chest as Oakley's face appears in my mind. The real blood heir. *The real grandchild of Julius DeVil.* I am nothing but a fraud here.

Alek's gaze drops to my dagger, watching as I spin it between my fingers and he shakes his head, desperate for some way out of this. "I . . . I—"

"I need a name, Aleksander. Who's behind these attacks on Oakley

Quinn?"

He spits at me, a nasty sneer pulling up the corner of his lips. This desperate attempt to save himself quickly morphing into obvious guilt. "I'll never tell you," he spits. "You don't deserve to stand there. You're weak, pitiful. You'll run Empire into the ground."

"A name, Alek," I repeat, taking another step, a lion closing in on its prey. "Give me a name and I will make this quick."

His eyes become frantic, trying to watch us all at the same time. In a desperate bid for freedom, he whips around and bolts toward Sawyer, a dagger in his hands. We pounce like the fucking hungry carnivores we are.

Instead of shrinking away from Alek's blade, Sawyer embraces it, stepping into him and moving like lightning. He's untouchable, like a fucking ghost in the night, simply playing with his toys.

There's nowhere he can run from us, and in the blink of an eye, we're right there, his back against my chest and my blade at his throat. His dagger clatters to the ground as a sick enjoyment brings me to life. "I'm not going to ask you again, Alek. Give me a name."

"Rot in hell like your piece of shit father."

I let out a heavy sigh, realizing I won't be getting what I need, and with that, I draw my dagger across his throat. I let his body fall heavily to the ground, then with a small nod to the boys, we turn and walk right back out the front door.

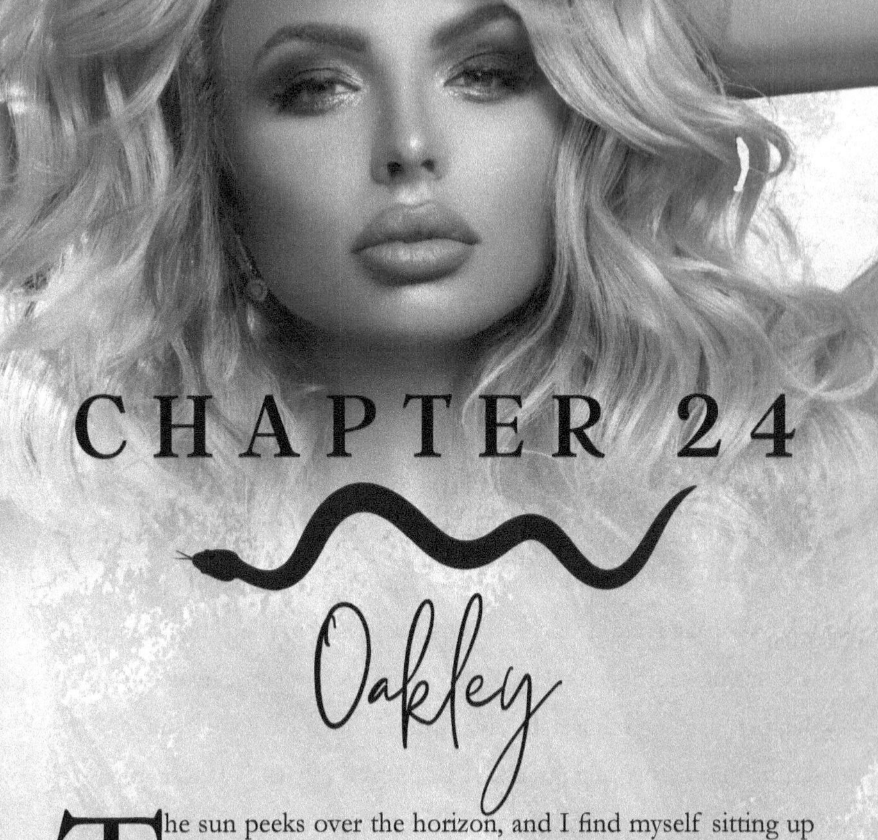

CHAPTER 24

Oakley

The sun peeks over the horizon, and I find myself sitting up in bed, staring out the massive floor-to-ceiling window. The view from Zade's home is like nothing I've ever seen, and while it remains the same day in and day out, I can't help but feel as though it's always something new.

Bright rays of golden light stretch across the sky, cutting through the city, and a low blanket of clouds creates the most stunning contrast, making me feel like a queen as we hover above it all. I could sit here for hours on end, simply watching as the sky changes around us.

Glancing at the small clock on the table, I realize it's barely past six in the morning. I let out a groan, squishing my head back into my pillows and pulling the blankets up to my chin. It's way too early to be awake. I stayed up late with Dalton until I crashed on the couch and somehow woke up in my bed. I can only assume he carried me in here like a perfect gentleman.

A strange warmth spreads through my chest at the thought of this unusual connection I share with him. He betrayed me in the most brutal and ugly way, and yet when he's around me, that's exactly where I want to be. There's something about that cocky grin and all-too-confident demeanor, but the bullshit that flies out of his mouth—what can I say? The guy makes me laugh, makes me want to start enjoying this time with him and forget about the ugliness of his betrayal.

My gaze remains locked on the view, and as the sun continues to rise in the morning sky, I realize falling back asleep is never going to happen. Letting out a sigh, I throw my blanket back and trudge to the bathroom before taking care of business. Only as I stand in front of the mirror, my gaze shifts over the remaining bruises on my throat and the healing cuts on my wrists, and I find myself way overdue for a little self-care. And no, I don't mean that I'm about to rub one out in the bathroom. I need to be pampered.

Spying the oversized shower behind me, I peel off Dalton's shirt and search through the cabinets for anything I can use to help me feel like a woman again. Coming up with nothing but a loofah, razor, and men's shampoo, I realize this will have to do until I get a chance to collect the rest of my things. Though something tells me that will take longer than anything has the right to.

Taking my borrowed things, I slip into the shower and scrub my body before putting every effort into making me feel alive. I wash my hair and scratch off the last remaining remnants of my shitty midnight blue nail polish, and by the time I step out of the shower, I feel like a whole new person.

I take my time doing my hair and getting dressed in a cropped cami and a pair of sweats that are so comfortable, they should be illegal.

It's very rare I wake up this early. Not wanting to let the day slip away from me, I venture out into the penthouse, wondering exactly what my limitations are on my imprisonment here. Am I strictly confined to the penthouse or do I get free rein of the hotel and its amenities? I mean, I googled this place yesterday. There's a huge resort-style pool on level three with a cocktail bar full of daiquiris, and if I'm going to be here, then I might as well live it up in style. Besides, I could never afford to stay in a place like this on my own.

The penthouse is quiet, though I don't expect anything else from four overbearing, giant assholes. They'll probably sleep till three or four in the afternoon before coming out simply for the love of frustrating me.

As I head toward the kitchen, I find myself trailing past the boys' bedrooms instead. Dalton's and Sawyer's are empty, and my brows furrow, wondering where the hell they could be. Not interested in going anywhere near Zade's room, I wander toward Easton's, the only room with a closed door.

Surely they wouldn't leave me here alone. Not after my little performance of following them into Empire.

My curiosity gets the best of me, and before I can mentally scold myself, my fingers curl around the handle, and I gently push the door open to find Easton fast asleep in bed. I watch him for a moment, my gaze lingering on the bandage across his shoulder. I've been checking on him as much as possible, but let's be honest, he's not the type of guy who wants someone doting on him and making sure he's taking his painkillers.

I go to close the door when his rumbly voice breaks through the silence. "Need something?"

I cringe and shake my head. "No, sorry. I didn't mean to wake you," I tell him. "I thought you might have all taken off. Dalton and Sawyer aren't here, and I didn't want to risk what would happen if I accidentally woke Zade."

He peers up at me, amusement in his eyes. "So you took your chances with me?"

I step into the doorway, leaning against the frame. "Something like that," I mutter before biting the inside of my cheek and letting my gaze drop to his shoulder again. "How's it feeling?"

He gives me a blank stare. "Like someone shot me."

My gaze drops, guilt brimming in my chest. "I'm sorry," I murmur. "I know you didn't ask for this. If it weren't for me, you never would have gotten hurt."

Easton laughs and gives the slightest lift of his chin. "Come here," he says, sitting up in his bed and putting a lot of effort into making it look as though the movement doesn't pain him.

Striding across the room, I drop my ass on the edge of his bed, but he reaches for me and curls his strong arm around my waist, hauling me up onto his lap with my knees on either side of his strong thighs.

I pause, staring at his gorgeous face. We don't have a relationship like this. We have nasty comments and broodiness, but certainly not intimacy. And this right here . . . well, shit. This feels intimate.

His hand drops to my thigh, pushing higher until it's right up at my hip. "You don't need to apologize for me getting shot," he tells me. "In my line of . . . work, getting shot at is just part of the territory. It happens more often than not."

Reaching forward, I brush my fingers over the bandage before letting them linger on his warm chest. "I don't like it."

His intense stare meets mine, and I suck in a breath as his hand travels higher, slipping up to my waist and around my back. He pulls me in, rocking me forward so that my pussy grinds against his hardening cock. "Nobody said you had to," he murmurs, his lips barely a breath from mine.

I crave his touch, his kiss, but he doesn't give it to me. Instead, he lets the tension grow, desire building deep inside of me. "You have my drawing tattooed on your back," I state, my tone low and breathy.

His eyes become hooded and my heart starts to race. "Couldn't let such haunting beauty go to waste," he says, taking my hips and rocking me back and forth.

My head tips back, pleasure building deep inside me as his words settle into my chest, not ready to start decoding the secret meaning of why he did it.

He reaches up, curling his fingers around my throat, his thumb stretching up to my jaw and forcing me to meet his eye. "You're going to fuck me, Oakley," he commands in that low, brassy tone, making butterflies swarm in my stomach. "Is that clear? I want you to take those fucking clothes off and sit that sweet little cunt on my cock. I wanna feel you ride me. I wanna feel you squeezing around me."

Need floods me, and I grin down at him. "Oh, I don't think you're ready for me yet."

"Really?" he questions, his brow arching as he slips his hand inside the waistband of my pants and finds me bare beneath. He cups my pussy and without warning, slides two thick fingers inside me. "Because it seems like you're more than fucking ready for me."

His fingers curl and massage inside me, and I grind down on them, the blissful pleasure already building. The need for him is like never before. His grip tightens on my throat, forcing me to meet his stare again. "Now, Oakley. Take those fucking clothes off and ride me."

Oh lord, take the wheel.

The need to please him rocks through me. I grip the fabric of my shirt before peeling it over my head, feeling his heavy gaze lingering on my tits. Before he can do a damn thing, I raise my hips off him and hook my thumbs into the waistband of my pants to get rid of them, kicking them aside before lowering myself back on Easton.

His eyes blaze with hunger and I watch as he releases that thick, veiny cock from his pants. "Fucking ride me, Pretty," he mutters. "Slide down on my cock, nice and slow. Let me feel how fucking warm you are."

Fire burns through me as I move into position, feeling his tip at my entrance. I slowly begin to sink onto him, my gaze locked on his dark one. I take my time, feeling him stretching me, sinking lower and lower as our gazes remain locked, the intensity and tension growing rapidly between us.

He fills me to the brim, the growing hunger in his eyes only making me want to please him more. I start to rock my hips, my pussy grinding down against him. I move slow but purposefully, teasingly rising up only to instantly drop back down, my pussy clenching around him.

His fingers uncurl from my throat and sail down my body, brushing over my tits before dropping to my waist. He reaches around me, gripping my ass, and as his head tips back with undeniable pleasure, I feel like a fucking queen.

"Fuck yes, Pretty. Fuck me just like that."

His words do wicked things to me, and I give it my all before reaching down between us and pressing my fingers to my clit. I rub tight circles over the aching bud, making my eyes flutter with a deep satisfaction. I watch as Easton's gaze drops, watching just how I like it. "Fuck, that's hot, Pretty," he tells me. "Give me more."

I do just that, lifting my hand and skimming my fingers over my tits, feeling my nipples harden beneath my touch. He groans and pulls me in, closing his mouth over my pebbled nipple, his tongue rolling over it as I cup the other, gently squeezing.

I find the perfect pace that sends us both into overwhelming fits of pleasure, and I feel that familiar tightening deep in my core. "Oh God," I moan, riding him as though I'll never experience something so brutally raw and pleasurable again.

He sits back, one hand on my hip as the other reaches to his bedside table, his fingers curling around a small black object. I think nothing of it until he opens it, and I realize it's a pocketknife. I falter, pausing as I look at it with nervousness. "Don't fucking stop," he warns me in that silky tone that has me picking up my pace again. "Keep going."

I keep my eye on the black blade, the anticipation building in my chest. But I don't dare stop, keeping both of us right on the edge. I fuck him harder, his sharp hiss of breath only spurring me on as I feel my orgasm ready to take me higher.

I ride and grind, and as Easton lowers the blade to my thigh, I suck in a breath. "Keep moving, Pretty," he says with a grunt, clenching his jaw as he gets closer to the edge. "Don't fucking stop."

The blade cuts into my thigh, and a sharp squeak tears from the back of my throat. "Don't focus on the pain," he says, thrusting his hips, his cock driving deeper into me. "Focus on the pleasure."

Letting out a breath, I take my mind away from the blade and focus on the feel of his cock deep inside me, stretching me wide and sending me into a world full of bliss. The blade sails down my thigh, biting into my skin, an inch, maybe two, and I use that pain to fuel my pleasure. Blood seeps from the cut, trailing down my leg and making a mess in his sheets, but he doesn't stop. And I realize I don't want him to.

I have no doubt he would stop if I asked him to. Despite everything these guys have put me through, when it comes to Easton Cross, I can trust him.

Easton lifts the knife and brings it back down in the opposite direction, the sharp blade effortlessly slicing through my skin. This line is shorter, cutting through the other, and as he lifts the blade off my thigh and peers down at it, I realize it's a cross.

Easton Cross.

He's branded me with his name. He claimed me, made me his.

A thrill shoots through me as my gaze lifts to his. The pleasure becomes too much, and I come hard, my orgasm tearing through me.

My toes curl and I clench my eyes, feeling a million shots of electricity pulsing through my body. My pussy clenches around him, convulsing erratically, and as Easton's thumb presses to the cross on my thigh, soaking in my blood, he comes with me, shooting hot spurts of cum deep inside me.

He groans and lifts his bloody thumb to my tit, swiping it across my skin and leaving a trail in its wake. "So fucking gorgeous," he mutters as I try to catch my breath, slowly coming down from my high.

He reaches over to his bedside drawer and pulls it open, taking out an array of bandages and gauze. He cleans me up, and I keep my stare on him, watching every little thing he does. "You branded me," I mutter, feeling as though the words need to be spoken out loud despite us both knowing damn well what just went down.

"Mmhmm," he says, lifting his gaze. "So when you fuck Dalton and Sawyer, they'll know you're mine."

Well, shit.

He finishes cleaning me up, and just when I think he's done with me, he nods toward the door. "Come on," he says, going to get up. "Let me make you breakfast. Then as soon as you're fed, I'll be laying you out on the fucking dining table and eating that sweet pussy."

Yes, sir. Who the hell would say no to that?

Getting out of bed, we trail out to the kitchen, cutting back through the massive penthouse. As we walk in silence, I'm struck with a realization. This man I just rode is a callous killer, a cold-hearted murderer. They all are, and yet here I am, their promise to protect me from their world the only reason keeping me from making a break for it.

By why?

What do I mean to them? Why put their life at risk for me?

Why even care?

Zade is about to become the leader of the whole organization, and yet he's been lumbered with babysitting. It doesn't make sense. There's something more to this, something they're not telling me. And you can bet your sweet ass I'm going to find out.

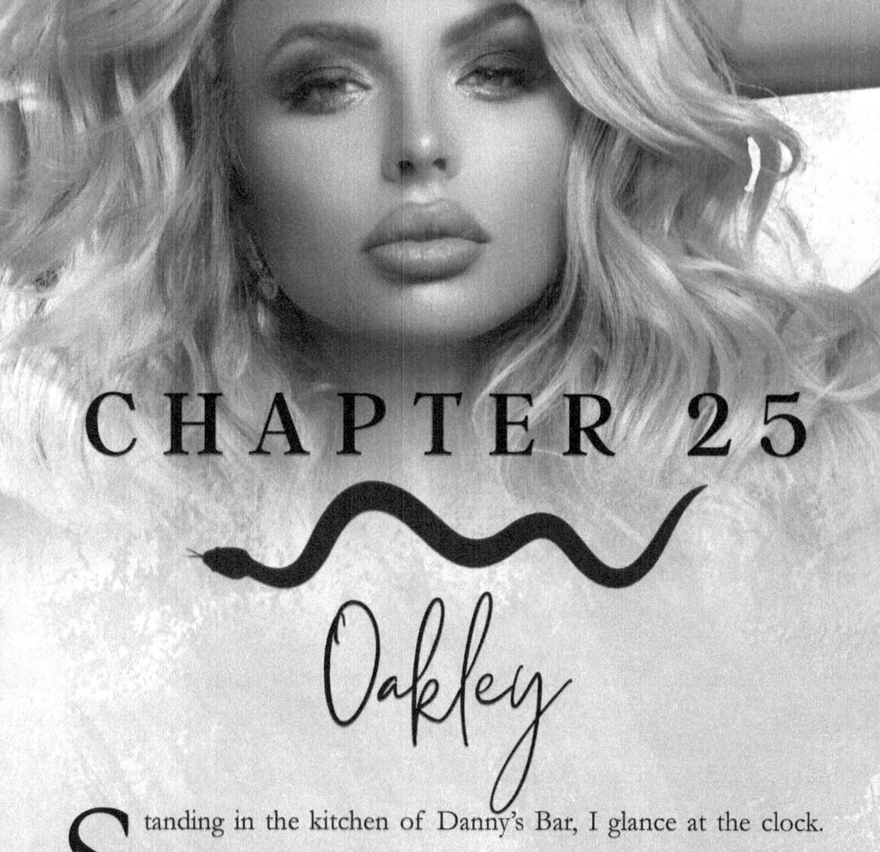

CHAPTER 25

Oakley

Standing in the kitchen of Danny's Bar, I glance at the clock. There's twenty minutes until we close, and with both Heather and Hannah working the near-empty bar, they didn't need me hanging around. Yet here I stand, hovering in the kitchen, pretending as though I'm helping out while staring at the back door.

Zade, Dalton, and Sawyer chill out by the bar, and I have no doubt they're watching my every move. But out here in the kitchen, slipping through the back door and taking off wouldn't be hard.

Since the minute I questioned their intentions, I haven't been able to get it out of my head. I need to know what they're keeping from me, need to know how a nobody like me ended up on the radar of a multi-billion-dollar organization. I'm going to figure it out if it's the last thing I do.

Zade appears a little more chilled out today. Apparently it has something to do with finding the man responsible for giving out my name, but as usual, not one of them was forthcoming with the details.

The boys got back to the penthouse a little after Easton and I finished our breakfast, and with me wearing nothing but one of Easton's shirts, all three of their gazes dropped to my thighs. Sawyer seemed curious while Dalton looked as though his friend just stole his toy on the playground. Zade though, he looked irritated. He gave Easton a scathing glare, then walked away. Apparently he'd had a long night.

Glancing at the clock, I realize I've wasted another five minutes staring at the door when I should have been bolting through it. This is a stupid idea. Almost as bad as hiding in the back of Zade's Escalade, but this time I have a plan. I mean, it's not a great one, probably a little reckless and underprepared, but it's a plan nonetheless, and I fully intend to see it through.

Letting out a shaky breath, I grab the trash bag to give me a reasonable excuse to be out back in case one of them comes looking for me, and I shoot out the back door.

My heart races. They're really going to kick my ass for this.

Dumping the trash bag, I make a break for it.

My feet pound against the pavement, racing through the streets and down back alleys, heading toward the college campus. I see it up ahead and search the windshields of every passing car for that magic little word—

Uber.

Most days, they're everywhere, but nearing 10 p.m. on a Wednesday night . . . I might be shit outta luck.

People come and go, getting home from their nights out while others are only just leaving campus after spending the night buried deep in textbooks. A black car pulls up, and a couple barrels out of the backseat, and the second I spy the Uber sticker in the back window, I make my move.

I wave him down, probably looking like a moron, and watch as the driver puts his window down, probably not used to this level of desperation. "You okay, Miss?" the driver questions, glancing around behind me, probably checking to make sure I'm not being followed.

"Please, I need a ride," I rush out. "It's not far."

He looks hesitant, glancing at me and then back at his app, probably scanning it to see if any better offers pop up. "This isn't how this usually works."

"I know, I'm sorry," I say, remembering my tips that are still buried in the apron I've forgotten to take off. "I can pay you in cash."

He mutters something I can't make out, clearly not happy about this, before finally letting out a sigh. "Alright, get in," he tells me, watching as I scramble into the back seat. "Where to?"

"I—" I cut myself off, not sure how to describe where I need him to take me. It's not like I can say, *You know that secret door hidden deep in the old train tunnel where a super-secret organization likes to party, fuck, and murder? Yeah, take me there.* "I'm not sure of the name of the road, but I can direct you. It's only about ten minutes from here."

He nods, finally pulling away from the curb, and I use this moment to try and calm my racing heart. Taking slow, deep breaths, I give him directions until we're pulling to a stop in the abandoned parking lot by the old train tunnel.

The driver glances back at me, concern etched on his face. "Miss, are you sure you wouldn't like me to drop you off somewhere a little . . . safer?"

Letting out a shaky breath, I shove my hand into my apron pocket and grab a bunch of cash, handing it over. It's probably way too much, but I'm grateful for his help. "I wish I could ask you to drop me off anywhere but here, but unfortunately, this is what my night is going to look like."

His brows furrow, clearly not sure what to make of that, but he takes my cash anyway and gives me a hesitant nod. I quickly thank him, and before I convince myself to back out, I push the door open and clamber out onto the street. The driver watches me a moment longer, and I give him a tight smile to reassure him that everything is alright until he finally pulls away.

I can practically feel his eyes on me through his rearview mirror as he drives away, but I don't have the time to waste waiting for him to disappear. Turning on my heel, I make my way toward the old tunnel, glancing back over my shoulder to watch as the Uber's brake lights come on.

Dread settles in the pit of my stomach, and I silently will him to just forget about me. A second later, he comes off the brakes and hits the gas, deciding I'm no longer his problem. Letting out a relief-filled breath, I quicken my pace, moving closer toward the tunnel until I'm stepping through the darkened entrance. The same chill I felt last time sweeps over me.

Somehow it feels colder in here tonight. I hate that I'm about to do this, but I'm not getting any answers from the boys. It's time I seek them out myself, regardless of the dangers in doing so.

Despite knowing trains no longer use these old tunnels, I stick to the side, my fingers brushing along the cement wall as though it can somehow keep me safe. My eyes are wide, and I search through the darkness for the old maintenance door. It was about a ten minute walk last time. By now, the boys would have already realized that I'm gone, so I need to make this quick.

Picking up my pace, I hurry through the tunnel until I come across the familiar door, almost striding right past it as it blends in with the concrete. My breath comes in hard, fast pants, and I can't tell if it's from nerves or if I'm just really out of shape, but I don't have the time to find out. Remembering just how heavy this door is, I push against it, putting my whole body into it. Only, the fucker doesn't budge. "What the hell?" I mutter, trying again only to get the same result.

Frustration burns through me, and a thorough scan over the door reveals a small keyhole I didn't notice before. I mentally curse myself for not thinking this through. Last time the door opened for me because the boys left it unlocked, and I'm only now realizing they must have done that on purpose. Of course the door isn't going to magically open for me. It's a secret society, for fuck's sake.

Groaning loud, I slam my fists against the door, trying to release just a bit of the frustration building inside me. I clench my jaw and glance back up the long, dark tunnel, feeling deflated. I'm not ready to give up yet, but what choice do I have? I'm not getting in there without that key. Not to mention the two other security measures on the other side of this door.

FUCK!

Shaking my head, I feel my shoulders droop. As I go to take my first step, I hear a soft click coming from the other side of the door. My heart kicks into gear as nervousness flutters through me. It could be anyone on the opposite side of the door. Hell, it could be the asshole responsible for the attacks on my life.

I try to figure out what the hell I'm going to say. Do I tell them my name and request a meeting with the dude in charge, or do I lie and tell them I've been hired for a few happy endings?

Time runs out as the door swings open before me, and a tall older man steps out. He's handsome, in a suit that has me almost ready to call him Daddy, and familiar green eyes, but there's something in them that has me shrinking away. He stares down at me, clearly knowing I'm not supposed to be here. "Can I help you?"

I nod. "My name is—"

"I am well aware of who you are, Miss Quinn," he says, watching me through a narrowed gaze, his stare knowing and dark. "What I want to know is what you're doing here?"

Trying to display a show of confidence, I raise my chin and look him dead in the eye. "I've come to get answers."

"Answers," he repeats.

"Yes," I state. "If you are well aware of who I am, then I'm sure you're also aware that over the past two weeks there have been multiple attempts on my life by the people of this organization. The guys who claim to want to protect me aren't giving me the answers I'm looking for, so I'm taking matters into my own hands."

"I see," he says. "And these guys who are protecting you. Are they aware you're here?"

My stomach clenches, torn over how to respond to this. If I say no, he becomes painfully aware of just how alone and vulnerable I am. But if I say yes, he might be reluctant to tell me anything in fear of this information getting back to them.

Taking my chances, I shake my head. "No, they don't know I am here. But I suspect they will come looking soon."

"I don't doubt that," he says, stepping out of the doorway and making space. "In any case, you better come in. You don't know what kind of monsters lurk around these tunnels."

He waves me through the door and my hands start to shake. I give him a curt nod and step past him, not comfortable with having this strange man at my back, but I'd be damned if I'm staying out there in the shadowy tunnels now.

Walking into the dimly lit corridor, he waves me toward the first set of stairs that lead down to the strange golden gate. I put one foot in front of the other, swallowing the feeling of dread that only gets worse with each step.

Reaching the bottom of the stairs, he leans around me and slips a old, brass key into the lock and pushes the gate open. "After you," he tells me.

I nod, not trusting the look in his eyes. I hesitantly take a step out in front of him when a black bag is yanked down over my head and tightened around my neck. I scream, reaching out to grip the material as scuffles reverberate off the walls around me. Someone pulls my hands tightly behind my back, and while I blindly try to resist their strength, it's no use. Something hard collides with the side of my head, knocking me to the ground and with a deafening ringing thundering through my ears, my world fades to black.

CHAPTER 26

Oakley

A burst of ice-cold water against my face rips me from unconsciousness, and my eyes spring open as I gasp in shock. Looking around the room wildly, the reality of my situation tears through me, and I struggle against my bound hands.

I'm in a hardback chair with my legs and wrists bound to the seat, and the man with familiar green eyes paces before me in the darkened room. My heart races, fear eating at me as I quickly realize this is the same dungeon where Zade brutally murdered the doorman from the ball.

My stomach clenches, and I keep my eyes on the man. I never should have come here. I should have trusted the boys, but instead, I've walked right into this man's trap.

"You snake! What do you want with me?" I spit.

The man laughs. "Oh, I must admit, I am very sorry for all of this. I am not a callous person by nature, but you showing up here like this has put me at quite an advantage. One I simply cannot allow to slip through my fingers."

"What are you talking about?"

"Goodness, girl," he says, belittling me. "So many questions, so little time."

"Who. Are. You?"

His brow arches in surprise. "Wow. Out of everything you want to know, that's your priority?" he muses. "Okay, I'll play. My name is Nikolai Thorne. I am—"

"Sawyer's father," I gasp in horror.

"Indeed," he says with a nod, almost looking impressed that I've put the pieces together so quickly. Not that it's hard, considering they have the same green eyes and share a name. "I believe you've had the pleasure of getting to know my son over the past few weeks? I do hope he's been on his best behavior."

My brows furrow. What the fuck is this guy's deal? He's got me bound in the murder dungeon but wants to discuss his son's behavior? "Your son likes to fuck and is hung like a horse," I tell him bluntly. "That's about all I know of him."

Nikolai presses his lips into a hard line, clearly not too impressed by my crass words or his son's willingness to fuck the chick he's supposed to protect. He doesn't respond to me, and I let out a heavy sigh. "I highly doubt you went to all this effort of getting me down here just to talk about how well your son can get me off," I mutter. "So why don't you go ahead and tell me what you really want with me."

"You're right. I suppose I owe you an explanation before I end your life," he says, crossing the small space and leaning up against a table filled with things I can only assume are used for torturing innocent souls. "You see, there's something special about you, Miss Quinn. Something not many people are aware of."

My brows furrow. "What are you talking about?"

"It's important to me that you know I am loyal to the blood. I would never disgrace Empire by committing such horrendous acts of treason. However, this is not a typical situation. I have been backed into a corner, and for the sake of this organization and the strength of its future, I am only doing what is right."

Tears well in my eyes as I watch Sawyer's father, and I can only describe him as heartbrokenly resigned to this fate. "And ending my life is what's right?"

He nods regrettably. "As I said, I am not a callous man by nature, and my loyalty to the blood has been my only purpose in life. I have raised my children in my image, to follow in my footsteps. Once word gets out about what I have done here tonight, I will be sentenced to death, but I know my son will fall into his place and finish what I have started."

"Okaaaay," I say slowly. "I think you've skipped a few things. I'm not following."

Nikolai takes a heavy breath before pushing off the edge of the table and striding back toward me. "You, my sweet girl," he says with a strange adoration in his eyes, kinda like in the way a young girl would look up at her idol. "You are the only living heir of Empire, this magnificent organization that is home to so many. The blood which runs through your veins is what we were built on. It is what has ruled us for the past hundred and fifty years, passed down from generation to generation. You, Oakley, are the rightful heir."

My jaw drops. "You're hearing yourself, right? Do you know how insane this sounds? I'm sorry, but you have things twisted. I don't know anything about Empire, what it is or what it stands for, and no offense, but I really don't want anything to do with it. Besides, Zade DeVil is the heir, not me. Because his father was the leader."

"The only problem is, Lawson DeVil was never supposed to lead our people. He does not possess the blood, but you know who did?" he asks me, a sparkle hitting his eye. Sharing the privileged information of his beloved society really gets this man going. He looks like he could come in his pants with excitement for being the one who gets to break this news to me. "Your father, Matthias Quinn."

I shake my head, horror blasting through my chest. "No," I say, feeling sick at the thought of my father being involved in this. "My father had nothing to do with this world."

"On the contrary," Nikolai says. "Your father was deeper in this world than anybody I've seen come through here. He was the bastard child of Julius DeVil, Zade's grandfather, conceived by another who was not his wife and then abandoned at birth. Julius went on to adopt a child with his wife. That child was Lawson DeVil, Zade's father. Lawson was, for all intents and purposes, Julius's son, but he did not possess the same DNA. The blood of Empire does not run through Zade's veins. You, however, as Matthias's only child, do. You are the heir to Empire, Oakley—the rightful heir. Not Zade DeVil."

"But you . . . You said you were loyal to the blood."

"I am indeed. I have always been loyal to the blood. Things shifted over a decade ago after Lawson discovered the truth of his lineage and learned who your father truly was. He knew he would lose the power he possessed and be stripped from Empire." He gives me a pointed stare before continuing. "Lawson was a proud man, and the thought of losing everything he loved was something he could not bear. It was for that reason he slaughtered your father so no one would discover the truth. And that is exactly why I must do the same now."

Panic tears at me, and I stare up at him with wild eyes, desperation clear on my face. "Please," I say, my hands shaking as my heart races in my chest. "I'll do anything you want. I'll disappear. I'll leave Faders Bay and never look back. I don't want anything to do with Empire, except to be as far away from it as possible. Just let me go back to my life in Missouri and you'll never hear my name again."

"I'm sorry, Oakley. It does not work that way. You have the blood, and despite your lack of interest, you have a duty to Empire," he states. "If you live, you will be forced into power, and I simply cannot accept that. A woman ruling over this world, no matter how capable you might be, would destroy us. We would burn to ashes."

"So, you're going to kill me simply because I was born?"

"That," he says, "and other reasons."

"Such as?"

He lets out a breath as though explaining all of this to me is beneath him. "Zade DeVil is strong and possesses all the qualities of a fine leader. He is callous and cruel while also compassionate and forgiving when he needs to be. He will do well as our leader despite not belonging in power." Nikolai rubs a hand down his face as though lost deep in thought. "I was happy to let this go. The restless members of Empire would have eventually taken you out. But as you sit here before me, I am presented with a unique opportunity."

"Dare I ask what that is?"

"You see, if you die, Zade will not be able to complete his leadership ritual and Empire will be left to fend for themselves. We would indeed crumble. And despite the respect I have for Zade, as a man I've watched grow and mature, I cannot allow a fraud to lead Empire."

I shake my head, feeling as though I'm stating the obvious. "But if you kill me, you have no true leader."

"In the wake of your death and Zade forfeiting his power, Empire will be presented with an opportunity to rise again with a new bloodline, a new leader, voted in by the people. Not a fraud who mistakenly inherited it, but a new seat of power who will preserve and carry on the traditions and rituals of this great organization."

I let out a sigh. I should have known there was more than he was letting on. "And let me guess, your name will be at the top of that list?" I question. "The great Thorne legacy."

A smile pulls at his lips, and I see the truth right there in his eyes. "I cannot deny how fond I am of the prospect."

My eye is drawn to the darkness across the room, and as if sensing my stare, a shadow moves toward us as Zade's low tone rumbles through the murder dungeon. "That was a nice story," he mutters as Nikolai whips around with wide eyes, his face falling in horror. "However, I'm sure you understand that I cannot allow you to do this."

"Zade," he breathes, shaking his head and backing up, clearly knowing who has the upper hand here. "I didn't intend for this to happen. She showed up here and the opportunity presented itself."

While keeping his gaze on Nikolai, Zade stops by me and reaches into his pocket, producing a knife similar to the one Easton used to brand me. He moves in behind me and effortlessly cuts through the tape, freeing my hands before passing me the knife, indicating for me to release my ankles.

"No matter your reasoning, Nikolai, this is the highest level of treason," Zade states as I madly free my legs and get off the chair, half hiding behind Zade. "You have proclaimed your intention to murder the only living heir of Empire for your own gain. You have shown disloyalty to your people, to the blood, and to your brothers. On top of this, you have confessed your intentions to tamper with the process of our most sacred ritual, ensuring I cannot complete my task and rise to power, staining your family's name and reputation."

Zade indicates to a pair of cuffs on the table behind Nikolai, and he reluctantly swipes them off the table before cuffing his own wrists, pain in his eyes. "I should have your head for this right now," Zade tells him. "However, out of respect for Sawyer, I will allow this to go to trial in front of The Circle."

Nikolai's head whips up, his eyes wide and filled with horror. "No," he rushes out. "A trial is a guaranteed death sentence."

"Yes," Zade agrees. "It is. But a trial allows you the opportunity to say goodbye to your children, your wife. You have been a great role model in my life, Nikolai, and I will not deny that this betrayal hurts me, but I'll show you the respect you have shown me over the years and offer you this one kindness. I suggest you take it."

Nikolai nods and with that, Zade pulls out his phone and makes a quick call. Within seconds, a large man who looks like some kind of hired security barges through the room. He strides right up to Nikolai, and I can't help but notice that even in the worst of situations, Nikolai is still polite.

"Harrison," he says with a nod. "How are the children?"

"They're doing well, Nik," the guard says before gripping the back of his arm. "Come on. I'll take you down to the cells."

As the man escorts Nikolai out of the murder dungeon, Zade's tight grip clutches onto my arm. He pushes me in front of him, quickly making his way out of the dungeon and up the stairs, much like we'd done the other night. Despite how terrified I am of being here, I've never been so happy to see Zade DeVil.

He doesn't speak a word as he leads me out of the Empire compound, through the long walkways, and back to the gold-plated gate. It's not until our feet hit the pavement of the old train tunnel that he throws me up against the wall, his rock-hard body pressed against mine. "What the fuck were you thinking coming here?"

I scoff and shove him hard, and I'm surprised to find he actually takes a step back, allowing me space to come back at him. "Me? Get fucked, Zade. You knew I was the fucking heir of Empire and you didn't say a damn thing."

He laughs. "Why the hell would I say anything?" he questions. "Thirty fucking days and it's all mine."

I step into him, ignoring the way he towers over me with that intimidating stare. "One problem, big guy," I murmur, raising my chin and letting him see the challenge in my eyes. "I'm the rightful heir. I could take it all away."

Zade scoffs. "You'd have to prove it first."

"Honestly? That's what you've got?" I question. "Someone stands before Empire and makes a bold claim like that and you don't expect an organization like this to take a DNA sample? Really now, I'm disappointed."

"In the real world, yeah. That's exactly how it would work, but not here. I dare you, walk back into that compound and tell them exactly who you are. Tell them what Nikolai told you and see how fast you get a bullet between your eyes."

I clench my jaw, anger burning through me. "Hear me when I tell you, Zade DeVil. I will take Empire from you. I will take your power and destroy you with it."

He grins at me, taking my waist and pulling me in hard against his wide chest. He stares into my eyes, my defiance making something come alive within his dead eyes. "Go ahead," he challenges. "But the only way you're getting it is if you take it from my cold dead hands."

CHAPTER 27

Leaning forward, I brace my elbows against my knees as Dalton, Cross, and I stare at the numbers on the elevator, impatiently waiting for Zade to bring Oakley back to us.

None of us could have seen just how hard it was going to be to keep this chick alive. The way she keeps escaping us . . . It's as though she's asking for someone to slit her throat. Does she not understand just how brutal this will be? Our world is not for the faint-hearted. It's vicious, cold, and powerful, and she's shitting all over it as though they'll never be able to touch her.

I swear, Oakley Quinn is fucking hot, but if she tries to escape us like that again, I'll make her remaining days hell on earth. Sitting in that bar and waiting for her to finish her shift, not knowing she'd slipped out the back door . . . Fuck, she made a fool of us all.

We split up. I went to the apartment complex, Dalton and Cross checked the streets, and Zade went to the compound.

We received a text from him forty minutes ago stating he'd found her, and now I'm itching for her to show up so I can give her a piece of my mind. I don't know why I'm so worked up about this. I should've been able to calm myself by now, but the frustration keeps building. Keeps blasting through my system like a fucking hurricane.

In thirty days she'll be gone, so tell me why the fuck the idea of her being in danger makes me feel like tearing the world apart to get her back? We don't even talk. I fucked her a few times and it was phenomenal, but as far as our encounters go, that's about it. It doesn't make sense for me to be so messed up about this.

The elevator *dings* its arrival, and we're on our feet before the door even opens. Oakley walks out first, her gaze locked on the ground, and it's clear she's received some kind of hell from Zade. Out of all of us, she drew the short straw to be found by him. That motherfucker would have made her wish for death. I can only imagine the bullshit that went down when he found her.

Zade follows her out of the elevator, and step forward, ready to let her have it when Zade holds up his hand, cutting me off. "Sawyer, stop," he says, a strange tone in his voice that has me pausing mid-step. "We gotta talk."

The fuck? Talk?

My gaze cuts to Oakley, wondering if this has something to do with her before turning to Dalton and Cross, who wear the same confused expression. "What the fuck is going on?" I question, unease settling into the pit of my stomach. I've known Zade since we were kids, and he's never once told me we need to talk.

He hesitates, and I see from the look in Oakley's eyes that she knows exactly what this is about. But she wouldn't dare speak a word, not when Zade has already made his intentions clear to take point on this. Neither of them look at Dalton or Cross, making it clear that whatever this is has everything to do with me.

"I found her at the compound," Zade starts. "She was in the basement, tied up, wrists and ankles bound."

"The fuck?" Dalton spits, his back stiffening and he looks over Oakley, making sure she's in one piece. "Who?"

Zade's stare remains on me. "Your father, man," he says, a hint of anguish in his eyes. "He wanted to kill her to keep me from completing the ritual."

My brows furrow and I shake my head. "Nah, that's not right. Have you met my father? He's a prick at the best of times, but he doesn't make fucking power plays like that."

Zade rubs his hands over his face and walks into his dining room, turning his back to us and bracing himself against the table. "There's more," he states, pain in his tone. "Something you all need to know."

Oakley hovers awkwardly by the elevator before shuffling slightly closer, not wanting to miss whatever's about to go down in here.

Zade takes a heavy breath before finally turning to face us, an acceptance that doesn't belong flashing in his hard stare. "Despite everything we've been told and knew to be fact, I am not the heir of

Empire. The blood does not run through my veins."

"What?" Dalton grunts, glancing around to make sure we're all equally confused. "What are you talking about?"

"Her," Zade mutters, turning a filthy stare on Oakley. "She is the heir, the only living heir, and it's why her name was put forward for protection."

My gaze snaps to Oakley, taking her in with disbelief, trying to wrap my head around what Zade just said. Oakley is the heir. "How is that even possible?"

Zade shakes his head. "A secret adoption after my grandparents failed to conceive an heir. My father didn't share my grandfather's DNA." He turns that stare back on Oakley. "But apparently she does."

Cross narrows his gaze on Oakley, and I've seen that stare a million times before. He doesn't trust her. Doesn't trust that she has been forthcoming with what she knows. Now, he has just what he needs to believe she's been keeping things from us. "What is he talking about?" Cross mutters, his tone low and lethal, making Oakley swallow.

Oakley raises a brow at him, not liking the way he watches her. "Don't look at me like that, Easton," she spits, his name sounding like an insult on her lips. "This is all brand new information for me too."

Wanting to get this over and done with, Zade continues. "My grandfather had an affair that resulted in Oakley's father. His mother died shortly after birth and he was adopted into a different family. When my old man heard of this—"

"Let me guess," Dalton cuts in. "He saw to it that this dirty little secret could never get out."

"Exactly," he confirms. "Point of the story, Oakley is the rightful heir."

I try to put the pieces together, attempting to figure out how my father could possibly be involved in any of this when it all starts crashing in, horror twisting through my gut. If he had Oakley bound in the basement, that means he had intended to take her life. But that doesn't make sense. My father would have railroaded Zade to protect the blood. He'd dedicated his life to his loyalty. He would never have harmed her. Not unless there was some kind of ulterior motive.

"What did my father want with her?" I question, no longer interested in the *who's your daddy* conversation.

Zade presses his lips into a hard line and sets his gaze on me.

"Just tear it off, man," I tell him. "Give it to me straight."

He nods, his loyalty and friendship to me put above all the other bullshit. "Your father intended to kill Oakley to keep me from being able to complete my ritual," he states, the words coming out of his mouth sending hot coals down my throat and into my gut. "He committed treason, Sawyer. He betrayed his loyalty to the blood by professing his intention to strip Empire of our last remaining heir in the hopes I would forfeit my position as leader, leaving Empire defenseless. We would have crumbled."

I shake my head. "I . . . I don't understand why he would do that."

Cross steps toward me and meets my stare. "Because without an heir or anyone in leadership, he could have manipulated his way into power."

Zade nods, confirming exactly what Cross has said. I let out a heavy breath, knowing damn well my father is about to lose everything. "What do we do?" I ask, looking back at Zade. "If The Circle finds out about this, he's dead."

"I'm sorry, Sawyer," Zade says, that anguish returning to his tone. "The Circle already knows. He'll be put to a private trial."

My chest sinks as I stare at Zade in horror. "No," I say, shaking my head. "You can't fucking do that. It's a death sentence."

Zade takes a step toward me, a coldness seeping into his eyes. This is the man who's about to become the leader of Empire, not the friend I grew up with. "You know damn well had that been any other Circle member, I would have slit his throat right where he was standing. Out of respect to you and your family, I gave him a chance to prove himself. And at the very least, a chance for you all to say goodbye."

I step into him, shoving him hard in the chest. "You're fucking killing him," I spit. "Where the fuck is he?"

Zade closes his eyes for a brief moment, struggling with the decision he's made. "He's in the cells," he tells me. "You know just as well as I do you won't get access."

"Let him go," I demand. "You have the power to do that. Override the trial. You can't let this happen to him. To me. Please, man. My father practically raised you."

Regret lingers in Zade's eyes and desperation has me balling my hands into fists. "It's in motion, Sawyer," he tells me, trying to remind me of how these things work, but I don't want to hear it. I know it all too well, and right now, everything is working against me. My father will be executed, and there's not a fucking thing I can do to stop it.

Dalton grunts from across the room. "Our best bet is getting Zade into power. Make sure he gets through this ritual and then he'll have enough pull to try and save him."

I stare across at Zade, seeing nothing but the coldest betrayal. "You sentenced him to death," I mutter, my chest heaving with grief and knowing I have to be the one to break this to my mom and Cara. "You fucking killed him. You might as well have taken your fucking knife and slit his throat."

"Sawyer, I—"

My arm rears back and I let it fly, nailing the fucker right in the jaw. The second my fist lands home, it's like a rollercoaster of wild emotions spasming through my body. I hit him again and again, each punch more devastating than the last, but he just stands there and takes it like a fucking man. He's punishing himself, knowing just how desperately we both need this.

I hear Oakley's gasp of horror, but it doesn't slow me down. I take out my frustration, my pain, my grief, giving it my all until Cross finally intervenes, keeping me from taking Zade's life just as easily as he took my father's.

My knuckles bleed, and Oakley steps toward me with wide eyes. As I take in her pitying and broken stare, I can't help but push her away. Striding toward the elevator, I hear Dalton's voice behind me. "Where are you going, man?"

I scoff, my heart shattering in my chest. "I have to go tell Mom and my sister that my father is about to be executed by my best fucking friend."

"Shit," Cross mutters as I slam my hand down over the elevator call button, the doors opening immediately. He turns to Dalton and quickly nods. "Go with him and make sure he doesn't try anything."

I step into the elevator, my stare locked on Zade. I hope like fuck he knows to sleep with one eye open.

CHAPTER 28

Oakley

aking my way out into the living room on Saturday morning is like stepping out into the land of the dead. Zade sits on the couch, staring out the window. His face is cut up and bruised, and I can't even begin to understand how much pain he must be in. But what he's feeling is nothing compared to what Sawyer must be going through.

Easton, on the other hand, has been holed up in Zade's home gym, unable to form a single sentence. No one has heard from Dalton or Sawyer since they left. Apparently, the key to working out your frustrations isn't filthy, wild sex after all. Someone should have told me.

An icepack rests on the coffee table in front of Zade, and I let out a sigh. It's the third time I've had to replace it, and not once has he thought to actually pick it up and put it on his face. I can't stand Zade at the best of times, but watching him stand back and allow Sawyer to beat the shit out of him wasn't easy. There was something vulnerable about it. Something raw and honest.

He was very clearly punishing himself for the role he had to play last night. Sentencing his best friend's father to death like that couldn't have been easy, and there was clearly a struggle between duty and what he felt was right. But as I've heard so much lately, the traditions and rituals of Empire are blah, blah, blah. Does anyone even care about their ridiculous traditions? Fucking snooze fest if you ask me.

Though I can't lie, I'm intrigued by the idea of all these traditions. Sounds kinda like witchcraft to me. Every time their rituals are brought up, I can't help but listen a little closer while imagining Bonnie Bennett from *The Vampire Dairies* performing some fucked-up type of old magic. Something tells me I'm a little off, though. In reality, it's probably just a bunch of old men chanting in a circle. I just wish I knew what this ritual is that Zade has to perform to claim his leadership. All I know is that it's got something to do with me, and so far, anything in this fucked-up organization that's had my name attached to it hasn't been good.

Letting out a sigh, I get up and stride across to Zade before scooping up the melted ice pack and really trying not to roll my eyes. Despite being well into their twenties, some men just refuse to mature. "I'm going to order something to eat. Do you want anything?" I ask, hesitant to try talking to him after my daring escape yesterday. At some point, I suppose I owe him a thank you for saving my life, but I doubt he's in the mood to hear it today.

"Mmm," he grunts, not lifting his gaze away from the window.

Not having the energy to try and force a better response out of him, I turn on my heel and stalk toward the home gym, wondering what the hell these guys did with their lives before spending every minute of every hour babysitting me. I'm almost certain Dalton, Sawyer, and Easton don't actually live here. Not that I've specifically seen anything to suggest they don't, but it just makes sense.

Moving into the doorway of the gym, I catch Easton's gaze across the room. "Hungry?"

All I get is a brief shake of his head, but hey, it's a shitload better than the response from Zade. At least I can say I tried. If they die of hunger in the next few hours, it's not on me.

Making my way back out to the main living area, I cut through the kitchen to the phone hidden in the butler's pantry and dial the number for room service—a number I'm becoming all too familiar with. "Concierge desk," says my favorite voice in the building.

"Benny," I cheer. "Me again."

"Ahh, Miss Quinn," he says. "Didn't I just get you a bacon cheeseburger for breakfast? You couldn't possibly be hungry again."

"What can I say, Benny? Adrian's food is just that good."

He chuckles and I grin, knowing my flattery will get me anywhere I want to go with the concierge of the fancy DeVil Hotel. Knowing how it bugs Zade when I make friends with the staff, I quickly put in my order and wait patiently at the table as though I were actually eating at the five-star restaurant.

A knock sounds at the door ten minutes later, and my gaze slowly rolls toward Zade on the couch. "You gonna get that?" I question, not prepared for the onslaught of death glares I get every other time I've tried to open the door, followed by the lecture reminding me how stupid I am for blindly opening the door when there's a target on my head.

Zade doesn't respond, and I let out a huff, getting up and hurrying to the door before making a point of glancing through the peephole. Recognizing the bellboy, I open the door and reach for the tray in his hands. "Miss Quinn," he says with a polite nod.

I glance up and meet his eyes, more than prepared to return a friendly smile, only this time there's a tightness in the set of his jaw and his gaze is filled with nervousness. Anxiety wafts off him like a bad smell, and I hold his stare a little longer, both our hands gripping the tray. "Everything okay?" I ask.

He forces his smile to become more genuine. "Oh yes," he says. "Everything is wonderful. Enjoy the rest of your day."

My brows furrow and I watch as he quickly scurries away, something he usually never does. Most of the time I struggle to get him out of the penthouse, especially when Zade is around. He always wants to talk, constantly searching for Zade's approval, but today is different.

Not wanting to get caught out in the open for too long, I pull the door closed and head back to the dining table, setting the tray down. I reach in, grab my Diet Coke, and quickly take a sip before opening the lid off my lunch. My back stiffens as I gape down at the black Empire envelope that stares back at me, the glossy E shining against the black paper.

Nervousness rattles me, and I pick up the envelope, flipping it over to check if there's anything on the back. It's bare, but I hold it up anyway. "Hey, check this out," I say, realizing exactly what the bellboy was nervous about.

Getting no response from Zade, I peek over my shoulder at him only to find he's not actually there. Feeling like an idiot for talking to myself, I glance over the envelope again, wishing just the sight of it didn't make me feel sick.

Needing to know what's inside, I flip it over and break the seal. I find a calling card, exactly the same as the one I first found in my apartment, and let it fall to the table before fishing out a note.

It's folded in half and I quickly open it to find black smudged ink scrawled across the paper.

One cannot flourish in the power of Empire without first giving his soul.

A sacrifice to be made, an innocent life to be lost.

In sixty suns and sixty moons, he shall sacrifice an innocent in the hour before dawn.

Her still beating heart carved from her body, he shall offer it to the sacred fortress.

For this is his offering to his Empire. This is his sacred ritual to bind him in blood.

What the fuck is this?

My heart races as I scan over the note. A second, third time. Fourth, and then a fifth.

This couldn't be what Zade needs me for. This couldn't be the ritual he's been talking about because that could only mean that he's been keeping me alive, protecting me from these cruel, vicious attacks, just so that he can be the one to carve my beating heart right out of my chest.

Sixty suns. Sixty moons. How long has it been since he murdered his own father?

In the dungeon, Nikolai said that Zade cannot rise to power without completing his ritual. I'm his golden ticket to secure everything he's ever wanted, and all I have to give is my life.

They've been lying to me this whole time, drawing me in and forming these connections, making me want to trust them. And I fell right into their trap, yet again.

Fool me once and that's on them, but fool me twice . . . well shit. I won't allow it to happen. I won't sit back and allow myself to become sliced and diced for someone else's twisted games. My life is not a bargaining tool. It's not there to be used at someone else's will.

I have two choices. One, I can disappear. All I need to do is make it past the night of the sixtieth moon and ensure Zade cannot complete his ritual. My life will be saved, and Zade will forfeit his claim to leadership. Then I can bitch out, run as far as I can until they eventually catch up to me. Or two, I can be the daughter my father raised me to be and take what's rightfully mine.

I am the rightful heir, and the power of Empire is right there, waiting for me to take it.

My father lost his life for this, and now that I finally have some answers, I can make this right. And when I do, Zade DeVil better watch his fucking back.

With my decision made, I glance around Zade's penthouse, making sure the coast is clear, and without a second thought, I slip the note and calling card into the back pocket of my jeans and walk straight out the front door.

Using the fire escape, I take myself down a few levels before cutting across to the main elevators and taking it all the way down. Reaching the lobby, I keep my eyes wide, searching around me for whoever might have left me this note.

Stepping out into the street, I move past the valet parking when the attendant turns to me, a welcoming smile on his face. "Ahh, Miss Quinn," Joe says, another person I've become familiar with over the past few weeks. "Going somewhere? Can I fetch you a car?"

I look around, staring out at the busy streets as I shake my head. "I, umm—"

A sharp pinch stings the side of my neck and I whip around to Joe, watching as that welcoming smile morphs into a sinister grin. "Sleep tight," he says as a car pulls up to the curb. He opens the back door, and just as my body becomes too heavy to hold myself up, he pushes me inside, closing the door behind me as I succumb to the darkness.

The loud clang of banging metal echoes through my pounding head, and I open my heavy eyes. The ground is cold beneath my body, and I try to sit up, peering through the fog and realizing I'm in some kind of prison cell.

My heart races and I shift to my knees, trying to crawl across the darkened cell, but my body is too heavy to hold up. I cry out as I fall, desperately trying to pull myself back up.

My hand closes around the metal bar, and I drag my body across the rough stone, my jeans catching and ripping on the stray rocks. Gripping the bars with both hands, I pull myself to my knees and try to catch my bearings.

Where the hell am I?

"HELLO?" I call out, the sound pounding against my skull as I try fruitlessly to shake the bars. "Please, someone, help me."

I try again and again, defeat gripping my chest and squeezing tight. Tears stain my dirty face, and as I cry out once more, my desperation knowing no bounds, I hear a haggard voice coming from across the room. "Give up, girl," the man says, his voice thick and dry as though he rarely uses it. "No one's coming for ya."

My gaze cuts around the cells as I grip the bars tighter, hauling myself to my feet and staring into the shadows of the neighboring cells. I see a faint outline of a man hidden in darkness, and nervousness starts to pound in my chest. "Wh . . . where am I?"

"Doesn't matter," he responds in that gruff tone. "Once you're in here, there's no getting out."

Falling back to my knees, I drop my face into my hands, tears streaming down my face as hopelessness claims me. I had a plan. I had a life I needed to save. And now I'm nothing but a sitting duck, just waiting for someone to come and end it all. Whether it be the person who's been organizing these vicious attacks or someone much closer, someone I thought I wanted so desperately to trust.

"What's your name, kid?" the man says in a bid to distract me from my tears, his tone disinterested and bored.

Wiping my cheeks with the back of my hands, I mutter my name over the lump in my throat. "Oakley Quinn."

"No," comes a whoosh of breath, accompanied by the sounds of heavy chains dragging along the stone. I look up at the cell directly across from me and watch as a pair of dirty hands lock around the metal bars before a face appears through the darkness. "No, it can't be," the man says, a hint of desperation in his raspy tone. "Tell me it's not."

My brows furrow as I peer into the darkness, trying to make out the man's face. I pull myself back to my feet when I finally see him. I suck in a sharp gasp, my breath getting caught in my throat as I see the ghost of the man who's haunted my dreams for nearly twelve years.

"Dad?"

THANKS FOR READING

If you enjoyed reading this book as much as I enjoyed writing it, please consider leaving an Amazon review to let me know. https://www.amazon.com/gp/product/B0B2Q6MYXV

EMPIRE EXTRAS

Empire Pinterest Board
https://pin.it/6DZLmZN

Cara's Smut_XPERT Bookstagram
https://www.instagram.com/smut_xpert/

Playlist
https://open.spotify.com/playlist/1NBPuMI15YFObcqC-716Qf0?si=fcb9db9b46084fa1

STALK ME!

Join me online with the rest of the stalkers!!
I swear, I don't bite. Not unless you say please!

Facebook Reader Group
www.facebook.com/SheridansBookishBabes

Facebook Page
www.facebook.com/sheridan.anne.author1

Instagram
www.instagram.com/Sheridan.Anne.Author

TikTok
www.tiktok.com/@Sheridan.Anne.Author

Subscribe to my Newsletter
https://landing.mailerlite.com/webforms/landing/a8q0y0

Hive Social!
@SheridanAnne

MORE BY SHERIDAN ANNE

www.amazon.com/Sheridan-Anne/e/B079TLXN6K

YOUNG ADULT / NEW ADULT DARK ROMANCE

Broken Hill High | Haven Falls | Broken Hill Boys

Aston Creek High | Rejects Paradise | Boys of Winter

Depraved Sinners | Bradford Bastard | Empire

NEW ADULT SPORTS ROMANCE

Kings of Denver | Denver Royalty | Rebels Advocate

CONTEMPORARY ROMANCE (standalones)

Play With Fire | Until Autumn (Happily Eva Alpha World)

PARANORMAL ROMANCE

Slayer Academy [Pen name - Cassidy Summers]

www.ingramcontent.com/pod-product-compliance
Lightning Source LLC
Chambersburg PA
CBHW050745190726
48285CB00005B/1539